THEY CAME

RAIN

Christopher Coleman

CHAPTER ONE

"COME ON, BABY! PUT a little weight on it! I wanna get at least two drinks in me before Dante's closes."

Amber Godwin spun the volume control of the Ford Ranger's radio to ten, and then she quickly sprung to her knees and faced her boyfriend, grinning. She linked her fingers and looped her arms over Derrick Zamora's head, resting her hands on his opposite shoulder, oblivious to the danger such a maneuver might pose while traveling sixty-five miles an hour in the middle of the night.

"You wanna get me a little drunk tonight, right?" she asked with a coquettish lean of her head.

Derek smiled, keeping his eyes on the road. "Every night."

Amber leaned in and gave a schoolgirl kiss on Derrick's cheek, and as she pulled the innocent peck away, she let the tip of her tongue linger for several beats before running it slowly across Derek's jawline to his mouth. As their lips met, Amber kissed her beau gently, allowing her tongue to roam there for a moment, wandering in and out of Derrick's mouth.

Derrick shifted in his seat, the bulge in his pants beginning to form; but he kept his eyes locked on the road, leaning hard left to keep visibility past Amber's head.

"So, then you gotta drive faster, baby. If we get there too close to last call, that hulk Bo at the door ain't gonna let us in."

Derrick pulled away, re-focusing. "I understand Amb, but the city line is coming up, and I'd rather not end up at the bottom of the ravine." He reached over and turned the radio down to a volume barely audible.

"Why'd you do that?" Amber asked, her lips an inch from Derrick's ear.

Derrick glanced down at the radio, not really processing what he'd done. "Oh, sorry. Habit."

Amber rolled her eyes and plopped back to her seat. "Christ, this town," she lamented. "I swear to God. Got us all programmed like a bunch of freaking robots. Can't listen to the radio. Can't have a cell phone. It's like we're stuck in 1945."

"I know, baby, but let's at least wait until we get past the—"

"Derrick!"

Derrick spotted the cause of the exclamation a half-second after Amber's cry, and, instinctively knowing the calipers would lock if he panicked, he pressed slowly but firmly on the brake pedal, thumping the grill of the truck through a pair of orange cones before bringing the pickup to a lurching stop less than fifteen yards from the gaping chasm in the middle of Interstate 91.

Amber pitched forward but avoided crashing into the dash; her face was now lit with intrigue, unconcerned with how close they'd come to their deaths. "Pull up closer," she said.

Derrick took several deep breaths and turned toward Amber. "What? Are you crazy?"

Amber frowned and opened the passenger door, and then she walked toward the sinkhole, now rapt by the giant crater.

Derrick rolled the window down and stuck his head out, following Amber with his eyes. "If I was you, I'd think about stopping right about there."

"I've never seen one of these before," Amber said, her gaze still on the giant crater. "And by tomorrow it'll probably be fixed. Just give me a minute."

"It's just a hole, Amber. Ain't no big deal."

Amber finally turned back toward the truck and smiled. "So you're saying all holes are the same?" She put her hands on her hips and cocked her head to the side, questioning.

Derrick laughed. "Ain't saying that, baby. I ain't saying that at all."

Amber smiled. "Well, good. And just pull the truck forward a little. I can't really see it without the light."

Derrick sighed. "Fine, Bambi."

Derrick ducked his head back into the car and shifted the truck to park, and then he pulled the Ranger forward until he could just see the rim of the hole, at the point where the asphalt had cracked and now bent inward toward the center of the earth like a gaping mouth.

Hell of a place for this to happen, he thought.

Highway 91 was the only way in to Garmella, Arizona—and the only way out—and as Derrick looked to his left a few yards past the sinkhole, he could see where the shoulder of the road dipped dramatically to the left, and, just a few steps past the guardrail, became a steep embankment that led to the ravine below, leaving only a precipice on the western side of the road. To the east, on the right side of the hole from where he sat currently, was a forty-foot high wall of rock that hugged the interstate for several miles down the mountain. Derrick had always thought the landscape a welcoming entrance to the town, the tight road suddenly opening up into a picturesque flatland of homes and trees and distant mountainscapes. But for tonight, and at least for the next few days, he assumed, despite Amber's faith in the efficiency of her state's public works, the geography of the area would make the town a prison. Until the road was repaired, no one was driving in or out of Garmella.

That was fine with Derrick, though, he and Amber's partying plans for the night notwithstanding. The farthest he'd ever been from Garmella was Phoenix, and that was when he was a junior in high school and Pima made it to the 2A state basketball championship game. And even that trip had just been overnight. His family barely went on vacation when he was a kid, and when they did, it was either a weekend trip to the Grand Canyon or to some national park in Flagstaff.

But Derrick Zamora had a truck now, the single inheritance he'd gotten from his grandfather following the old man's sudden death over the winter, and as soon as the summer was over—or when he'd saved enough cash to last him a month or two, whichever came first—Derrick was heading east. If he and Amber were still a thing by then, which he truly hoped, he'd invite her to come along, but either way, come September, he was gone.

Derrick parked the truck at what he estimated to be a safe distance from the sinkhole and opened the door slowly, and then he walked toward Amber, stopping a step or two back from where she stood, not even pretending to be as brave as she.

"Damn, Derrick. Look at that." Amber shook her head slowly in wonder, her eyes riveted to the crater below. "What do you think made it?"

Derrick shrugged. "I don't know. What do you mean? It's erosion, right? Water makes the ground underneath soft or something and then it collapses in on itself."

Amber raised her eyebrows and tilted her chin to her chest, now staring hard at Derrick as she grinned impressively. "Well, damn, Mr. Geography."

Derrick frowned, unconsciously deciding not to correct his girlfriend on her misapplied science moniker.

"It hasn't rained in three months though," she added absently.

Derrick pursed his lips and nodded. It was a good point; though, in truth, it was probably closer to two months than three since Garmella had seen its last significant rainfall. Still, Amber's argument was well-taken. Despite being in Arizona, theirs was a mountain town, seven-thousand feet up, with plenty of green and rainfall amounts that were about double the state average. Still, though, Garmella wasn't Seattle, and drought had descended upon the town of just under four hundred in late spring and had shown no signs of releasing its grip. And though Derrick was no geologist—Amber's impression of him aside—he was pretty sure sinkholes occurred in places where rain occurred with some frequency.

"So what are *you* saying?" he asked, genuinely interested in Amber's theories.

"About what?"

"You asked what *I* thought made the hole, now I'm asking you."

Amber puckered her lips and shrugged. "I don't know. I don't know anything about this stuff. I just think it's strange that the one road into this town suddenly has a big hole in it, right at a spot where the shoulder drops off a cliff and you can't go around and pick it up again."

Now Derrick was even more intrigued. He gave a broad smile. "So, Russians then?"

Amber chortled. "That's fine. Make fun. Your theory doesn't make any more sense than mine though."

"Yeah, well—"

"Derrick, look!" Amber pointed to a spot in the sky, in the distance over the mountains.

"I...what?"

"Kill the lights!"

"What?"

"The headlights! Turn 'em off!"

Derrick nodded obediently and then jogged quickly back to the truck, reaching through the window and twisting the small headlight control on the dash to shut off the beams. In seconds, he was back by the sinkhole standing next to Amber.

"You see it?" she asked, her finger still directing his gaze toward the heavens.

He squinted and stared toward the clear night sky, trying to find the source of his girlfriend's interest. He craned his head forward, shaking it slowly, and when he was about to give up and insist on the reveal, he saw it.

The sky, which had been garlanded with stars every night for what seemed like a year now, suddenly contained a void, a darkness over the horizon that Derrick barely recognized anymore. But it came to him in a moment, the recognition, and a grin the size of the crescent moon above drifted across his face.

Storm clouds.

"Damn, Derrick, is that what I think it is?"

"I sure as shit hope so."

"That's crazy, right? We were just talking about rain and then...man, it's beautiful."

The two young lovers—Derrick twenty-two, Amber nineteen—stood silently for several minutes as they watched the billowy black mass creep like ivy across the sky, methodically devouring each star in its path like a blue whale skimming krill from the ocean.

"We should maybe go," Derrick said absently, the instinct not to get caught in a rainstorm coming from somewhere deep in his gut. "Looks like it's gonna be quite the squall."

Not a second later, as if generated by Derrick's words, the black clouds lit to white as a surge of electricity exploded somewhere inside the gaseous form, sending horizontal bolts of lightning into the blackness.

Amber scoffed and shook her head slowly and with determination. "I'm not going nowhere, bucko. Are you insane? It hasn't rained in forever and this is too cool to miss."

"We don't have to miss it. I just think we should get back to town before the sky opens up."

"That's the point. The rain is gonna enter the town right here. And I wanna be the first one in Garmella to feel it."

Derrick rubbed his forehead and sighed, feeling the burn of frustration rising in his chest. Amber's stubbornness had always been a weirdly attractive character trait, but it also made their relationship difficult at times. She never let a rude waitress or clerk off the hook without a comment, and he'd been thrust into more than a couple of fistfights because of her inability to let a catcall fall by the wayside. He loved Amber, but he knew she would have to change—at least a little—if she was going to become Mrs. Zamora one day. Once he left Garmella, Derrick had goals and milestones he planned on hitting with each month and year that passed, and he couldn't have Amber Godwin questioning every move he made along the way. Maybe when it was time to go and he set the rules down clearly and passionately with her, she would fall in line, change her ways and commit to growing with him. He hoped so, for both their sakes.

For now, though—tonight, at least—he was content to revert to his common pattern of compliance and let Amber dictate the way the night would go. It was about to rain after all, so not a night for fighting.

"Fine, but I'm going to move the truck to the side of the road. I don't need some Speedy Gonzalez smashing into the back of me on his way out of Dodge. All the good these damn cones did."

Amber seemed not to hear Derrick, her attention still spellbound by the atmosphere beyond, where the clouds were now a three-quarter blanket of black, with the leading edge pulled back from the sky, leaving the moon and a cluster of a dozen stars still uncovered.

Derrick backed the Ranger up until he'd cleared the rock wall on the east and then drove slowly to the opposite shoulder, parking the truck along the guardrail on the edge of the drop-off. The truck's headlights were still pointing toward the hole, though from a bit further away now, not quite illuminating the sinkhole with the same level of light as before. He exited the truck and walked back toward Amber who was now tilting her head up, face toward the sky. She lifted her hands and brushed back her long auburn hair from her face, and as the first large drops of rain fell on her forehead, she began to laugh.

Derrick stopped about five paces from Amber and stared at the girl with a certain mild wonder, struck by her youth and beauty as if seeing her for the first time.

"Listen." Amber clucked her head forward now, turning her neck slightly as she put her ear to the sky.

Derrick obeyed and heeded the night, and immediately he heard a muffled whooshing sound rising from the valley like a distant wind. It was barely detectable at first, but within seconds, it built to the noise of a rushing river.

"Look!" Amber pointed to a spot in the road past the sinkhole.

There was only blackness there, but Derrick could feel in his bones the cascade of rain just beyond, only yards away now, approaching them like a stampede of horses, growing louder with each second that passed.

The showers ravaged Amber first, as she was still several paces ahead of her boyfriend, and Derrick could barely contain the pangs of desire that blossomed in him. "Dammit," he said to himself, grinning at the girl's irresistibility.

Within moments, Derrick was caught in the torrent as well, the cool feel of the droplets on his skin almost inexpressibly refreshing, orgasmic. He felt the urge now to run to Amber, to squeeze up behind her and press his damp body against hers, to celebrate the return of rain to Garmella in some physical, quasi-sexual way.

But he calmed his loins quickly, deciding instead to keep his current distance, to allow each of them to take in the magic of the rain independently. Derrick never took his eyes off Amber, however, and though he could barely see her anymore—the visibility in the pounding storm now almost zero—he could still see her silhouette in the shine of the headlights. He took two steps forward, clearing his eyes and forehead as he did, and when he removed his hands from his face, he saw what appeared to be a flow of dark shapes emerging from the sinkhole only a few feet away from where Amber was standing.

Derrick wiped his eyes again, frantically this time, blinking in frustration and incredulity, trying to will his vision into a clearer view of what was happening ahead. The sight was still blurry, but the shapes remained, as black as the sky itself, and they appeared to be crawling—climbing—the movements of an animal, their thin, wiry limbs pulling their bodies from the hole with ease, the haziness of their forms never coming into focus.

Derrick tried to make sense of the shapes, attempting to keep his focus on the blackened shadows, his heart and lungs now in overdrive, threatening to shut down his brain if it didn't come up with an answer soon.

But before his mind could reconcile the forms in the sinkhole with the reality of the world, the shapes suddenly stopped, and those that had already emerged quickly disappeared into the night, drifting away like smoke from a chimney.

Derrick forced himself to move, running forward until he was again at the edge of the hole next to Amber. He stared into the bottomless chasm in front of him, his chest and throat as tight as a corset as he craned his neck forward, trying to make some sense of what he'd just seen. But there was nothing there, and he stared off to his left now, taking a couple steps in the direction the shapes had appeared to be moving before they vanished.

"Amber," Derrick said, his voice dreamy and confused as he continued to search the landscape, staring straight ahead now at the road that wound down the mountain beyond the sinkhole, "we need to go." He snapped his eyes back to his left again, expecting the forms to be approaching from that direction, or to see them simply standing there at attention, ready to attack. But there was nothing other than the blur of the soaked night.

It was just a trick of the light, he thought. *Amber hadn't seen the movement, so maybe it was the vantage of his position, just a strange shadow caused by the rain and headlights.*

But Amber had been looking to the sky, basking in the rain, so she wouldn't have seen the forms at her feet even in the light of day. It was no trick of rain and refraction; Derrick didn't know what he'd seen, not exactly, but whatever it was, it was real.

But what? What could even come close to fitting the description of what he had just witnessed?

"You felt the rain," Derrick barked. "Let's get on the road now."

Amber ignored the command and instead lifted her arms high now, reaching her hands toward the sky as if offering some type of pagan prayer to the gods. She stood this way for several moments and then began to spin in slow dervish circles, laughing.

"Amber, we *need* to go," Derrick repeated, sternly now. "And you need to take a couple steps back."

As if to torment Derrick, Amber sauntered even closer to the sinkhole so that she was now only a step or two away from the rim, her head still to the sky, oblivious.

"Amber!"

Derrick moved in to grab Amber, slipping on the lunge, the rain having brought to the surface oils that had lain dormant for almost ten weeks now. But he regained his footing quickly and grabbed the girl at her wrist just as she was about to take another step back, one that, were it not for Derrick, may have been the last purposeful movement she ever made in her life.

"Jesus Christ, Amber! What the hell are you doing?"

"What?"

"*What?* I just saved your fucking life!"

Amber snatched her wrist from Derrick's hand and then pushed him backwards, both palms in the middle of his chest. "The fuck off of me, Derrick. What the hell are you doing, huh?" She squinted and shook her head, disgusted. "Goddamn, man, you're so...ugh. Just leave me alone. If you're so freakin' scared of the rain, get on out. I'll be fine here by myself."

"You almost fell in!" He paused. "And I saw..." He hesitated again, trying to recall the images he'd seen earlier in the sinkhole. Only a couple of minutes had passed since then, not more than three or four, and already he was doubting whether he'd seen anything at all. Maybe it was some eruption of underground oil, he now considered. Or a tree that had been growing underground, one that, once the sinkhole was formed, slowly made its way to the surface, even accelerating now through some layer of dirt that the rain had softened. Perhaps the latent tree had even caused the sinkhole, Derrick pondered, which would have explained its occurrence despite the lack of rain.

None of that made sense, of course; if it was oil or a tree, either would still be visible right now. Derrick was grasping.

"I'm not even close! Look!"

She was a yard away, if that. "I'm not going anywhere," Derrick said, trying to bring the conversation down a peg, though, in the pouring rain, his words were drowned, and he had to project his voice, making all of what he said sound like yelling. "Just be careful. It's wet now and it's hard to see the edge of the hole." He checked the sky again. "And in a minute or two, the moon'll be covered and then it's going to be pitch black."

"'K, dad," Amber replied, sneering. "I'll be extra careful."

Derrick shook his head, annoyed, but he kept his eyes on his girl. Amber was flexing her stubbornness muscle to its full capacity, but he was still responsible for her, and if anything happened to her at that sinkhole, the blame would fall fully on his shoulders, just as it should.

Amber shook her hair out now and reached down to the hem of her shirt, crisscrossing her arms at her chest and then lifting the garment over her head.

"What are you doing, Am?"

"I'm getting naked. What's it look like?"

She reached both hands around to the clasp of her bra now, but as she was about to snap it loose, she stopped in the middle of the motion, standing frozen for just a moment before taking a step backwards.

"Derrick?" she said, her voice trembling, teetering on a cry.

"What is it?" Derrick's voice was the masculine mirror of Amber's, shaky and frightened, and the dark shapes from minutes ago snapped back to the front of his mind.

"I saw something, Derrick. I...Just now. Just in the distance. I don't know what, but—"

"Where?"

"I...I don't know. Just...through the rain. It was blurry but...I don't know what it was. I don't even know...what it could have been."

Derrick grabbed Amber's arm again, gently, and this time she let him guide her away from the hole, and they both walked slowly backwards for several paces before finally turning toward the truck which was still parked along the guardrail on the embankment.

They picked up their pace now until they were almost running, following the beckoning glow of the headlights.

They were close now, less than ten yards from the truck, when a long, thin shape passed in front of the dual beams, stretching a shadow over the pair before instantly disappearing into the dark.

They both stopped instantly.

"Did you see that?" It was Amber, nearly hysterical. "What the fuck was that?"

"It was...I don't know. A deer maybe. I saw it earlier...I—"

"You saw a *deer* earlier? Or you saw *something?* Cuz whatever I saw back by the sinkhole wasn't no deer. And that sure as shit wasn't one either." Amber was yelling now, crying, and Derrick raised his hands in front of his face, palms out in a pressing motion, signaling for her to calm down.

"It's probably Omar and Kenny fucking with us. That's why they're not hanging—"

But before Derrick could finish his bolstering statement, the form reemerged in the headlights, this time stopping in front of the beams, looming in the glow, presenting itself as a towering silhouette at the front of the truck.

It wasn't Omar or Kenny; that much Derrick knew for sure.

"Derrick?" Amber squeaked.

Derrick squinted toward the shape, his eyes simultaneously filling with the driving rain and tears of panic. The shape appeared almost featureless in the shafts of light, at least a foot taller than Derrick, and it stood erect—almost perfectly—so straight and still that it appeared as much like a tree as a man.

Yet despite its symmetry and body design—which was familiar, recognizable as something resembling a human, with shoulders that arched high above its long torso and arms that hung like frozen branches down past its waist to the middle of its upper legs—it was blurry, formless at times, the black outline bleeding constantly into the air, yet recollecting back to form just before lingering too far.

Derrick tried desperately to make sense of the image, to place it within the context of all he knew to be scientifically possible. It was alive, there was little doubt about that; Derrick had seen it move, as did Amber. It had crawled from the pit like some misty crocodile, and Derrick quickly reminded himself that he had seen at least two more, though the things had been so close to each other it was difficult to tell where one creature had ended and another began.

The rain began to ease slightly now, and Derrick could now make out the being's head a bit more clearly, even noting the outlines of features, though nothing he could definitively call a face.

"What...what do you want?" Derrick asked finally, yelling the words, instinctually taking a tone that was assertive, aggressive, though through the rain his voice sounded timid to his own ears, impotent.

The creature stood motionless, giving no indication that it had heard Derrick at all. Its position directly in the front of the truck eliminated any chance of Derrick and Amber using the Ranger as a means of escape, so, for just a moment, Derrick considered grabbing Amber's hand and running with her back down the road toward town. If the thing wasn't going to allow them passage to the truck, then they could try to jog the seven miles home, walking when they became exhausted. It would be the trek of a lifetime, in the pouring rain at night with some skeletal black form lurking in the dark behind them, but at least it would give them a chance.

And that led to another possibility: that perhaps this thing standing before them *wanted* Derrick and Amber to flee, that its purpose was to frighten them off, allowing it to carry out whatever secret reason it had for being there.

But Derrick quickly reconsidered the flight notion, remembering again the other pit creatures he had seen and that were possibly lingering somewhere beyond the light. With that scenario, strolling along the dark mountain road on foot probably wasn't the best play, at least not immediately. Besides, they had eyes on this creature, so, until he had no other choice, he would see out this showdown.

The young couple stood their ground for what seemed like ten minutes but was probably closer to two, neither speaking as they studied the form, both barely breathing, waiting for the black shadow to give even the slightest jerk or flutter.

And then, as if triggered by some unseen signal, the creature's head twitched just a hair, down and to the left, as if it were noticing some sound or motion coming from behind. The movement left a puff of residue lingering in its wake, floating in the air for just a moment before finding its source again.

The movement seemed benign at first, but only seconds later the stalk-like figure bent forward at the waist and twisted its body in a long sweeping motion until its torso was turned entirely around so that the shape was facing the truck.

The creature's back was to the couple now, and the instinct to run again emerged in Derrick's mind. But, as if reading Derrick's mind, the thing took two long strides to its left and was suddenly out of sight again.

"Shit, Derrick!" Amber cried. "Where is it? Shit!"

Derrick said nothing in response, his stare still frozen on the void left by the creature. But the thing hadn't left for good—Derrick could still hear it in the night—and then, suddenly, the headlights of the Ranger flashed wildly toward the sky, and the flash was immediately followed by the sound of the truck rocking back to the ground before settling.

There was a lull of silence, five seconds perhaps, and then the headlights scattered again as the truck was turned upside down, flipped to its roof in one smooth motion. Derrick stared in wonder as his vehicle balanced for just a moment atop the guardrail and then toppled down to the ground on the opposite side of the barrier.

"Oh, god!" Amber whimpered, a verbal acknowledgement of the strength required to push four thousand pounds of metal and rubber up over a guardrail.

Derrick watched helplessly as the vehicle rolled back to its tires on the other side of the rail, completing a revolution; but the force of the thrust was enough to send the Ranger another quarter turn so that it rolled again until the driver's side door was flat on the ground. This time, however, the body of the truck caught the slope and the pull of gravity below, and in a wink, the pickup plunged from the landscape into a freefalling plummet down the side of the mountain.

"No!" Derrick yelped, a desperate response that included a combination of the loss of his truck, the inhuman strength of whatever monster was before them, and the help-less situation in which he and Amber now found themselves.

Amber screamed, bending at the knees as she did, putting her full energy into the shriek. And then, without another thought, she turned toward the road and ran, taking the choice about what to do next into her own hands.

Derrick watched her go, as if witnessing her in a dream, desiring to call her name but incapable of producing the sound lodged deeply in his throat. He turned back to the monster now—unconsciously settling on the word for the moment, as he was aware of no other one that could truly de-scribe it—hearing the final sounds of his destroyed truck set-tling at the bottom of the ravine resonate up the mountain.

Derrick searched the night for the monster now, trying to locate the spot where it had been only seconds earlier, but it was gone. Without the illumination of the headlights, it was possible that it was standing right in front of him, blend-ing in with the rain and darkness.

Derrick spun frantically, rotating a full three-sixty, searching desperately for the black vision that had twisted his innocent evening with Amber into a nightmare. But he couldn't find it, and, spurred by instinct and despair, he ran forward toward the ground where the beast had stood only seconds ago. He stopped when he reached the edge of the drop-off, looking first down into the ravine and then along the ridge in both directions.

Nothing.

Then, in the darkness of the night, perhaps a hundred or so yards from where he stood, Derrick heard a scream. It was high-pitched, feminine, a sound that was a mixture of both fear and agony.

Amber.

He turned toward the road again, his eyes wide with terror and helplessness as he listened to Amber's cries quickly choke to silence.

Derrick closed his eyes, squeezing them tightly now as if trying to force himself to wake from a terrible dream. He stood that way for five seconds or so, during which time his mind quickly switched back to survival mode, trying to find a way out of the horror of his situation. Derrick finally opened his eyes again, and when he did, instead of seeing the sheer cliff face that ran the length of Route 91, his vision met the black torso of the monster from the sinkhole.

It was only a foot or two from Derrick, and before he could unleash a scream to match the one Amber had released seconds earlier, the creature's arms whipped forward with a speed that was unlike any animal that existed on the planet, though its murky shape seemed to dull the quickness just slightly.

Derrick felt only the slightest prick of cold on his face, but as the mysterious creature held his face in its hands—claws that were like cages at the end of some nightmarish scarecrow—his mind suddenly slipped from that moment of unimaginable terror and began to flood with visions and experiences from his twenty-two years on earth. Millions of memories and ideas invaded his brain all at once, most of which he'd thought were long erased from his hippocampus, never to be resurrected again.

Derrick was no stranger to psychedelics, having eaten more than his share of mushrooms in his short lifetime, most during the summer after senior year; and though those encounters were met with quite a bit of success—good trips being his definition of the word—nothing came close to the voyage his mind was on at that moment. It was a deconstruction of his being.

An unraveling.

But as quickly as this deluge of recollection arrived it was gone—his lifetime in a few seconds—and Derrick was now back in the moment, standing at the edge of a pit in Garmella, staring at the face of something long, black and terrible. Not ugly or hideous, the way one might describe a monster from a nightmare, but blank, absent, as vacant from life as anything he could imagine.

Suddenly its empty face formed slight contours near its chin and forehead, something resembling the features of a face, and then the lined wrinkle at the bottom opened slightly, as if to speak. But the words Derrick heard came not into his ears, but to his mind.

"Tell me your evil."

Derrick felt his breathing accelerate, his face flush as beads of sweat built at the top of his forehead. He knew instinctively what the thing was asking of him, knew it as clearly as he knew the date of his birth. How he was so sure he couldn't have said, but the torrent of his lifespan seconds earlier had everything to do with it.

But he couldn't dredge up the memory—never—so he clarified, instinctively stalling. "What do you want?"

"Tell me your evil."

Derrick shook his head, the pain of the memory fighting to get to the forefront of his mind, fighting to come out for its master's survival. But Derrick was vigilant, keeping himself distracted. "No," he whimpered. He was crying now, shaking his head, pleading. "No."

The cold pressure of the creature's hand turned warm, and then, as if the monster were a lightning rod in a thunderstorm, its hands sent a bolt of pain that encompassed the entire mass of Derrick Zamora's skin and bone and tissue, devolving his body from a thing of cellular life into a statue of black carbon death.

Seconds later, the creature moved its hand from Derrick's face to his neck and then dragged his corpse to the edge of the Route 91 sinkhole that had appeared as if magically only a day earlier.

And there it waited patiently, for just a minute or two, until the second of the three black forms appeared through the rain, hauling with it the carcass of its own kill, that of Amber Godwin.

Each dropped its lifeless prize into the pit, minding it no longer than the two or three seconds each body took to flop from the precipice into the endless cavity.

There was no time to savor, no time to appreciate. They were there to collect.

And collect they would.

CHAPTER TWO

THE RUMBLE FIRST CAME to Josh Carter in a dream, deep-toned and gloomy, a sound that was obviously generated by the lumbering stomp of a distant T-Rex marching through the dry ground of a fern forest. Josh didn't have visual of the creature, but he could picture the slow, searching swivel of the beast's head, its huge mouth brushing against lush, overhanging branches, jaws locked in a sinister, smiling overbite as it hunted, seemingly with glee.

And then something deeper in the boy's mind roused, sending an alert to Josh's cortex, signaling that the rich, bass sound from the forest had, in fact, come from somewhere else in the endless stretch of time and place and was caused by a thing larger and vaster than the sum of all the prehistoric reptiles that had ever lived.

Josh opened his eyes and was now facing the door-side wall of his bedroom. His breathing was frantic, his tee shirt damp with sweat. In a moment, his eyes adjusted to the dark and he could now see the perfect completion of Mike Trout's swing, the poster of Josh's idol having been tacked to his wall two years earlier, eye-level at his request. The slugger's powerful follow-through brought a sudden feeling of comfort to the eleven-year-old resident of Garmella, Arizona.

Josh's vision dipped to the foreground now, to his nightstand, where a digital clock read 12:12. The symmetry of the time felt somehow peaceful, and it helped further to bring him down from the terror of being hunted by an eight-ton killing machine.

He rolled a quarter-turn to his right so that he was now on his back, and he lay staring at the ceiling. He took several deep breaths, closing his eyes as he did, and with each exhalation he relaxed a little more.

Brrmmmmmmmm.

The rumble again, this time sustained for several seconds, and Josh's eyes flashed wide, his heart regaining the tempo from seconds earlier. He sat up straight in his bed and lifted his chin high, his mouth slightly open as he tilted his right ear toward the window of his bedroom trying to locate the sound, praying it had been caused by the thing upon which his mind had already settled.

He swung his legs to the floor gently and stood, putting as little weight as possible on the cold, hardwood planks, not wanting the groaning floorboards of the old house to mask the distant sound, fearing he would miss the noise when it returned.

A flash of light outside followed by *Boom!*

This time the noise crashed into Josh's room like the cretaceous monster from his dream, and he lurched back onto his bed, scooting rearwards on his mattress until he slammed his back against the headboard, causing an even louder blast.

Thunder—there was no mistaking it this time—and it was followed in a moment by the plopping twang of drops against his window.

It was raining. Finally.

Within moments, a door down the hallway opened and seconds later a ribbon of light appeared beneath Josh's door.

Excited whispers drifted into his room now and he stared with anticipation at the handle of his bedroom door as it turned clockwise.

The door pushed open.

"Josh!"

Ray.

"Hey, what's going on in here, buddy? What was that thumping sound?"

Josh shook his head in silence.

Ray Bronigan walked into his stepson's bedroom wearing the smile of a villain. He leaned in close to Josh and put his hand on the back of his head, pulling it forward gently, lightly grabbing a tuft of hair at the back. "It's raining, buddy. Can you believe it?"

Ray lingered at eye level for a moment longer, hoping to elicit the joy from the boy that he, Ray, was feeling. Not receiving it, he frowned and stood tall and then walked to the bedroom window, pushing aside the plain white drapes that shielded the beauty of the dark, clouded sky. He stood there with his arms crossed, unmoving, only inches from the glass, rapt by the approaching storm.

Josh watched his stepfather curiously, with a dusting of fright, wanting both to join him at the window and for him to leave immediately.

Ray turned back to Josh again and flickered his eyes. "Should we go outside?"

Josh opened his mouth to speak, but his jaw hung lamely, unsure about how to reply.

"It's too late for all that."

The response came not from Josh but from his mother, Deedee, who stood leaning against her son's doorframe, a tattered Sun Devils t-shirt hanging loosely down to her thighs, an unlit cigarette dangling from her lips. Her voice was groggy and annoyed, the words themselves dismissive as she attempted to ignite the flame of a bright pink plastic lighter.

"And y'all'll just get all wet anyway and make a mess in the hall. And guess who'll have to clean that up? Just wait til morning. Makes no sense goin' out there now."

Deedee Bronigan finally spun the metal wheel of her Bic with enough force to bring the lighter to life, and then she dipped the open end of the cigarette to the dancing flame, singeing the exposed tobacco of the Winston Light to orange before instantly inhaling and releasing a plume of smoke to the shadows. The relief in the sound of her breath was like that of a diver coming up for air.

"Might not be raining in the morning, Dee," Ray snapped back, now facing his wife of eight years, two of which—years five and six—had been spent divided by a thick layer of polycarbonate glass while Ray served his time for a class 2 felony theft conviction. "Ain't rained since April last I recall, so I don't expect we should put too much faith that this storm's gonna be a two-day monsoon."

Deedee scoffed a cloud of smoke into Josh's room, another trivialization of her husband's notions. "Do whatever you want, but Josh has to go to camp tomorrow, so I don't want him all tired in the morning. And he gets sick from being out in that rain, that camp's gonna call me, which means I'm the one that's gonna have to leave work." Then, as an addendum, she added, "Lord knows you ain't gonna wake up and go get him."

Josh thought the reply was a bit mean, unnecessary, searching for a fight. Ray had the reputation of a troubled past, but he'd kept straight for the past couple of years, and he'd been called back for a second interview at the Grieg, working on the maintenance crew, which would be the first real, sustained employment he'd had since getting out of the pen. Still, Deedee gave the man little slack, and she took the chance to expose Ray's vulnerabilities at every opportunity.

Of course, Ray wasn't much softer with his criticisms of Deedee, though perhaps a little more reluctant to offer them as pointlessly. In any case, the battle usually began with a throwaway line similar to the one his mother had just offered, and once it was out, it landed like a grenade, precipitating at least an hour of verbal gunplay.

"What's that supposed to mean? Why you gotta—"

"I'll go out with you if you want, Ray," Josh interrupted, addressing his stepfather by name for what felt like the first time in his life. The word 'Ray' felt foreign in his mouth, even though he said it aloud all the time, talking to his mom or his friends at school or whatever.

Ray let his glare linger on Deedee, who seemed not to have the least bit of concern for the scar she'd left on her husband. Finally, he dipped his eyes to Josh and frowned and then took a deep breath as he closed his eyes, keeping them shut for several seconds as he cleared his mind. He then shook his head slowly, methodically. "Nah, your mom's right. It's late. Wouldn't want you catching nothin.' Probably be raining when you wake up anyway. Like she said."

Ray said nothing else as he walked toward Josh's bedroom door and gently pushed past Deedee, who did a kind of *ole* as he passed. She turned back toward Josh, grinning and shaking her head.

"Get some sleep, little man. There's Eggo's in the freezer for breakfast. Chocolate chip, I think. Mrs. Demartis'll be here at seven—I'll be long gone by then—so make sure you're ready to go."

Josh nodded. "I will."

Deedee gave an obligatory wave of her hand to clear the smoke from her son's room and then blew a kiss toward Josh as she closed the door.

Josh waited for the door to latch and then leaned back on his mattress again, replaying the exchange that had just occurred between his mother and Ray as he studied the ceiling above him. It was going to get worse, he knew that, and at this point, as much as he understood the strain it would put on his mom for a few months, and perhaps longer, he just wanted them divorced.

But in two more days he wouldn't have to worry about that relationship anymore, at least for the rest of the summer. Dwayne Carter arrived from Amarillo on Sunday, and Josh would be going back to Texas with his dad until school started again.

Josh had no memories of living with his father, he and his mother had divorced before Josh's second birthday, and for all he knew, his parents' relationship was no better than the one between his mom and Ray. But Josh felt more of connection with his dad than he ever did with his mom, and though he would never say it aloud—to either of his parents—he'd always wished his dad would have gotten custody of him.

The thought of his father's arrival suddenly instilled a new energy in Josh, and, having heard the door to his mother's room close—with no ensuing argument between his mom and Ray carrying over from his room to theirs—he slipped out of his bed and walked to the window, standing in the spot where Ray had been only minutes earlier. He stared through the falling rain to the outline of the mountains in the distance, absently wondering if water was falling on the other side as well. His eyes then dropped a level closer, but still to an area several miles out, landing now on the huge dark radio telescope that rose like an alien spaceship from the earth. Despite its distance and the density of the rain, the outline of the massive disc was distinct, imposing, taller than any tree in the area and by far the most recognizable feature of the landscape.

Josh scanned the surroundings closer to his own home now, bringing his gaze in gradually, his eyes slowly adjusting to the graphite outlines of barns and silos and windmills that peppered the vast acreage of the Tanner farm, the immense piece of land that shared a small border with his family's humble property.

Despite Josh's wish to live with his father, and his anticipation to go back to Texas, Josh was mostly happy living in Garmella, even with the angst caused by his mother and Ray. It was a small town in terms of permanent population, but it saw a fair share of visitors and vacationers, and there were three kids in Josh's class whom he could call a 'real' friend, as well as another handful with whom he got along fine. And there was even a girl, Rebecca Minor, whom he liked and she him, though at his age, he didn't really know what that meant as far as next steps.

But what he really wanted was to live in a new house, a different house, and there was little he could imagine that he wouldn't have given to live in the house next door on the Tanner farm. Compared to his own residence, which was a drab, powder blue rambler that sat on an island of dirt at the end of a rubble driveway, the Tanner farm was a rolling vista of rocky green beauty, with a serpentine creek that seemed to meander everywhere on the property, and teams of horses and cows luxuriating in paradise, roaming and running and eating to their hearts' delights. And the torture of it was, of course, that this was no setting on a television show or picture in a book; the farm was the backdrop to Josh's life, the property line mocking him only thirty or so paces from Josh's ground-level bedroom.

So, every morning when he woke and scanned the beginning of his day through the back window, Josh's eyes would land first on the dirt patches of his own backyard, taking in the rusted playground and broken gate that seemed to scorch his retina each time they met. But within seconds, as he lifted his gaze just six inches or so, the magic of the Tanner meadow came into full view. On breezy days, the tall reeds of lush grass would sway elegantly, watching magnanimously through the fence at the brown weeds sprouted randomly around Josh's yard.

Thoughts of the crisp farmland suddenly overwhelmed Josh, and, almost in a panic, as if compelled by some spiritual force of nature, he gripped the base of his window and lifted it to its full width, immediately relishing the fresh, foreign smell of the rain that rushed into his room like a ruptured dam of moist oxygen.

The sensory experience nearly brought Josh to tears; he hadn't realized until that moment how much he missed the element of rain. Ray had been right—Josh had known it in the moment—they should have gone out together in it. They should have spent the rest of the night splashing and laughing and soaking up as much water as they could. What that would have felt like!

Josh closed his eyes and listened now to the sound of the pattering drops. There was simply nothing like it. Not just the slap of water on the concrete patio or the clatter upon the siding, but the vibration of the droplets in the air, the *shush!* through the sky. It was indescribable, really, truly magnificent.

Josh put his nose against the screen now, wishing he could stick his face through the opening and feel the water fall directly on his head and face. With his eyes still closed, he allowed his neck to go limp and his forehead to drop forward, pressing now in a relaxed state against the screen. And, as if his wish to feel rain had been spoken to a genie, the mesh partition, already torn and weak at every corner, popped forward, dropping limply to the backyard, landing on the muddy ground without a sound. The barrier between his room and the world was broken, and the crisp wet air of nature quickly replaced the hazy staleness of Winston smoke.

Josh lurched backward and instinctively looked to his door, waiting silently for the sound of his mom or Ray to open their own door again and then make their way back down the hall. There would be less enthusiasm this time—Josh had no illusions about that—and the promise of a whipping would surely accompany the scolding, though the threat would never come to pass.

He gave it a few more seconds, praying the silence would continue. If they weren't arguing, they were either sleeping or doing adult things, both of which meant whatever he did for the rest of the night was of little concern to them.

Josh put his head out the window now, instinctively sticking out his tongue like a snake. But the eave above him extended too far from the roof, and any potential relief was caught in the cluttered gutter and was directed toward the mangled downspouts.

He grumbled and then stuck his hand out now, extending his torso through the opening so that his belly was now on the sill. Still, he could barely reach the place in the void where the sheets of water began, so he took one last peek toward the bedroom door and then lifted his leg to the sill and put his foot out the window, and then he quickly brought the other over and climbed through the opening until he was standing on the ground in his backyard.

He was still under the eave as he lifted his face to the sky, watching the huge drops come down at him in slow motion, emerging from the darkness like tiny, oval invaders the moment they reached the halo of the dim security light that came from the Martinez' house, their neighbors to the right.

Josh looked off to the Tanner Farm now, and as he prepared to take his first steps toward the barrier fence, to climb into the farm where he would enjoy the storm from the setting of his dreams, an object above the shed in the Martinez yard seized his attention.

Josh squinted and craned his neck forward, intrigued by the strange figure, which was thick and hazy, wavering slightly in the night.

"The heck?"

The Martinez house was slightly smaller than Josh's, but unlike his own family, the Martinez' took pride in their abode, keeping it up as nicely as anyone in the neighborhood, and one of the few families on the block that kept any semblance of a lawn. Such an achievement in Garmella required a good deal of work from Mr. Martinez, which meant working in the yard most weekends, as well as owning an inventory of garden tools and mowing supplies which he kept neatly in his shed.

And it was the shed that was now the source of Josh's attention. Atop the shelter, at the far end from where Josh stood in his yard, there seemed to be a dark cylinder rising from the roof, sticking up from the shed like a stove pipe chimney, even smoking slightly.

Except it's a shed, Josh thought. *Sheds don't have chimneys.* And besides, Josh had been looking at that shed for years, and he knew there was nothing on top that fit the description of what he was looking at currently.

Except there was tonight.

A bird?

Not likely. Not only did it make no sense for a crow or raven or some other black bird to be perched there at that time of night, the shape of the figure didn't fit either. It was too straight. Too thin. Certainly not an owl. And if it were a bird, its feathers were disintegrating slowly into the air.

Josh looked back to the farm and the dark wet fields beyond, weighing again whether to make the trespass, and when he looked back to the shed, to reconsider the shape again, it was gone.

"What the...?"

He walked toward the structure now, slowly, reluctantly, unconsciously forming an explanation for his middle-of-the-night presence in the yard of his neighbors. He quickly decided if Mr. or Mrs. Martinez happened to be up at this hour and were staring out at the rain—the same way he had been and probably many of his neighbors were—he would just give them the truth. He wasn't really doing anything wrong—other than trespassing, he supposed—and if they did catch him, the bonus was he could find out what he'd seen on the roof of the storage shed.

Josh was only a few steps from the structure now, his eyes remaining fixed on the roof and the spot where the shape had been. The rain was still driving, but the closer he got to the Martinez house, the better his visibility became.

A crackle of wood to his left.

Josh stopped and spun toward the sound, gasping as he did. He immediately began to backtrack towards his house, fearing that whatever had made the sound was somewhere in the tall grass of the Tanner Farm, stalking him, though he was likely safe with the fence in place.

He kept his eyes fixed on the land past the fence line though, now expecting a coyote to appear, perhaps even a bear, which he'd heard from Ray still roamed in parts of Arizona, though whether Garmella was one of those parts Josh was unclear.

But both of those possibilities were quickly eliminated when Josh spotted the shape from the roof again, just over the property line of the farm. Except now the shape was moving, its blurred form drifting away from him, moving at a quick walking pace. Josh's eyes soon adjusted to the darkness of the field, and he could now see the shape he'd seen above the shed was attached to a much taller shape, one as black and hazy as the head above it. It continued moving quickly through the grass, heading north, deeper into the Tanner property.

Instinctually, Josh ducked low, though there was nothing to truly hide him other than the night, and he watched in terrible fascination as the creature ascended the gradual slope up toward the Tanner house, in the direction of the Grieg Telescope.

Despite every impulse in his body telling him to run back inside, to wake his mother and Ray and describe what he'd seen in the Martinez yard and the Tanner farm, he decided to follow the form. If he didn't, he knew no one would believe his story, just as he wouldn't have believed them if the roles were reversed.

He let the black form take a few more steps into the grass of the Tanner farm, and when he heard a desperate moo-ing sound from a cow several yards away, Josh walked to the fence and climbed over, and then he began to follow.

CHAPTER THREE

CONSTRUCTION ON THE Johann Grieg Radio Telescope began in 1985 and saw first light in October of 1991. The six-year build time was almost two full years ahead of schedule, and, as a result, millions of dollars under budget, a pleasant combination of specs that was almost unheard of anywhere in the world for a project so large. By early 1992, the geniuses who had designed the telescope had it perfectly calibrated and adjusted for efficiency, and by summer of that same year, the mammoth device was in full operating mode, scanning the skies in search of signals from galaxies of almost unimaginable distances.

"You know that damn thing is searching the whole universe for noises?" Henry Kellerman had asked his son rhetorically one day during the first week of operation, scrunching his face while he stressed the word *universe*, as if perhaps he'd heard the description wrong and was now looking to his son for a correction.

But Jerry Kellerman's dad had been pretty close: the universe was the arena of the Grieg Telescope, and though the device obviously had its limits, to hear the people who knew about such things tell it, it was nothing short of a scientific wonder. The massive metal receiver was almost as tall as the Statue of Liberty—and twenty times as heavy—its wide, concave face positioned in a relentless stare toward space, ready to receive even the slightest of electromagnetic waves that might drift to Earth from the heavens.

"I heard some buzzing around the dish today," Jerry's dad would mention in passing to his son at least a couple times a year. And then, with a look both grave and thoughtful, he would ask, "Think an alien farted?"

Even when he could see the punchline coming from a mile away, Jerry would genuinely laugh at the joke every time, and even today, at forty-one years old, as he sat in the 4x8 guard gate at the only checkpoint of the Grieg compound, he still couldn't help but crack a smile. He missed his dad terribly, even now, almost a decade after his death. Jerry supposed it didn't help that he worked only steps from where the man had collapsed and died from a massive stroke during his morning crew meeting one spring day; the shared workplace meant the memories of the man often came in floods.

Yet, despite the monotony and boredom that accompanied his particular job, Jerry considered the work important, and this importance gave him a sense of satisfaction. And though the telescope and the barren acres on which it had been situated might have been relatively dull and unchanged since his childhood, the town of Garmella had evolved into a very different place since then. The town was always beautiful—a hidden gem in the mountains of Arizona that few people even knew was there for most of its existence—but with the construction of the Grieg telescope, the place had become somewhat of a local tourist destination.

It wasn't just the telescope itself that drew people in now, however, though there were still plenty of people who came for the science of the thing alone. In the summer months, geeks from as far east as Texas and the Oklahoma panhandle came to take the tour of the compound, which, in Jerry's opinion, was rather unspectacular as guided tours went.

It was the indirect effect of the telescope, however, that had given the town its main notoriety, and because of this effect, Garmella was now a small-town version of a sideshow attraction. For the Johann Grieg Radio Telescope to be effective—at least to the degree that it was intended—it required the air and space surrounding it to be completely absent of competing radio signals. And in the late seventies when the plans were drawn, and into the late eighties when construction began, the mass use of cellular technology did not exist. The science of the telescope was as advanced and progressive as anything on earth at the time, as were the minds developing it; still, a greater technology was on the horizon, and no one at the time saw the ubiquity of cell phones that was to come.

When a decade later the world was devoured by a plague of craned necks and swiping fingers, it was far too late to change the location of the telescope to a place more isolated. The result of these colliding technologies was that a ban was placed on cell phone use anywhere in Garmella, as well as on any other type of radio frequency. It wasn't ideal for the residents of the town—as even things like microwave ovens were frowned upon—but to outsiders looking for a spot where they could drop off the grid, Garmella was just the place.

Jerry looked at his watch—12:30 am. He had another four and half hours until his shift was up, and he could already feel his eyelids getting heavy. The truth was, of course, if he had really wanted to spend his shift curled up in the back of his pickup truck napping, no one would have known the difference. It was one of the many advantages of living in a quiet zone: if someone really wanted to check up on you, they had to do it in person.

But that wasn't Jerry's way. In the four years since he'd worked at the facility, except for the occasional nodding off on a particularly tough night, he'd never done anything other than what he was paid to do. His father had been a part of the first maintenance crew that oversaw basic upkeep and repairs on the telescope almost thirty years ago, and, as corny as such a connection might have seemed to most people, it was important to Jerry that he respected that legacy.

Pop! Pop!

The sound was like gunfire and came from above him, on the roof of the guard booth. Jerry sat straight in his chair, placing his palms flat on the desk in front of him, preparing to push himself up and dart toward whatever danger was producing the sound. He maintained the pose for several seconds, listening for the racket again, and a moment later the plunks came down in rapid fire, splattering above him like exploding acorns.

Jerry took a deep breath and sighed, and then he began to laugh.

"Ho-ly shit," he whispered, nodding with glee now. "It's about damn time."

He opened the booth door slowly and took the shallow step from the curb to the pavement, never taking his eyes from the dark sky as he walked out into the one-lane road. His mouth was agape as he scanned the night sky like the telescope looming above him in the distance. He wandered a few more steps until he was standing directly in front of the mechanical barrier arm, but the light from the booth was making visibility difficult, so he walked several more yards from the gate until the glare faded and all he could see was the wavy charcoal of the firmament above.

Rain. He almost couldn't believe it. He'd stopped looking at the weather outlook in the paper weeks ago; but still, if rain had been in the forecast, he would have heard about it from somewhere. He ate breakfast at Carla's Diner almost every morning after his shift—including the prior morning—and if the forecast had called for rain the next day, he certainly would have heard about it from that crowd.

Huge pellets of water were now splattering into his face and eyes, and within seconds, the drops became a deluge of heavy sheets. Jerry blinked several times, clearing his vision of the relentless moisture, and then he ran his hands through his hair and shook his head, spraying the area like a dog drying from a dip in a creek. Then, as if the vibrating motion triggered an area in the reasoning portion of his brain, he was reminded that he had no spare uniform to don—either in the booth or in his truck—and that sitting in soaking wet clothes for the rest of the night was probably not the best way to spend his shift.

He turned back to the booth now, and as he took the first step of retreat to the gate, a shadow, as tall as it was thin, entered the frame of the gate's rear window and then disappeared.

Jerry stopped so quickly he almost tripped over his feet, catching his breath with the same abruptness, releasing a gasp that was some mixture of confusion and terror. He wiped at his eyes again, trying desperately to clear the rain, no longer concerned with the drenching of his uniform. He swiveled his head slowly back and forth, trying to locate the dark shape again, but he knew in the blackness it was a useless task, and that only the light of the guard gate had allowed him the vision.

He turned toward the auxiliary maintenance building now, a long flat structure that was about the width of a small elementary school. The building was about forty yards from the gate and in the direction which (the man?) he'd just seen was heading. A dull orange glow came from a bulb above the entrance, giving a radius of light that stretched to the far corner of the structure.

Jerry took a deep breath and began to walk toward the building, and within moments he was only a few paces from the door. He looked back to the guard gate, the oasis of light there seeming to beckon for his return, offering the safety of its steel construction and illumination. But this was his job, his duty, and if someone had wandered onto the compound, it was his responsibility to find and apprehend him.

Jerry reached to his waist and wrapped the fingers of his right hand tightly around the handle of his baton, the weapon hanging holstered from his hip like an appendage. He stood directly in front of the door to the brick maintenance building now, and as he placed his left hand on the knob, the image of the dark shadow came to his mind again.

What had he seen exactly?

Jerry's brain flooded with ideas, none of which quite made sense. The thing was too tall. Too shapeless to be a man. It had looked as if the trunk of a tree had passed by the window. *Maybe that was it*, he thought. *The sudden onset of the storm had uprooted a tree and blown it past the booth. It was odd, for sure, but not impossible.*

But the tree explanation didn't fit. The speed at which it had crossed the window was too slow, the direction too upright and even. And there was a human movement to the shadow; Jerry hadn't seen anything resembling a head or torso, but as he replayed the two-second event in his brain once more, he thought he had seen...arms?

He shook his head once more, this time erasing his speculations, trying to focus on something closer to reality, though, in truth, he was at a loss. Despite the movement, whatever he had seen didn't quite meet the human test, and it certainly didn't fit the description of any animal he'd ever heard of anywhere in the world, let alone one that existed in these parts.

Jerry lingered under the awning of the structure for a few seconds, taking a moment to let the droplets of rain clear his face, and then he turned the knob to the door and pushed in.

He waited a beat before stepping inside the maintenance building, and as he lifted his foot to enter, he heard a crackling noise come from somewhere to his right. The sound was slow and deliberate, footsteps, fifteen yards or so down from the door, near the exterior corner of the warehouse at a spot where the light offered just the dimmest sliver of visibility.

Instinctively, Jerry unholstered his nightstick and turned to the sound, squinting as he tried to locate the source in the darkness of the early morning. His eyes fought to adjust to the shadowed corner, searching for some type of clarity in the fog of the downpour.

And then he spotted it again, the shape from moments ago, a figure so tall and thin it reminded Jerry of one of those stilted Mardi Gras walkers, the ones who dressed in bizarre masquerade costumes and marched in long, awkward strides through the streets, towering over the throngs of equally bizarre parade characters.

But this figure wasn't adorned in any bright peacock colors, nor did it move with any of the wobbly treachery of a stilt walker. Instead, it moved as if pushed along by the wind, with no swing of its arms as it strode. Jerry could just make out the outline of limbs against its torso, though its entire body was distorted by the rain, an image that didn't quite make sense but was the only explanation that was reasonable.

Jerry put his hand to his mouth, staggered by the sighting, feeling both nauseous and incontinent, his eyes filling with the burning tears of terror as he watched the cloudy creature cross the open gravel lawn in front of the warehouse before marching on toward the side of the building.

"Oh, Jesus," he whispered, the quintessential quiver of fear accompanying the words. There was little question in his mind now that whatever he had seen float behind the guard gate, and which was currently moving toward the back of the maintenance house, was organic. Animal. Alive.

Jerry stood stunned for several seconds, petrified and awestruck as he subconsciously tried to calculate the size of the black monster. Its head—or at least the portion of the creature that was highest up on its body, as he could see no clear definition of a head in the darkness—was only a couple of feet below the roof, which meant its height was closer to seven feet than it was to six.

Jerry took three deep breaths now and put his hands to his chest, his palms flat, fingers spread as if physically trying to slow the beating of his heart. He had to relax or he would hyperventilate, and he wasn't in the best shape anymore—never had been, really—and an episode like the one he was experiencing tonight could be the thing to send him to the grave if he wasn't careful.

It could just be a prank, he thought. It would have been an elaborate one for sure, and he couldn't think of anyone who had the time or the motivation to pull off such a stunt, but it was still a possibility, and, as he considered it further, it was one certainly better than any explanation involving a seven-foot-tall shadow creature.

Jerry pulled out his flashlight now and clicked it to life, and then, with the conscious thought not to replay in his mind what he'd just witnessed, he headed in the direction of the corner around which the figure had just vanished. He kept his chin high as he walked, looking toward the roof, thinking he might even glimpse the beast over the edge. But he had no visibility there, not really, and the thing wasn't quite that tall anyway, so Jerry increased his pace, walking briskly now, eager to discover both the truth of the sighting and, if what he had seen was indeed something dangerous, to deal with it. He was a big believer in the notion that the anticipation of a problem was usually much more debilitating than the problem itself, and the sooner you confronted it, the quicker it resolved. Of course, he usually reserved that idea for problems of the intellectual or emotional kind, but still, the same principle applied with physical confrontations as well, especially being a security guard where confrontation was pretty much the job.

The telescope.

The thought of the multi-billion-dollar piece of equipment that sat elevated above the town suddenly inspired Jerry, energizing him with the reminder that he was the first and only line of defense against would-be vandals or thieves. It was his *raison d'etre*—the reason for any security position—so if he wasn't going to put up a fight tonight, what was the point of him being there?

With this new sense of duty now lodged in his mind, he took off in a gallop to the side wall of the warehouse, and the moment he reached the corner, he stopped for just a moment before turning it, the baton out in front with one hand, the flashlight in the other.

He scanned the torch quickly but steadily from left to right, immediately seeing that the side of the building was empty. Jerry moved quickly now to the next corner, this time barely slowing as he turned left, his eyes darting as they investigated the long exterior wall that formed the rear of the shed.

Nothing.

He took a breath for what seemed like the first time in minutes as he stood staring down the length of the structure. He turned to his right now, away from the building, staring off to the first row of trees that began about a hundred yards from the warehouse and continued on for over four miles, rising gradually up the mountain before plateauing into a clearing in which the telescope sat watching the skies unceasingly. Jerry considered now the possibility that the thing he'd seen had simply kept walking into the woods and was perhaps hiding there for now, waiting for daylight. If that was the case, Jerry would never find it tonight, and he would have no choice but to log the event, call it in to the company, and report it to the new kid, whose shift followed his in the morning.

But he would wait to call the sheriff, at least for now, at least until he could come up with some explanation for what he'd seen, something to relay to the officers when they arrived.

Jerry returned his focus back to the warehouse and then jogged the length of the back wall, turning the corner that led to the last uninspected side of the rectangular building. As expected, he found only empty gravel there as well, so he continued along the side wall until he had completed his circumnavigation of the structure and was again at the front door, staring at the entrance as if it were a portal that led to another world.

The door to the warehouse was still open, Jerry having left it that way when he went to investigate the shadow figure, so he grabbed the knob once again and pulled it shut, relishing the sound of the thick bolt latching as it entered its metal hollow. He turned to head back to the guard gate now, and in that moment decided to make his call into the sheriff, (no cell phones were allowed in Garmella, but thank god for good old landlines), and as he began to walk to the booth, the dullest of thuds came from behind the door, a sound so gentle that on any other day it would have gone unnoticed.

Not tonight, however. Definitely not tonight.

Jerry closed his eyes, his back still to the door, his body resisting the urge to turn around again. *Just keep walking. Make the call first and then, if you still want to, you can go back and check out the noise. Or better yet, don't. Just wait for the guys with sidearms to show.*

The internal conversation happened in a half-second, and Jerry reminded himself that it was him leaving the door open that had likely invited in the source of the noise, a squirrel or raccoon or some other scurrying creature. The whole space was a clutter of shovels and tools and a thousand other things that could have made the noise.

And if he hadn't already seen the shadow creature, that's what he would have assumed.

"I can't call this in without knowing first," he said aloud, shaking his head as he spoke, as if understanding in the moment the wrong decision he was making.

And then an idea came to him, one he'd never considered in four years on the job.

Jerry turned and ran toward his F150 parked in the lot just in front of the guard gate, reaching it in seconds and quickly unlatching the tailgate, dropping the short rectangular door flat, exposing the bed and the gun locker tucked neatly against the right side. He fumbled in his pocket for his keys, blindly finding the correct one and inserting it into the lock in one fluid motion.

Three guns filled the locker—two rifles and a shotgun—and Jerry instinctively pulled the latter, feeling the close-range capability of that particular weapon would be the better choice. Firearms were technically forbidden on the job, and not issued by the company as part of the guard kit, so anything that happened once he picked up the gun would be all on him. But that was fine. If it turned out whatever he'd seen was some kind of nighttime mirage, the stretched-out shadow of an animal or some other trick of the light, well, then, no harm, no foul.

But if his eyes were true, and there was some mutant black creature lurking around the telescope compound, the shotgun would be just the thing, and he would gladly pay the price for violation of protocol.

The rain was still falling steadily, but the downpour was light now compared to the onslaught of ten minutes earlier, and in the distance, Jerry could now see the stars above him once again and the clear demarcation of clouds and sky.

Jerry lifted the gun chest high, and though he already knew the gun was loaded, he broke the chamber just the same, revealing the two red shell casings that indicated the weapon was ready to go.

Then, before he took a step toward the warehouse to begin the hunt, he stopped, doubt suddenly flooding his mind.

This is not a good idea, he thought. Weird sightings or not, it wasn't an excuse to break procedures.

"What the hell am I doing?"

Jerry took a deep breath and then lay the gun back down on the truck bed, wiping his face clear of the rain for the millionth time.

"Relax, brother."

He had seen something suspicious—*someone*, perhaps—that was all there was to it at this stage. And, per procedures, he had investigated the issue, and, despite perhaps some hazy visual evidence to the contrary, he couldn't find anything to report. In such cases, protocol required him to call in the incident to HQ, or, if it was an emergency, to call the police.

This didn't qualify as an emergency, he figured now, so he would start with his company, and when he called it in, his description could be as vague as necessary. He didn't need to come off sounding like someone who'd just escaped from a mental hospital, especially not to the people who signed his paychecks.

It looked like a man, I guess. I don't know, tall. 6'9 maybe. He was black, but not in the sense of race. This last part didn't make much sense, so Jerry figured he would just leave that off altogether, as he wasn't sure exactly how to explain it.

But for all Jerry knew, that was all he'd seen. The thing's height was unusual but not impossible, and maybe its color and shape truly was just a trick of the darkness, some bizarre phenomenon that occurred with the rain and light from the guard gate, and later with the bulb above the warehouse. Or maybe his eyes were going. Or his mind. Those were not impossibilities either.

Jerry left the gun laying in the bed and snapped closed the tailgate, and then he turned back to the guard booth, having made his final decision to retreat there and make the call into the company.

He took a deep breath, nodding with satisfaction at the sober judgment he'd just come to, and as he looked up toward the guard station where the phone awaited him, standing in front of the barrier arm was the creature, and this time there was no question that what he was seeing was real.

The light from the booth illuminated the outline of the slender being, making it appear as a giant silhouette, so tall and black it was as if a hole in the atmosphere had been removed, sliced with a jigsaw, perhaps, revealing behind it only the darkness of space, albeit one that was draped in smoke and haze.

Panic erupted in Jerry's gut with twice the level from earlier, causing him to retch up a tablespoon of vomit that he instinctively spit to the side as he continued to stare wide-eyed at the shape in front of him. The lump in his throat was massive, constricting, and he swallowed it slowly as he reached his hand back to the latch of the tailgate. Without taking his eyes off the black form that stood unmoving by the guard gate, he pulled up on the latch and dropped open the small door once again, easing it down this time, fearing any sudden noise might trigger the thing to attack.

Jerry felt his hand around on the ripples of the metal bed, but he couldn't immediately locate the weapon, so, in what was surely less than three seconds, he turned his head back to the truck, finding the shotgun almost immediately, just an inch or so from where his hand had been searching.

He skated the gun toward him and lifted it, gripping it with both hands now as he slid the dual rounds into the chamber. He rotated back toward the creature, his legs ready to approach now, his will ready to fire and kill.

But by the time Jerry turned, there was no longer any distance to cover, and the weapon in his hands was consumed by the black mass in front of him, forcing Jerry to drop the shotgun to the street, leaving him stunned and defenseless.

The creature was upon him, standing above him like an enormous charcoal statue, its head, which to this point had been barely recognizable as such, tilted forward, the shape of it drifting in and out of form, as if eager to escape its master yet never wanting to get too far.

Jerry could see the vague contours of a face now, and for the briefest of instances, he felt a pang of satisfaction at verifying that what he'd seen earlier skulking behind the warehouse was in fact something other than a man. He wasn't crazy, it turned out, just unlucky.

Ripples near the top of the thing's head appeared now, small, distinct creases that began as thin lines and then separated into what Jerry could only have described as eyes. These were the first true features of the form, verifying that it was indeed alive, animal.

And then wrinkles of contortion appeared below the eyes, narrowing the thing's face into an expression that resembled not quite anger, but something that dared to be rejected, the look a male lion gives to another stray male as it passes the pride from a distance, the precursor to attack.

A second later, the black monster shot its arms forward and grabbed Jerry, maneuvering him like a doll, using its large thin fingers to completely envelop the security guard's face and head, leaving only a narrow gap through which he could see a hole in the beast's face open, creating something akin to a mouth. The feature was invisible to Jerry until that moment, and it revealed a cavernous void that was nearly as black as the thing itself and seemed to go on for eternity, like a tunnel into space.

The strength of the creature was like nothing Jerry had ever experienced, and as the first words started to emerge in a plea for his own life, the history of his existence to that point suddenly inundated his mind.

Most of what he saw came so fast that it was gone before he could grasp the memory, but some images lingered, sparking the remembrance. His game-winning double that sent his team to the county middle school championship. Helen Doherty's hand down his pants in the back of the Cineplex when he was fifteen. His father's funeral.

And Isaiah Adakai, the boy he'd left for dead on the road on February 9th, 2003.

And, of course, perhaps even more frightening, the accompanying image of the headline that appeared in the paper two mornings later, along with an article that pled for the public's help in locating the car responsible for the fatal hit-and-run.

Jerry was drunk that night, there was no question about that; he'd had at least two too many. He could barely figure out the gear shift of his Mazda, and when he finally got it into reverse and pulled out of the parking space at Delaney's, he nearly clipped the only car left in the lot that was parked at least ten yards behind him.

But Jerry had also convinced himself over these last seventeen years that even if he had been as sober as the pope that night, it wouldn't have made a difference. It was so dark. And the kid was on a bicycle at two-thirty in the morning! Maybe even drunk himself, he sometimes rationalized, though there was little evidence to support that notion. And even though the kid had been hugging the shoulder as closely as possible when Jerry came up behind him, when Jerry sped up to pass him, the kid suddenly lurched the bike to the left, at just the wrong time, right at the moment Jerry was on his hip. There was nothing to be done, drunk or not.

Jerry heard the dull crunch of Isaiah's head hitting the pavement, and he knew from the sound alone that, if he wasn't dead, he was never going to live a worthwhile life again.

Jerry knew in the moment to stop, of course, even with a BAC that was certainly north of .20, and even with the full understanding that any consequences he would face were certain to be severe and life-changing. But he never slowed, never even checked his mirrors, except to see if there were any headlights in the distance, anyone behind him who would have seen the accident or the shattered bike and teenager on the road and the car speeding off into the distance.

But there had been no one on the road that night, only he and Isaiah Adakai, the latter of whom would be laid to rest that next weekend, the case of his manslaughter unsolved.

Jerry had thought little about Isaiah in the past few years, but he relived it now as if it were happening in the moment, along with the rest of his joys and pains over the years, none as highly pitched as that one, however.

And then from the void of the creature's mouth he heard a voice, toneless and guttural, as if patched together with the words of dead pirates.

"Tell me your evil."

Jerry heard the voice clearly, knew the true nature of the request in an instant, but his mind simply wouldn't allow the revelation to be spoken aloud, his conscience having committed to the secrecy of the incident years earlier.

"No," Jerry answered, his voice both distant and defiant.

There was a pause in the creature, a settling of its strength and motion, as if it were allowing Jerry the opportunity to answer again.

But Jerry Kellerman never reconsidered the refusal, and the last conscious thought he had just before his body froze into a solid block of black was that if he'd been pressed to say what was happening to him in that moment, he could only have described it as being killed by the Devil himself.

CHAPTER FOUR

RAMON THOMAS HAD ARRIVED in Garmella only three days after graduating from the police academy. A life-long resident of Arizona, he rode into town smiling and eager, delighted to have found employment in his home state, and in a town less than an hour from the one in which he'd grown up. Deputy of Garmella, Arizona wasn't his dream job exactly, but it was one on which he could cut his teeth, where he could learn the real-world lessons of being a cop before moving on to a place that offered a little more challenge and variety. Scottsdale or Mesa, maybe, and then someday, hopefully, Phoenix.

But that plan had been laid out over eight years ago, and Ramon was still in Garmella. He held the position of sheriff now, so there was progress made on that front, but still, the tiny quasi-tourist town of Garmella wasn't the place he had pictured himself when the decade came to an end. In fact, he'd even said as much during his job interview, the sheriff at the time, Dwayne Malone, smiling and nodding as he listened to Ramon's ambitions. Ramon had thought the man sincere in the moment, encouraging, but he wondered later if the sheriff's looks were patronizing, as if he'd heard similar pipe dreams from rookie officers his whole life.

But Sheriff Malone was long gone, and Ramon was king cop now, and though he wasn't uncovering billion-dollar drug rings or solving gangland murders on a daily basis—or ever, really—he was kept busy enough, especially during the summer months when the tourists trickled into town at a modest but consistent rate. For some, the absence of mobile phones was an invitation to live as though there were no rules at all, as if Garmella were some throwback Shangri-La, or perhaps a frontier town of the early West, where any depravity the mind could conceive was permitted. Most of that impiety involved controlled substances, of course—and not the kind that grew naturally in the hills—but there were other sins as well, and Garmella was not unaccustomed to the occasional aggravated robbery or sexual assault.

"What's the word on that sinkhole, Glo?" Ramon asked, standing at the threshold of his office, his hand gripping the frame above his head. "Got hold of DPW yet?"

Gloria Reynolds was one of four officers under Ramon's command, and the most senior amongst them, both in terms of age and time on the force. She was in her early fifties and had been with Ramon for just over five years. Additionally, she was probably the hardest working of the bunch, though, truthfully, that wasn't saying much. There was Luke and Randy Carson, brothers, two years apart and with the same glaring weakness, namely the inability to understand basic commands of their superior officer. They were fine boys, Ramon supposed, but they had a long way to go to reach their potential, and he never felt completely comfortable giving them an order that involved on-their-feet thinking, which, in policing, was a bit of a problem.

And then there was Allie Nyler, certainly the smartest of his officers, mid-thirties and next in the seniority line. But Allie's ambition had flatlined less than six months into the job, and though Ramon couldn't prove it (nor did he have any real desire to), he knew this lack of motivation could be traced back to a long line of empty bottles, ones that were designed to hold both booze and pills. At least twice a week she showed up hungover, and though she was subordinate and followed most orders to a tee, her lack of enthusiasm for the job kept her from being truly effective.

"They said they knew about it and that they'll send someone up to assess the damage tomorrow. Didn't give me a time though."

"I should hope they know about it; I called it in almost two days ago. What's the hold up? Why tomorrow?"

Gloria shrugged. "That's just what they said."

Ramon sighed and gave a small quiver of his head, a signal of frustration at both the DPW and at Gloria, who, though hard-working, was a little too pleasant sometimes. An agreeable temperament was an asset when dealing with the public, but inside the local government, sometimes you needed a little snap.

"And I don't need an assessment," Ramon added. "I need a damn mixer truck up here and a load of cement."

"I told 'em that, but they said it's not that easy. Said they need to see how deep it is and if it's still sinking. Shit, I bet they don't even get to it until next week."

Ramon glared at Gloria, his jaw clenched. "I don't want to hear that, Gloria. We've got a whole lot of people heading here starting next Saturday that will be none too happy if that's the case. None too happy at all. And the non-residents who are here now and are stranded? They're gonna be even less happy. This ain't a damn ski resort; no one expects to get trapped in Garmella."

Gloria shrugged again. "Want me to call 'em back? Maybe they can put in something temporary. A little bridge or something."

Ramon frowned and gave Gloria a crooked look, not quite following how exactly her speculative bridge would work. But he let it go and continued to lament the problem in silence.

The sinkhole was a mess, no question about it, having opened up with no warning at some point over the last couple days, nearly killing Brian and Regina Simms and their two kids as they made their way out of town, off to the Grand Canyon for a couple days.

Thankfully, the Simms' had avoided catastrophe and reported the damage to Ramon on their way back into town; but their Canyon plans, along with the rest of those in Garmella with aspirations of getting out of town, had been put on hold until further notice.

Ramon had called in the incident to DPW within a half hour of Brian's alert, but Garmella was a small town, remote, and the Department of Public Works in Apache County wasn't exactly a Swiss watch factory. He'd had to call several times just to speak to a live human and then was rewarded with a classic sing-songy explanation about how Ramon's wasn't the only town in need of maintenance. *Spring and summer are tough, you know, all that driving on the roads takes its toll.*

Ramon got it, but summer hadn't officially started yet, and Garmella was unique in that it didn't have alternate routes in and out of town. It was this characteristic, Ramon believed, that should have sprung his crisis to the top of the priority list.

"And don't forget: it's audit weekend."

Ramon closed his eyes and put the heels of his hands to his forehead, and then he slid them in opposite directions until he reached his temples, stopping there and pressing lightly before gliding his palms down the sides of his face. "It can't be that time already?"

Gloria nodded. "Been a month. In fact, I think I saw one of the trucks already. Must have come in a few days ago, before the sinkhole."

Ramon gave Gloria a confused stare. "Can't remember the last time that happened." He pondered the unusual practice further. "Guess they think people are starting to figure out their schedule."

Gloria shrugged. "I wouldn't have even known they were here 'cept I happened to be coming out of Sonny's right when it was coming in."

"At night?"

Gloria nodded.

"Hmm."

One weekend a month—weekends being more opportune since people were most likely to be at home on Saturday and Sunday—the Grieg Observatory sent a team of monitor trucks, typically no more than two or three, to patrol the streets of Garmella in search of anyone violating the town's transmission agreement. It was supposed to be a secret to the citizens when they arrived, but anyone paying even the tiniest bit of attention could have figured out the schedule and when they were coming.

The trucks rarely came in early though—Ramon thought it a few years since the last time that had happened—but perhaps they had without Ramon's knowledge, as they weren't obligated to tell him when they were coming.

The white pickup trucks came loaded with detectors the size of refrigerators in their beds and usually began their patrols around dawn on Saturday and continued slowly and silently through the streets, all day, almost daring anyone to test their detection abilities.

And people always did.

The violations came mainly in the form of cell phone use, and of those, the vast majority were committed by out-of-towners, most of whom claimed they didn't know the rules despite the miles of signage along 91 alerting them to the town-wide ban. Technically, the Grieg monitors had no legal power of enforcement, but Garmella received a rather generous annual compensation from the lab, a sum agreed upon when the telescope was first commissioned, and, in return, the town had agreed to legislate for radio silence, with the authority to issue an ordinance violation to anyone who broke the rules. To date, Ramon had only written a handful of such violations during his eight years; a stern warning was usually enough to prevent repeat offenders.

And these days, the quiet airwaves of the town *were* the attraction, a novelty, so anyone who couldn't tolerate being away from social media for more than an hour usually didn't pick Garmella as a weekend destination.

"Well, not really my problem if the rest can't get through," Ramon said. "Nothing I can do about a hole in the ground. Man, I can't wait for the day when they can just send drones in or something."

"Drones? Isn't that radio signals or something? I think that might defeat the purpose."

Ramon snickered. "Yeah, I guess that's right."

He walked from his office into the main area of the station, dumped a quarter cup of cold coffee into the small kitchenette sink across the hall, and then he strolled to the Mr. Coffee for a refill. In mid-pour, he could see Allie Nyler pulling up to the station, and Ramon reflexively glanced to the clock on the wall. 5:21. Late.

He set the pot and his cup on the counter and walked to the glass window front of the station where he stood with his arms crossed, watching Allie fumble herself together as the sun began to rise behind her, stretching her eyes clear as she examined her face in the rearview mirror before tying back a quick, ragged ponytail. She then shrugged a huge breath and made her way inside the station.

"Morning, deputy," Ramon blared before Allie had even closed the door.

"Morning, Sheriff," Allie replied, her eyes focused forward, not yet ready to meet those of her boss. "Sorry I'm late."

Most days when Allie was late, which was at least twice a month, Ramon offered some type of rebuke, the severity of which depended on his mood that morning and usually ranged somewhere between a lecture on punctuality to the veiled threat of suspension. But today he didn't have it in him. He had too much on his plate already to spend the effort correcting Allie Nyler's behavior. Besides, in his heart,

Ramon knew the reprimands only made him feel better and were doing little to improve Allie's circumstances in life. She had a drinking problem—maybe drugs too, he wasn't entirely clear on that—and nothing he said was going to change it.

"You been out to the sinkhole on 91 yet?" Ramon asked.

"I thought Luke and Randy were gonna set up the block," Allie replied quickly. "Figured you gave it to them last night?"

Ramon put his hands up in mock protection. "I'm not blaming you for anything, Allie. Just asked if you'd been out there?"

Allie opened her mouth to argue but then seemed to think better of it; instead she frowned embarrassed by her defensiveness. She shook her head. "Sorry, Sheriff. No, I haven't been out there. Want me to check it out when the sun gets up? See if it's spreading or whatever."

That hadn't been Ramon's implication, but now that Allie had mentioned it, it sounded like a good idea. He had intended to give it to the Carson boys, as Allie had announced, but he hadn't seen them yet today and they weren't due in for another hour. "Why don't you. I set some cones out but we need something a little more permanent. A sign at least. And make sure there's no mountain of cars piled up coming *into* town either. Hopefully, DPW had at least enough sense to close the road at Simonson. Anyone who gets past that town is gonna have a hell of three-point turn to get back down the mountain."

Allie nodded, and then, as if the idea of a lifetime struck her, her face lit into a broad smile, her eyes gleaming. She stretched her arms wide, shoulder height, palms to the sky. "How 'bout that rain last night? Huh?"

Ramon and Gloria both whooped in unison, having forgotten to discuss the momentous occasion amongst each other.

"I swear I thought the roof was gonna come in at one point," Gloria shrieked. "It's been so long I barely recognized the sound."

"It was a barrage," Allie added. "Came hard and fast and then was gone within the hour."

"Sounds like most of your boyfriends."

Allie squinted at Gloria, hands on hips, trying to squeeze back a smile that ultimately erupted into a blaring laugh.

Ramon blushed, keeping clear of that part of the conversation, and when the locker-room portion sputtered, he added awkwardly, "I can't believe my home phone wasn't ringing off the hook with accident reports. I figured people would be sliding and crashing all over town."

"It's still early," Allie answered. "I'm sure the calls are coming soon."

Just as the words finished leaving Allie's mouth, the phone on Ramon's desk rang, and he looked at Allie and Gloria suspiciously, as if he were on some hidden-TV prank show and they were both in on it. Each smiled and shrugged.

"Sheriff Thomas," Ramon answered.

"Hello, I...uh...I'm not sure if you're the right people to call, but um...I think there might be a problem."

The voice on the other end was male, young, maybe only a year or two out of his teens. His voice pitched up at the end as if his statement were a question, another indicator of his youth.

"What's your name, son?"

"Riley. Riley Tackard."

Ramon knew the Tackard name, though not anyone named Riley. That wasn't unusual, though; the Tackards seemed to have a never-ending stream of family members up at their place beginning in the middle of May and running all the way through September.

"What can I do for you, son?"

"Um, I'm working over here at the Grieg for the summer. At the telescope. I've been here only about two weeks, I guess, since school let out. I'm working the guard gate."

Ramon wasn't aware of this, but he also wasn't entitled to know about everyone who arrived in town or where they worked. "Welcome to Garmella, Riley. What seems to be the problem?"

"The guy that works the shift before me—Jerry...I can't remember his last name..."

Ramon knew Jerry Kellerman well, well enough to consider him a friend even, though it had been a while since he'd seen him socially. "It's Kellerman. What's going on, Riley?" He felt that first bubble of disquiet form in his gut, the dull, queasy boil that arises when trouble is somewhere in the distance, marching steadily forward like a somnambulant soldier.

"He ain't...isn't here."

Ramon processed the report in an instant, picturing the layout of the Grieg at the guard gate, reconstructing the grounds of the compound, considering the many possibilities of where Jerry Kellerman might have gone, assuming he had made it there to begin with. "Is he making his rounds or something?"

"Uh...we don't really do rounds, I guess. We just kinda sit at the gate."

"What if you see something, Riley?" Ramon snapped. "Or hear something? Do you still just sit at the gate? Do you wait for the thieves to load up the telescope and drive off to Vegas or Albuquerque or Mexico City?"

Ramon realized his reaction was a tad over the top—and it made no sense regarding stealing the telescope, which was five times heavier than a California redwood—but Riley's reply had come off as slightly sarcastic, and Ramon was in no mood, already burdened with the weight of the day that lay ahead.

"I...I was just told if we see or hear anything to call it in. To my company. Or to you guys if it was an emergency."

This was right, of course, technically, but Ramon knew Jerry would never have followed that protocol to the letter, not without checking things out on his own first. Ramon backed off his hardline approach. "Listen, Riley, do you see his vehicle there? His truck? It's an F150. Gray."

"Yeah, it's here."

Ramon didn't know whether that was a good sign or not, but at least Jerry had shown up for work, which meant he wasn't lying dead in his house having suffered a massive stroke at his dining room table or something. "Is it where he normally parks it?"

"Yeah, I guess so. Front lot, across from the gate."

Ramon thought back to Riley's mention of the protocol. "Why didn't you call your company first, Riley? What made you call me?"

"I did call them. They told me to call you. They said it qualified as an emergency."

"Why's that?"

"Because of the truck. Jerry's truck. The tailgate was down when I got here, and his gun locker was open."

Now the boil of concern in Ramon's belly was at a simmer.

"And there's a shotgun on the ground right behind the truck."

Ramon's gut heated to a steady rumble at the last addendum, but Ramon kept his mind from racing, allowing instead for his brain to explore all the possibilities, to factor into the equation each of the elements Riley had just offered. At the moment, however, nothing came to mind that didn't involve distress.

The phone rang on Gloria's desk now and Ramon watched absently as she answered it, noting the wrinkled concern on her brow a few seconds later.

"All right, Riley, we'll send someone over. Have you been up to the telescope yet?"

"Uh, no. For what?"

Ramon closed his eyes and rubbed his hand across his eyes and forehead. "To see if there's been a breach, Riley. The point of you being there—of any guard being there—is to protect the telescope. And if Jerry wasn't there when you got there, that means someone could have entered the compound, right?"

There was silence on the other end, and Ramon could hear the fear in Riley's breathing. No doubt he'd been told the job was nothing more than an eight-hour session of reading magazines and doing crossword puzzles, with maybe a couple of credential checks throughout the day when the maintenance staff—of which there were very few—arrived for their day shift.

And ninety-nine percent of the time, that *was* the gig.

"It's okay, Riley, just stay at the gate. We'll get over there as soon as we can."

Ramon hung up and then watched Gloria do the same with her receiver almost simultaneously.

"What was that about?" he asked.

"It was Melissa Godwin."

"She's calling early."

"Said Amber didn't come home last night."

"Is that unusual? Isn't she still with that Zamora kid?"

"Yeah, but she said she can't get a hold of him either. She didn't sound too concerned, just wondering if we'd gotten a call that anything had happened. But then…"

"What is it?"

"I don't know. She hung up kind of abruptly. Like the phone went dead suddenly."

Ramon shrugged. "All right, I'll add it to the list. Maybe have Luke or Randy take a drive out to the Zamora house to see if anyone's there. Do you know if anyone else is staying there right now 'sides Derrick?"

"Not sure. He lives with his mom, Monique, but she's been known to disappear for a few days at a time."

Ramon nodded. "I'm sure them kids are shacked up there and hungover. Or maybe not yet home from doing whatever kids do nowadays."

Gloria grinned mischievously. "I think it's the same as they did thenadays."

Ramon snickered. "I'm sure. All right, let's send one of the boys out to Derrick's house anyway. Just to be sure."

"What was going on your end?"

"Issue at the Grieg. Jerry Kellerman's MIA. I'm gonna head up there and see what's what."

"MIA?"

Ramon nodded. "That's what the new kid said." He walked back to the coffee pot, finally replenishing his fix for the morning. "Didn't sound like a mental giant, this kid—some kin of the Tackards there for the summer—but I'm gonna check it out anyway. Jerry's not one to leave his post for nothing."

Ramon grabbed his hat and stepped out to the front parking lot of the station, breathing in the dampness of the night air that still lingered, only twenty minutes old now as the breaking sun shot in from the east. He scanned the street for a moment and then closed his eyes, studying the silence of the new day.

And then a thought struck him like a hammer, and he flashed his eyes wide. *Where was everyone?* It was early—most people were still in bed, for sure—but still, it was a weekday, and even though school was out, there should have been some cars on the road by now.

Ramon fired up his cruiser and sat in the driver's seat idling for a moment, considering again the troubles already on his slate for the day. *The life of small-town policing,* he thought. It was a good thing no one in town was expecting soon or he'd probably be scrubbing down and delivering a screaming newborn before the day was over.

He put the sprawling issues aside though, focusing instead on the task at hand—Jerry Kellerman—and then he shifted the car to drive and began his trek up to the to the highest point in Garmella, the point at which the only artery into town dead ended at the Grieg telescope.

As the small downtown area of Garmella opened up into the sprawling space of the mountain landscape, Ramon studied the scenery with fresh eyes, acknowledging the green leaves and white flowers popping all along the roadway, the glisten of last night's rain still glimmering in the morning sun, barely risen. That shine would be gone in a few hours, Ramon knew, but the sparkle of water was invigorating to him, as if he were drinking in the moisture with his eyeballs.

He passed the home of Winston Bell, a sprawling estate of stone and timber that blended seamlessly with the landscape, the hillside hugging it from behind with large trees that shrouded the house on all sides, giving it an almost camouflaged appearance. It was by far the largest home in Garmella, and Ramon always considered it the gateway to the Grieg, as it was the last private structure before the landscape flattened to barrenness, setting the stage for the desolate climb to the telescope.

Mr. Bell was unquestionably the town's wealthiest resident (Ramon always granted Winston the status of "Mr. Bell," mostly due to his fortune and age, the latter of which, conservatively, couldn't have been a day younger than eighty), as well as its most reclusive, though, since February, Ramon had seen him several times, personally making the drive to his house to issue yet another transmission warning.

But the man was rich—quite—and a hefty supplier of property tax revenue (not a small thing), and though Ramon had reached the point where Mr. Bell's infractions against the Garmella-Grieg agreement warranted a citation, to this point, Ramon had issued only warnings, about which Mr. Bell was always very appreciative. Nevertheless, at some point the agreement had to be enforced, and with the pressure coming down on him from the directors at Grieg HQ, that point had almost certainly been reached. Mr. Bell had lain low for the past couple of months, but the next violation would include a fine, at least, and possibly even a home inspection.

The thought of Mr. Bell's transgressions elicited a reminder to Ramon of the Grieg monitors who were scheduled to arrive some time tomorrow or the next day (and the ones which had apparently already arrived), and that thought brought him back to the sinkhole, which, he decided, needed the full thrust of his focus when he returned to the station. DPW needed an ass-kicking.

Ramon pulled up to the gate at the compound, but the guard house was empty; Riley Tackard was nowhere to be found.

The barrier arm was down, so Ramon parked his vehicle in the roadway directly in front of it and stepped from his car slowly, studying the scene with intensity, giving it the full three-sixty perusal before beginning his slow stroll onto the Grieg property.

He saw Jerry Kellerman's F150 in the lot across from the gate, the tailgate of the truck still down as Riley had described, and the shotgun still on the ground. *Good boy, Riley*, he thought; *leave the scene alone.*

On the back end of the guard station, parked vertically with the booth, was a tan Toyota Corolla, which Ramon assumed was Riley's, considering the out-of-town license plates. Colorado.

Ramon walked toward the warehouse beyond the gate, immediately noting the open door to the structure. He bristled with suspicion and placed his hand on his weapon as he approached, the sickening feeling from earlier emerging in his belly. He prepared himself to see the body of Jerry Kellerman strung up inside, and possibly Riley Tackard's beside him, but the warehouse was empty, save for the usual supplies and clutter, and Ramon took a deep breath through his nose, relaxing just a bit.

"Officer?"

Ramon spun now as his hand reached for his sidearm, snapping the .9mm from its holster in one smooth motion and holding it up at eye-level.

"Don't!" Riley Tackard cried, his voice cracking like a log on a fire.

Ramon lifted his hands away from his body, holding them high, point of his weapon to the sky, showing the rookie guard he planned him no harm. He grimaced. "Riley, I presume?"

Riley managed a nod.

"Good. I'm Sheriff Thomas."

Riley gave an understanding nod.

"Where were you just now?"

The boy was sweating, out of breath. "I...I was going to walk up to the...the thing. The telescope. Like you told me. But I just kept walking and the road kept going. I never made it. I didn't know it was so far."

The telescope was a good four and a half miles up the mountain, not a stroll most could take easily, and certainly not this kid, who, though young and thin, looked like he'd never run a hundred meters on any given day of his life, let alone hiked four plus miles up a mountain. "It's not really walkable, Riley. And I told you to stay put."

Riley said nothing and looked to his feet, shuffling them. "Why didn't you take your car?"

Riley shrugged. "I don't know. I've never been up there, so, like I said, I didn't know it was so far."

Ramon gave the surroundings another scan, squinting as he did, trying to take in some unseen clue that perhaps he'd missed upon first arrival. But he found nothing out of the ordinary, and he nodded to the guard. "All right then, today you get the tour, I guess."

Ramon and Riley began their trek up the mountain road toward the Grieg telescope in Ramon's cruiser, Riley sitting nervously in the passenger seat, already looking exhausted despite having several more hours of his shift yet to work.

"Didn't get much sleep last night?" Ramon asked.

Riley gave Ramon a guilty look, one that said perhaps he'd spent the previous night indulging in a few rounds with something strong and toxic, despite not looking of age to do so. And Ramon could only assume there were at least a few illegal substances sprinkled throughout the evening as well.

"Well, this is the kind of job where you need your sleep, Riley. Else sleep will come for you. Hard to fight it off when you're just sitting there doing nothing. Trust me; I've been on enough stakeouts to know."

Riley nodded. "Yes, sir."

Ramon gave Riley a quizzical look, appreciative of the formality the kid had just displayed. Maybe he'd misjudged Riley Tackard, he considered, though, in fairness, he'd never really passed judgement on his character to begin with, only his abilities.

"Do you think he's dead?" Riley asked, breaking Ramon's moment of sentimental thought.

Ramon chuckled, startled by the question. "Uh, if you mean Jerry, it wasn't my first guess, no."

"Then where is he? What other explanation could there be?"

"I don't know, Riley. You said yourself you never made it up to the telescope. Maybe he went up there himself."

"Then why didn't he take his truck?"

Ramon frowned and nodded, anticipating the question for which he had no answer. "I don't know. That's why were—"

"What was that?" Riley's words came out in a high-pitched chirp, though quietly, under his breath, as if speaking to himself.

"What was what?"

Ramon glanced to his right to see Riley turned fully toward the window, his stare directed into the thick woods that lined the entirety of the mountain road. His nose was pressed against the window like a child staring through the glass façade of a toy store.

"Riley?"

"Did you see that?" Riley spun his head toward Ramon for just a glance, his eyes bulging, pleading, and then he was back to the window. "In the woods there? Did you see it?"

Ramon had already begun to slow the cruiser, but the panic in Riley caused him to step on the brake pedal with a bit too much force, causing Riley to lurch forward, banging his left shoulder against the dash. The kid never wavered in his gaze, however, and Ramon quickly pulled the car to the side of the road, his eyes fixed to the woods, trying to find the mystery of Riley's focus. "What the hell is it, Riley? What are you seeing?"

Riley continued surveying the forest for several seconds before slowly breaking from his trance. He looked back to Ramon. "I don't think we should be stopping. Not here."

"You're acting like you just saw Bigfoot, Riley. I shouldn't stop?"

"No. You didn't see...let's just keep going." Riley was breathing heavily now, nearly hyperventilating.

Ramon lowered his tone and locked the kid's eyes with his. "Riley, relax. What did you see?"

"I don't know. It was black. And moving. Something...I don't know. I just—"

And then Ramon saw it too.

He raised his hand in a *Stop* gesture, cutting Riley off as he tried to bring into focus the figure wavering in his line of sight. There was just a blur though, a shadow, a second or two of motion perhaps twenty yards out beyond where the trees began. And then the scene cleared again, leaving only the lazy bounce of the leaves and branches.

Ramon blinked and shook his head in a quivering, clearing motion, stretching his eyes wide as he leaned toward Riley's side of the cruiser, staring through the window.

What in the holy F.

"You saw it, right?" Riley asked, nearly crying now, choking on his words.

Ramon nodded. "I...I think so. What *was* that?" His voice was dreamy, mystical.

"I don't know, man, but I'm not good with shit like this. This is not what I was promised."

Ramon ignored Riley, his mind flexing as it tried to process what he'd just seen. The figure was tall and angular, moving in what Ramon could only have described as a walking motion, though its form was somewhat amorphous. It was as if one of the trees had suddenly uprooted or broken off and then turned into some dusty version of a man.

But it wasn't *quite* that. The figure he had just seen was darker than any of the trees. Black, like Riley had noted, as if one of the existing trees had been consumed in a fire before suddenly morphing into human form.

Ramon drew his pistol and opened the door, and then he stepped slowly from his cruiser, keeping his eyes focused on the area of the sighting.

"Stay here," he told Riley, a command as unnecessary as telling the kid not to flap his arms and fly away.

Riley kept silent and nodded, but the minute Ramon was outside and clear of the car, he heard the *clunk!* of the locks depressing into their respective cartridges.

Ramon gave a half-glance back to the car, noting the issue for later if he needed to retreat, and then he marched forward into the trees, blowing out a long breath to relax himself.

Within seconds, he was in the deep foliage, the damp leaves brushing against him with every step, threatening to soak his clothes in minutes. The rain, however, had softened the ground, making his footfalls silent, which Ramon considered a small victory, though it also meant it would be difficult to hear whatever was moving in front of him.

Ramon turned left toward the upslope now, allowing his eyes to adjust to the clutter of trunks and branches and ferns that occupied the vista. The thing had been moving in that direction, up the mountain, and Ramon suddenly considered if there was much point blindly pursuing it under these conditions. To this point, what he'd seen was only a shadow, and, as he considered it further, it was obviously some type of animal, some rare woodland creature that his eyes (and Riley's) had misinterpreted. In fact, if Jerry Kellerman weren't missing at the moment, Ramon wondered if Riley would have even noticed the movement in the woods.

But Jerry *was* missing, and Riley *had* seen it. And Ramon had too. And whatever the shape was that he had seen—or shadow of a shape, if that's what it was—it was unlike any animal his mind could conceive.

Still though, it didn't change the folly of his pursuit. He wasn't prepared for a manhunt into the woods that formed the natural buffer of the Grieg telescope, especially not with Riley Tackard still quivering back inside the cruiser. The kid was his responsibility now, like it or not, and with this new sense of sobriety, Ramon lowered his weapon and turned back to the car. Within seconds, he was back at the passenger window, knuckling on the glass for Riley to open up.

Riley sat staring blankly through the window, his eyes half-closed, suspicious and disbelieving. He was shaking his head defiantly, the way a toddler would who's been told to eat his spinach.

"Riley, the quicker you open up, the quicker we get out of here," Ramon announced calmly, but with a tone that suggested those words would be the last ones he spoke with anything resembling civility. If he had to ask again, he was going to make sure his pistol was chest-high and visible.

"Riley!" Ramon barked again, lifting his hand to slap the window and emphasize his seriousness.

But as Ramon reared his open palm in a backhand motion, the crook of his elbow wrapped by his chin, he saw Riley's eyes suddenly dart past him and blossom, and then the shake of his head went from a gentle, disobedient tremble to a horror-filled quake. A large lump developed in his throat and the guard moved slowly away from the window toward the center console of the car, and then beyond it, until he was as far away from the passenger door as he could be.

Ramon swallowed down his own throat lump and then spun quickly back toward the woods. At first, he saw nothing, but then, as his eyes adjusted again to the green and brown and yellow of the forest, the image of the figure from earlier emerged like a mirage, this time standing as tall and still as a totem pole. Despite the clarity of the figure, however, the outline and form were nebulous, and Ramon doubted whether that was a characteristic of the creature or whether his vision needed attention.

"Jesus, Joseph, and Mary."

Ramon's words were a whisper, but they were spiked with terror, and before they had finished leaving his mouth, he was already sliding his body around to the front of the cruiser, his backside edging along the frame of the car until he reached the driver's side again. At that point, the tops of his thighs were against the left fender, his eyes never once leaving the sight of the creature.

"Open the fucking door, Riley," Ramon barked through locked teeth as he reached for the driver's side handle. The pitch of his voice was so low it strained his throat.

Riley's back was to Ramon, but Ramon could see the kid was still entranced by the scene outside, locked on the creature that seemed to hover amongst the trees like an ebony ghost.

Ramon directed his eyes back to the forest just as the black monster began moving forward, toward the car, and the instant his eyes landed on the beast, it stopped, now at least ten feet closer to him than before. Then, with little more than a second or two pause, the creature started moving toward them again, this time in long quick strides.

"Riley! Riley, open the goddamn door!"

Riley pressed his back hard against the driver's door now, the skin of his neck flattening against the window like a starfish. Ramon slapped his hand against the glass now repeatedly, never taking his eyes from the forest. Then, as if the ground beneath the black creature suddenly evaporated, the figure fell from Ramon's sight, dropping to the forest floor like a sea of coal cascading down a chute, leaving a mist of black in its wake.

"What the hell?"

It was on the ground now—Ramon could hear it shuffling through the leaves, crackling over the fallen branches—and he quickly moved away from the car, shifting into action as he did, his weapon now poised for killing. He took several steps back from the car and to his left, then forward around the hood, now moving in the direction from where he'd just come, toward the passenger side.

The sound of the rustling suddenly ceased, the creature seeming to sense the danger of Ramon and his pistol.

Ramon craned his neck dramatically over the hood, his eyes attempting to locate the crawling beast somewhere on the ground at the base of the cruiser.

Ramon was standing directly in front of the car now, and he glanced at Riley again through the windshield. The young man's face displayed a look that was both terrified and confused; his eyes were searching, desperate, as if trying to get his focus back on the approaching danger. But the form was too low, out of his eye line, and Riley, whose back was still pressed tightly against the driver's side window, leaned forward and began to move again toward his side of the car, trying to get a vantage of the thing somewhere below him.

Ramon kept his gaze on Riley, using him as a measure to determine for himself where the creature was exactly, watching the guard anxiously as he slid another couple feet toward the window.

Riley's body was pressed against the passenger door now, his knees planted on the seat, his eyes tilted down from the top of the window, scanning the ground.

Riley was frozen in his kneeling perch for two or three beats, his mind clearly racing as it processed the impossible sighting.

And then the destruction began.

Ramon heard the breaking glass first, the sound exploding through the air like a pail of gravel dumped onto a plywood table.

And then he watched in horror as Riley's head was instantly consumed in the clutches of the black monster.

What in God's name was happening!

The thing's hands were like dusty obsidian claws, unwavering as they pulled Riley through the broken side window with an ease that was almost beyond comprehension. Ramon could only stare in disbelief, and absently he conjured the image of a gorilla seizing a newborn baby from a stroller. He tried to bring the black beast into focus, but its form wavered in the air, fading into translucence and then back to solid every few seconds, never quite holding its figure long enough to be describable. And with Riley now standing in front of the creature, it made identifying the thing nearly impossible.

Ramon could only gaze at the sight before him, rapt in stunned amazement at the sight of Riley, who now stood before the creature like a child before a schoolmarm. His head remained in the thing's clutches, but he made no move to fight it. His attention seemed fixed, possessed.

"Riley," Ramon said, softly, barely a whisper. His mind was racing, losing its focus, irrelevant memories beginning to emerge.

Was the same thing happening to Riley? Only with more force?

Instinctively, Ramon closed his eyes and attempted to clear his mind, focusing only on his breathing and the feelings in his hands, techniques he'd learned through his practice of meditation which he'd taken up several years earlier.

Only a few seconds passed however when he heard the word 'No' uttered from Riley's mouth, followed by a full-throated shout. "No!"

Broken from whatever spell had been cast upon him, Riley was now struggling to free himself from the creature's grip, writhing in vain, now screaming, "Never! Never."

But there was to be no escape. In a movement that contained both ferocity and grace, the creature wrenched Riley Tackard's body backwards, twisting it as he did before discarding it to the ground like a cardboard box that had been opened, emptied, and broken down into a flat sheet.

Ramon was also now free of the images in his mind, whether through his own mindfulness practice or because of the creature's allowance he didn't know, but he moved quickly around to the passenger side of the car, his index finger now curved around the trigger of his M&P9.

But he was far too late.

As Ramon cleared the left fender of his cruiser, the black mass was already twenty yards away, slinking quickly toward the trees, smoky and amorphous as it faded into the forest, its total form growing in and out of focus like the shimmer of a desert road on a hot day. It moved in a slumping slither now, as low to the ground as a lizard, crawling crooked and gruesomely like some giant mutant stick bug, though with an ease of motion unlike any insect Ramon had ever seen. Its angular limbs and joints protruded in every direction, the monster so flat against the forest floor that the shape of the creature was barely distinguishable from the ground itself.

Ramon fired four shots in rapid succession toward the creature—two of which he was certain landed somewhere around the upper back of the thing—and then he sprinted the ten yards or so needed to reach the tree line again, firing as he went. But he lost sight of the beast almost immediately as it reached the denser sections of the woods where the foliage rose to nearly knee-height. Ramon stood still and listened to the clamber of its retreat for a few seconds longer, and then, as if it had never been there at all, all evidence of the figure disappeared into the trees like a whisper at sea.

Ramon stood staring into the thickets for a few moments more, trying to slow his breathing, simultaneously hoping it would re-appear and praying it was dead. And when it was clear that the black killer was not coming back, at least not at that moment, he turned back to the cruiser where the obliterated heap of Riley Tackard lay mangled in a bed of glass below the door.

Ramon walked quickly but apprehensively toward the kid, and when he reached him, he put a hand to his eyes as a current of nausea surged through his belly and chest.

Riley Tackard's body was twisted and broken, so destroyed and misshapen that the back of the guard's head was bent in a way that it was resting on his own calves. His clothes were shredded by the glass and talons of the monster and dyed with blood from his neck to his shoes.

But it wasn't the blood that had turned Ramon's stomach, or even the unnatural contortion of Riley's body; it was the color of the young man's skin. His entire face and neck—as well as his hands, which were the only other visible part of him—were consumed in blackness, as if he'd been pulled from a house the day after a fire, or had been caught at the epicenter of a lava-spewing volcano. Yet, the damage to his body didn't suggest it had come from burning or electrocution—where the skin melts away leaving only a smiling crisp skeleton—but rather, it was as if Riley's skin had been sucked of all its moisture and life. Like the cells themselves had been poisoned to death, desiccated to black.

"Jesus, my god," Ramon uttered, his hand across his mouth now as he continued checking over his shoulder every few seconds, his heart still pounding against the inside of his sternum.

He swallowed and reached through the broken glass of the cruiser, unlocking the door, and then he quickly opened it and grabbed the radio, depressing the call button.

He cleared his throat, trying to gather himself. "Gloria! Gloria, it's Ramon. Do you copy?"

Ramon released the switch and waited. Nothing.

"Gloria, are you there?" He paused again, still nothing. Then he said, "Allie, do you copy?"

Ramon wiped away the glass from the passenger seat and sat now, becoming increasingly unsettled by the lack of reply as he stared out to the forest, expecting the black figure to emerge at any moment.

"Dammit where is every—"

"Copy, Sheriff." It was Allie. "What's up, boss?"

Ramon let out a sigh. He closed his eyes. "Allie. Thank god. Where's Gloria?"

"Don't know, Sheriff. Haven't been back to the station yet. I'm out on 91 checking on that sinkhole. No pileups here, but there is definitely something."

Ramon ignored the cryptic tease for the moment. "Listen to me, Allie. Something's happened..." Ramon felt his voice racing and he calmed himself, not wanting to cause a panic, especially within his own ranks. "Something's happened up here at the Grieg. It's...there's a new kid—was a new kid—related to the Tackards. He was on duty this morning and now...he's dead. Jesus Christ, Allie; it happened right in front of me." Ramon swallowed. "You copying that, Allie?"

There was a moderate delay and then, "Copy that, Sheriff. It...it happened in front of you? *What* happened? What the hell went down?"

Ramon considered telling her the story, but he hadn't replayed the events yet in his own mind and thought it better to do so first before trying to describe it to someone else. "It's not..." He felt the sting of terror and despair creeping back in and he took a full breath, closing his eyes again as the cool morning air filled his lungs. He thought of the images that had sprung up in his mind, at just the wrong time, events in his life that he wouldn't have remembered if he lived another hundred years. If his mind had slipped like that at any other time in his work, he would have taken himself to the doctor immediately, figuring it was early onset dementia or some other mental sickness. But it had happened then, in the presence of something that couldn't exist on earth, something that had killed a boy who, Ramon was nearly certain, was also experiencing something hypnotic in his mind.

"It's not something I can explain to you...right now. I just need all hands on deck. I need you all up here now. Luke, Randy, you guys copying this?"

No reply from the Carson brothers.

"Where the hell is everybody, Allie?"

"Not sure, Sheriff. Haven't seen those boys at all yet today. I know that Gloria called them before I left, but I didn't hear any reply from them. And come to think of it, it was pretty damn quiet on the drive up here also. I'd even say *weirdly* quiet. I know it was early...or it could just be that nobody can get out of town today because of this giant hole in the ground so they're all staying put?"

Ramon hadn't seen any activity on the road either; it was as empty as the front of the station when he left. That wasn't necessarily unprecedented, especially for that time of day in a town as small as his, but it was unusual to be sure, and though he didn't yet have all the pieces in place at the moment, he knew it was related to the thing he'd just watched kill Riley Tackard before vanishing in broad daylight.

"All right, well I need you up here then, Allie. Immediately. And keep your head on a swivel. I'll keep trying the others."

"10-4 on that, Sheriff." And then, "Also, Sheriff, it looks like yours might not be the only fatality in Garmella today."

Ramon's heart stopped. "How's that, deputy?"

"I found that Zamora kid's truck. It's way the hell down in the ravine. And if he was in it when it went over, there's no way he's alive."

Ramon closed his eyes, suddenly feeling like he was in the middle of a horrible nightmare. "Any evidence of...bodies?"

"Not that I can see, but I'm thinking it's not too promising."

Ramon closed his eyes again and thought of Gloria's call from Melissa Godwin and her missing daughter. Ramon didn't think it too promising either. "All right, Allie, we'll do what we can, but as crazy as this might sound, I need you up here first. I'm heading up to the actual telescope, so meet me at the top. And like I said, be careful and don't stop until you get here."

"Copy that, Sheriff. Over."

"Over and out."

CHAPTER FIVE

RAMON PLACED THE RADIO in the cradle and stared at Riley Tackard's body, weighing his decision whether to drag it from the road or leave it be. He was disinclined to touch the corpse, not knowing exactly what the thing from the woods had done to the poor kid's skin. His flesh had been mutilated, turned to something resembling an old, dried banana peel, and if it had been caused by some type of poison or corrosive element, Ramon figured it probably best to keep his hands to himself.

He pulled the passenger door closed and then shifted left, taking his place in the driver's seat. He started the engine and gasped at the sound, the rumbling of the motor sounding thunderous now in the quiet of the trees. His nerves were shredded, hands shaking, and he drove slowly up the road toward the telescope, just fast enough to keep the car moving forward up the slope. His eyes searched the landscape like a hunter desperate for a kill, every wavering branch and leaf appearing as the matte black figure from moments earlier. He tried to bring the form to the front of his mind again, but already, only minutes later, it seemed like a thing that had come to him in a dream.

But it was real, unquestionably, and Ramon's gut told him the creature was heading to the telescope. Jerry Zimmerman had confronted it down by the guard gate, that much was obvious, and now, after his own confrontation halfway to the top, it seemed reasonable to assume the thing was working its way up the road.

Jerry.

In all the madness and destruction that had just occurred, Ramon had forgotten the reason he and Riley had been driving up the road to begin with. And now, as he considered the scene again at the gate—combined with the death of Riley Tackard—there was little doubt in his mind about Jerry Zimmerman's fate.

He absently thought of the monitor trucks now, how they were due to arrive that weekend, and he suddenly considered a connection between the murderous figure from the forest and the telescope which rose high above Garmella like a medieval castle. He couldn't imagine what that connection might look like, but he filed the correlation away for later anyway.

Ramon reached the plateau of the mountain in less than five minutes, and there the land became a barren flat mesa of dirt and concrete. He pulled his cruiser up to the giant base of the Grieg telescope and then eased the car right and continued driving, orbiting the gargantuan construction once, then again, circling it like a shark in the ocean before finally parking the car so that it faced outward to the single road leading up to the site.

Ramon clicked the radio again. "Allie." Pause. "Allie, you still there?"

Nothing.

"Gloria." Ramon's face burned with anxiety now. "Christ, is anyone working today! Somebody, answer me!"

Ramon gritted his teeth, seething, but he resisted slamming the two-way into the console and instead placed it gently back into the cradle. He took a breath and then disengaged the shotgun mounted beside him and gripped it tightly as he stepped from the vehicle, resuming his search of the landscape with a glare that was narrow and wary.

He walked with purpose toward the base of the telescope, without hesitation, the gun high, aimed, expecting the black beast to emerge from the lattice base at any moment, or to plunge down from the enormous dish like a drop of oil from a giant can. But he reached the metal base of the Grieg without incident, finding there only the bone white beams of the foundation, stark and bright in the morning sun, crisscrossing each other in perfectly engineered Xs.

Ramon continued past the telescope now and headed toward the trees, which were at least a hundred yards in front of him, shrouding the eastern perimeter like green columnar sentries. As he walked, he felt the openness of the area begin to press down upon him, and he knew if an attack were to come now, if the beast were to appear from somewhere in his blind spot, he would have only seconds to react and would need to be quick and perfect with the shotgun.

Yet Ramon, for a reason he couldn't have explained, doubted the figure would materialize in that way, not in the plainness of the base. The creature had come from the cover and camouflage of the woods, and Ramon assumed it had done so for a reason, that it thrived in cover and secrecy.

Regardless, Ramon picked up his pace until he finally reached the tree line, where the wooded edge of the vast forest provided him with a sense of security, false though it may have been.

He stopped and stared through the trees for several beats before beginning his trek around the perimeter, searching for signs of Jerry or evidence of the black figure. It didn't take long, however—less than a quarter mile or so—for him to realize the telescope's footprint was too immense, and that he, searching alone in this moment, was unlikely to find either. He couldn't focus his eyes or his mind, and every sound was giving him whiplash. He needed a team of officers to canvass the area, (a team which he didn't have, not on any day and certainly not on this particular morning), but Allie and the Carson brothers would have to do.

Ramon lowered his weapon and squinted into the bright forest, deciding at that moment to wait for Allie to arrive before making another move. At that point, they would do a quick search of the area and then head back to the station together. They would stop at Luke and Randy's along the way to see what the hell was up with those guys, and then at the station they would re-group, devise a plan. By then, Ramon would have worked out how to tell his story, and, if necessary, he wasn't beyond calling in help from the State barracks in Simonson if that's what it took. Especially if Derek Zamora and Amber Godwin were also dead. With three deaths in a day—one of them a murder—that was probably the right call to make.

Ramon was only a few steps into his walk back to the cruiser when he heard a shuffling sound in the leaves behind him, and he snapped to attention, pivoting on his heels, the shotgun at eye level now. He chambered a round and stepped back toward the woods.

"Who's there?" he called.

The rustle again, and Ramon now prepared his mind to see the shadowed beast again, the black form that shimmered and waved in the air like a latent image emerging on a piece of film.

Ramon called again and at first received no reply. But then, croaking from an area only yards from where he stood, he heard a voice. It was barely audible, sickly, but the word itself came through with perfect clarity.

"Help."

Ramon rushed toward the tree line and stopped, lowering the gun once again, and then he moved quickly through the brush, reaching the source of the distress call. It was a boy, shivering and cowering on his side, his back pressed against a fallen log as he unconsciously searched for warmth from the damp wood. Leaves and branches covered his body from head to feet, and only the bright red of his shirt, peeking through the gaps of brown and green, gave away the camouflage.

"Oh my god."

Ramon dropped to his knees and quickly removed his uniform shirt, and then he placed it across the child's shoulders, tucking it into his collar to complete the wrap. The boy blinked frantically up at Ramon, as if just waking from a dream, his damp hair flat against his head and face, leaves and sticks entwined in his locks.

"Sheriff?" he asked, as if not quite sure the image above him was real.

Ramon sighed, relieved, and then he shook his head in confusion. "Josh? Jesus Christ, son, what the hell are you doing out here?" He placed the gun down and gently pulled Josh forward, lifting him to a sitting position. "Are you okay? Are you hurt anywhere?"

Josh shook his head. "I dddddon't think so. Jjjjust cold."

"How did you get out here?"

Josh trembled again, a motion that seemed to Ramon to contain more than just cold. A combination of chill and fear.

"I...I don't really know. I jjjjust saw it. I saw it walking and...I kkkkept following. I ddddon't know why. I..." He trailed off, breathing heavily now as exhaustion set in.

Ramon closed his eyes as a strange feeling of gratitude fell over him, and then he looked to the heavens before focusing back on the boy. He was grateful to have found Josh, of course, that was nothing short of a miracle, but he was also relieved to know he wasn't insane. He hadn't truly considered that a possibility, but still, it mattered to him that there was someone else who had seen the thing too, someone alive who could validate his own story, assuming the creature was what Josh was referencing.

"I saw it too, Josh." Ramon nodded, wide-eyed. "I saw it too."

Josh stared hard at Ramon, frowning, his eyes full of tears, silently questioning the sheriff for an explanation about what they had seen exactly, searching for answers that Ramon didn't have.

"And then..." Josh trailed off, seeming to think better of what he was about to say.

"What is it, Josh?"

He stared back at Ramon sheepishly. "I...I thought I lost it. It was so hard tttto see in the dark. And the rain. But I just kept following it anyway. I just kept going in the same direction through the Tanner Farm. For miles, I guess. I didn't even know I was on the Grieg property until I...I'm sssssorry, Sheriff. I really didn't—"

"I don't care, Josh. You're not in trouble. I only care that you're safe. And that you stay that way. Does your mom know you're missing?"

Josh shook his head. "I don't know. I don't think so. I'm supposed to be at camp this morning. Mrs. Demartis was supposed to pick me up, bbbbut if I don't come out right away when she honks, she just leaves. And my mom is at work."

Ramon nodded, processing the prosaic day Josh had just described, so typical in the quiet town of Garmella, with kids and camps and carpools and work. Such routine seemed an impossibility now, an ideal that would perhaps never occur in this place again. *Was anyone at work right now? At camp? Alive?*

"I found it again though."

Ramon was back. "Found it?"

Josh nodded and then took a full breath, whimpering and shuddering on the exhale, his body still fighting to get warm. "I almost walked into it. It was right there in front of me. But even that close—only a foot away from it, maybe—it was so black I could barely see it." He paused. "And then it grabbed me."

"What?" Ramon put a hand to his mouth in shock, and the image of Riley Tackard's twisted back and frozen face instantly appeared to him again, mauled and charred to the point of unrecognizability. The young guard had been in the monster's grip for only seconds before being destroyed. How on earth, if the thing had grabbed Josh as well, could the boy still be alive? It was impossible.

"What grabbed you, Josh?"

Josh shook his head slowly. "Like I said. It was...I don't know. I...I can't really describe it."

"Did it look like...?" Ramon cut himself off, knowing that if he described to Josh what *he* had seen, it could lead the boy to reveal those same images in his retelling. "Just try, Josh. Just tell me what you saw." Ramon was eager now, fighting to keep his voice calm.

Josh began to cry now, and Ramon brought the boy in close to his chest, rubbing his shoulders, tugging his draped shirt tightly around his back.

"Okay, let's get you to the car. I've got warm blankets and I think a couple of Slim Jims in the glove box."

At the mention of food, Josh's eyes ignited, and he wiped his tears away, eager to get to the meat sticks. Within the minute, the boy was sitting in the back seat of the cruiser finishing off the first Slim Jim and already opening the wrapper of the second.

"Can you tell me what you saw now?" Ramon was seated beside Josh in the back. "If you can't, it's okay, but I just need to know if it was the same thing I saw." And then he added, "Because what I saw was *very* scary."

Josh turned toward Ramon on the word *scary* and nodded quickly, a lump forming in his throat. "It was...so black. So tall. But...I don't really know what it looked like. I've never seen anything like it."

Josh and Ramon had seen the same thing; that question was settled for good.

"It was like a vampire maybe," Josh added. "But...fuzzy. Without a real face." Frustration fell across Josh's face at his lack of vocabulary, but to Ramon, the description sounded as perfect as anything he could have expressed.

"And it touched you Josh?" Ramon asked. "You said it...it grabbed you?"

Josh nodded and dropped his eyes, tightening his shoulders into his torso; it was body language that suggested discomfort, an unwillingness to expand on his statement. Finally, he looked up at Ramon and nodded.

The boy was still shaken by his encounter, that was obvious, and Ramon knew there was the risk he would shut down altogether if pushed too hard. But Ramon's need for details was stronger than his sensitivity for a scared boy. At least in that moment. "Was there anything else? Anything you remember that might be important?"

Josh glanced at Ramon and then dropped his eyes in a flash. It was the move of guilt and shame, an affirmation of the question itself. Ramon had seen the look from suspects his entire career.

"What is it, Josh?"

Josh stayed quiet for several seconds, and just when Ramon thought he'd lost him for good, the boy said, "It talked to me."

For a moment, Ramon thought he'd misheard the boy, and he tried for several beats to imagine what other word Josh could have said that sounded like 'talked.' But he knew he had heard correctly. "Talked to you? Is that what you said? Are you sure?"

Josh nodded. "But it wasn't really talking. Not with a mouth like real talking."

"What do you mean?"

Josh frowned. "It was more like a thought that came into my brain. But I...I knew it came from the thing. Making me think about what it wanted me to."

Somehow, this explanation made more sense to Ramon than if the creature had actually spoken aloud. Maybe it was because it left open the possibility that Josh had imagined the words, but in his heart, Ramon didn't really believe that to be the case. He had had a similar experience, not of hearing a voice exactly, but the loss of control of his mind suggested some alternate power was at play.

"What did it say to you, Josh?"

Josh swallowed and began to shake his head, and then he started to cry softly.

"It's okay, Josh. Nothing is going to hurt you as long as you're with me. I promise."

Josh looked up at Ramon, his face squinted and confused. "You can't promise that, Sheriff."

Ramon wanted to smile, to be adult and reassuring, but the boy's words sent a chill of fear up his back. "Why do you say that?"

Josh scoffed. "Because it knows you too, Sheriff. It knows everyone."

Ramon searched Josh's face now, trying to find the meaning of his words somewhere in his eyes. But he could only find torture there, a grimness he'd never seen from a child before. He repeated his question. "What did it say to you, Josh?"

Josh was stoic now, his eyes narrow and sad.

Ramon nodded. "Go ahead?"

"My mind started going crazy. All of these memories started coming into my brain at once. It was... I don't know. I never felt anything like it. It was like every memory of my life in a second." He paused. "And after, that's when I heard it. That's when it talked to me." He stalled again and took another heavy breath, and then he locked eyes with Ramon. "It wanted to know my...my evil. Those were the words I...felt. 'Tell me your evil.'"

Ramon swallowed nervously as he attempted to process the boy's words, to make sense of them in the context of all he had witnessed today.

Evil. It was certainly a fitting word for the day.

"And did you answer him? Did you respond?"

Josh looked to his lap and nodded.

"What did you say?"

Josh lifted his chin and looked out his side window, gathering himself. After a few seconds, he turned back and fixed a cold stare on the sheriff. "I told it."

CHAPTER SIX

Six months before the rain

WINSTON BELL HEARD the sound of the approaching truck first, noting what an unusual time of day it was for anyone to be passing by his compound. The only consistent traffic he got up this way came from the mail truck and employees of the Grieg. But it was too early for the mail, and though it also seemed a strange time for anyone to be arriving for work—a little after 10 am—the rumble of the engine suggested it was one of the Grieg's maintenance men coming out to check on a problem, probably to do with rodents in the control room, Winston concluded cynically.

But when he gained a visual of the approaching vehicle, Winston got the sudden feeling that his day of peace and leisure was about to be disrupted. The looming truck wasn't one of the khaki green maintenance ones that Winston was so used to seeing, but rather it was off-white and plain, carrying a lump of rusty gray metal which rose from its bed like a tumor.

Winston caught his breath at the sight of the truck, more intrigued than anything else, wondering if he'd ever seen one of them so close to his estate. He knew about the audits, of course—he'd lived in Garmella for a decade now, after all—and he had seen the trucks on several occasions over the years, most often during one of his Sunday getaways when he simply couldn't stay in Garmella another minute. On those mornings—which hadn't occurred in over a year now—he usually took a drive down to Simonson for lunch, or even to Flagstaff when he was feeling especially ambitious, sometimes noting the monitor trucks cruising the side roads of the town like wolves outside a pen of goats.

But the trucks had always kept their distance from his property, a fact that Winston assumed was to do with his home's location, which was perhaps too far up 91 to make it worth their while to monitor. And though his house was the closest residence to the telescope, he lived in relative isolation compared to the rest of the town, and one home apparently didn't warrant its own monitor truck, especially, he concluded, if there had been no major frequency interruptions to raise the eyebrows of the monitors.

Winston sat rigid and still on his porch, in the same spot where he'd been now for over two hours already, enjoying the light bake of the sun and the cool air of the summer morning, the latter of which was already beginning to evaporate, threatening to unleash a typical blistering Arizona afternoon.

He continued spying the truck as it moved with pace down the interstate, alone against the backdrop of the desert, appearing like a wild mustang atop a distant ridge, out of context on the landscape despite its valid reason for being there, its nondescript metal frame somehow making it more unusual.

It was on its way to the telescope, Winston now reasoned, and though he had never seen one of the monitors ascend to the Grieg previously (though perhaps they had during his jaunts out of town), it made perfect sense, considering they were in Garmella every month for the sole purpose of keeping the airwaves clean.

Still, the truck made Winston uneasy, and he was unable to take his eyes off the vehicle. He held his breath as it neared the stretch of road that ran perpendicular to his driveway, willing it to pass by, moving his lips in a series of whispery commands which ordered the truck to continue on up to the Grieg.

"Keep going, keep going, keep going."

For the moment, it appeared Winston's will was indeed that strong, so persuasive as to move men and machine, as the truck seemed destined to pass by without incident and continue up 91 to the radio telescope.

But somewhere around twenty yards past the driveway to the Bell manor, when Winston was already in the middle of his exhalation of relief, releasing his grip of anxiety—a feeling which he couldn't quite understand in the moment—the red brake lights of the pickup flashed to bright, reflecting the rays of the eastern sun toward the section of wraparound porch where Winston sat.

The lights glowed for several seconds, a slow wink which registered like a beacon to Winston, and he felt the flush of blood swell to his face. He swallowed the lump in his throat and continued to sit motionless in his teak lounge chair, his eyes wide, anticipatory, one hand gripped tightly on the chair's arm, the other holding his coffee like a frozen server.

And then his eyes began to bloom as the red glow of the brakes suddenly deactivated and turned to white, and the truck began slowly to back up on the narrow highway. It reversed just ten feet or so past the driveway and then the front wheels pivoted to the right, and with that motion, Winston gasped.

The old man stood now, slowly, setting the coffee cup on the glass top of the patio table lest he spill it all over his shaking hand, and as the truck began to roll slowly toward his home, he watched it with a combination of curiosity and dread, anxiety and defensiveness.

What was the reason for this visit?

He'd done little more than turn on his coffee maker that day, and he certainly hadn't used any forbidden devices recently, not that he could think of anyway, nothing that would have warranted a warning or citation.

They were there for something else. Something dire.

A reasonable person would have assumed the visit was to offer some courtesy warning, a heads up about plans for increased monitoring or pending construction on the telescope. But within the last year, Winston's life had been robbed of reason, and his first instincts now contained the qualities of distrust, the assumption of injustice.

He sighed and cleared his mind, considering now that perhaps he *was* being cited. He didn't own a cellular phone, but he did have a radio, and maybe he'd unknowingly turned it on and was transmitting the signal at that moment.

But Winston was fairly certain any such citations would have come from the sheriff's department and not the monitors themselves, and there was little chance he'd accidently switched on the radio that was on the top shelf of his clothes closet. And besides, he knew by the rumble in his belly and the clutch in his chest that this visit was to do with something else. He didn't have much life left in him, but his intuition was strong, and he sensed that once the day ended, whatever was left of that life would be changed forever.

He closed his eyes and waited for the truck to arrive, and in less than a minute, the knock on the door sounded.

CHAPTER SEVEN

ALLIE NYLER HAD CLEARLY heard the fear in her sheriff's voice, and she wondered now if it was for the first time ever. Not that Garmella saw much in the way of terrifying events—it didn't—especially for her and her fellow officers, a force comprised of three men and two women, each of whom carried weapons amongst a civilian population that was overwhelmingly non-violent and law-abiding.

But there had been moments, a time or two when Ramon Thomas had faced situations that were beyond typical small-town affairs and would have petrified most people, Allie included. And in those moments, he had held his calm like a statue. One of these instances, Allie had seen with her own eyes.

Jennifer Gorman was eight years old when she was hit by a distracted driver as she crossed Drayton Ave, the impact causing her right femur to pop through the skin of her thigh like a chicken bone. Allie and Ramon had been first on the scene, not two minutes after, and before Allie could utter a single, useless question, something in the vein of 'Oh my god, what happened?!!,' Ramon had already ripped one of the shoulder straps from the girl's backpack and was wrapping a tourniquet around her upper leg like an army medic.

But what Allie remembered most about that day was Ramon's voice and demeanor, the way he had spoken to the third grader like he was telling her a bedtime story, ignoring her own screaming and the sickened shouts of the oglers around them. Later, Ramon had told Allie that it was the girl's screaming, in fact, that had kept him calm; the shrieks letting him know she was alive and functioning properly, at least from the waist up, and that whatever damage had been done below could be fixed over time.

And Ramon had been spot-on with that logic. Today, Jenny Gorman was alive and well and a three-sport star at Upper Apache Middle. It had taken several years of demanding PT to get her just right again, but right she was, happy and healthy and courting college coaches at the ripe age of thirteen. And Jenny had Ramon Thomas to thank for it.

So, on that morning, when Allie heard the shake in Ramon's voice over the radio, the distress and dread in his pitch, she felt more than just a wave of concern—it frightened her. The new guard at the Grieg was dead, that much she knew, and though she wasn't yet privy to the details of the incident—whether it was an accident or something else—she knew it must have involved something disturbing or grotesque, a scene horrifying enough to send her boss to the brink of hysterics.

Allie turned once more to the edge of the precipice where Derek Zamora's truck had gone over, giving one last suspicious stare over the guardrail into the ravine below. She then shifted her eyes to the rail itself and to the ground at her feet, then behind her to the road leading to the cliff, suddenly noting the lack of skid marks on the pavement. She also took note of the tire tracks in the dirt and how they were parallel to the cliff—not perpendicular, which would have made more sense.

She reexamined her theory now that Derek Zamora had been speeding—and possibly drunk—when he suddenly spotted the sinkhole, far too late, and then turned quickly to his left, crashing into the guardrail with enough speed to vault his Ranger over the barrier like Evel Knievel and down to the ravine below. The theory was sound, she supposed, but the pieces didn't quite fit. There was damage to the guardrail, but not the kind that would have come from the impact she imagined in her mind. And, again, the tracks along the side of the road ran in the wrong direction. Plus, if Derek had come upon the hole so suddenly, he would have slammed his brakes at some point, which would have left thick black marks somewhere on the street.

But Allie didn't have time to investigate the scene properly now; her Sheriff needed her, and, as insignificant as it seemed in the moment, she was determined to atone for today's late arrival—one of many indiscretions over the past few months—and to get back in her boss' good graces.

She jotted a couple of notes on her notepad, took a dozen pictures with her camera, and then returned to her cruiser, walking around to the rear of the car. From her trunk, she pulled out a yellow diamond sign that read 'Dead End' and a stack of orange cones which she set out in a tight row with the others across the width of the street, deciding that if these measures didn't prevent any more disasters, the fault was on the driver.

She stood in the road for a moment and surveyed the scene one last time and then let her stare drift up to the mountains in the distance. The sky was now as blue as sapphire, and a warm breeze rose from the valley and flowed across her face. Allie's eyes drifted to the sinkhole now and she instinctively averted her gaze before glancing back to the cavity, mildly curious about her own reaction. She took a few steps toward it, and when she was about ten feet or so from the lip, she stopped and looked back to the cruiser, her stomach suddenly clenched tightly with anxiety.

"What is wrong with me?" she mumbled.

She shook her head, trying to jostle her nerves back into place, and then she edged closer to the chasm, stopping again just a pace and a half away. She stood tiptoed as she craned her neck, trying to peek into the damaged concrete, to judge just how far down the abyss went.

She took one more step and was suddenly hit with a smell that was some combination of burnt flesh and ammonia; a nastier combination of odors she couldn't imagine.

"Jesus Christ. It's like a goddamn volcano for suicidal animals."

It made sense to Allie that a porcupine or badger—or maybe even an elk or mule deer—could have been claimed by the gap in the road and then gotten stuck in the crevice and baked by the Arizona sun. As she considered it further, she couldn't imagine a sadder thought.

"Sorry, fellas," she said, and then turned to head back toward the cruiser to leave for the Grieg.

Whoosh!"

The sound of whooshing air erupted from the hole behind Allie before she took her first step, and she pirouetted back to the crater and froze, her breath stuck high in her chest. She stared at the air above the hole like it contained the secrets of life, the noise blasting like a geyser of sound.

"What in the fu—"

And as quickly as the hiss emerged, it ceased, as if shut off by some valve deep in the earth, but before the mountain returned to the serenity of a minute earlier, a wailing noise called from the pit, low and distant, like a foghorn whose bell has been stuffed with mud. The howl faded in and out in a moment, but before the sound dissolved into the mountain, Allie heard what sounded like her name being called on the wind.

Allie felt a burn in her chest, the grip of fear again in her belly, but she fought it, shaking her head defiantly.

"No," she said. "I don't think so."

She refused to spend another moment analyzing this event—not today. Her mental issues, if that was the right term, weren't going to win this day. She turned her back to the hole and strode confidently back to the cruiser, slamming the driver's door aggressively and peeling out in a screech of the tires. It was time to follow her boss' orders and get on up to the Grieg.

Except there was somewhere else she had to stop first.

Halfway to the telescope, she spotted the POW/MIA flag that rose high above Luke and Randy's house—an emblem that their father, a veteran of the Iraq War, flew proudly. Her orders were clear—no stops—yet despite the sheriff's urgency, as well as her determination to turn over a new leaf, the decision to stop at the Carson house seemed the proper thing to do. The two minutes or so it would take to rouse and rally her partners would be worth it, especially if the scene at the Grieg was as bad as she suspected. Besides, the Carson

brothers should have been on patrol by now, and if something had happened to them, this was the time to find out.

As Allie neared the house, she noted Luke and Randy's
dirty black Tundra parked in the drive, as well as the Garmella Police Department cruiser, the fourth and last of the fleet,
a car which Luke and Randy shared between them. The vehicle was also confirmation that the boys had not yet left the
house for the day.

"What the hell are you guys doing?" Allie said to herself,
peering through the windshield as she pulled behind the
Tundra in the driveway. "Can't keep your damn radio on at
least?"

Allie exited the cruiser and walked to the front door
of the small, ranch-style home, giving two brisk raps as she
scanned the area around her, noting again the absence of a
single person on the street. Her gaze caught the Suarez home
two doors down, and she took note of the open front door,
as well as the first-barrier screen door hanging lifelessly by its
bottom hinge, leaving entry to the house wide open.

"What the hell is going on today?"

Allie knocked once more and then almost immediately
gripped the knob and turned, receiving the resistance of the
locked door. She scanned the layout of the grounds and then
walked tentatively around toward to the back of the house,
and as she cleared the right side of the small residence, she
gasped at the sight of a straw hat rising above a cushioned
chaise lounge. The chair was positioned on the stone patio so
that it faced the risen sun, away from Allie.

She assumed it was Terry Carson—Luke and Randy's father.

Allie took a breath, relieved to have eyes on someone at last. "Mr. Carson?" she called.

Allie kept her voice low, not wanting to startle the man, quickly silencing her radio as well. The man had been diagnosed with PTSD upon his return from the Middle East and on disability since, and though he seemed a congenial enough man—Allie had only met him a couple of times—she considered he may not be too appreciative of being snuck up on from behind by a relative stranger.

"It's Allie Nyler, Mr. Carson. I work with Randy and Luke."

There was still no answer, and Allie quickly assumed the man was sleeping. She took a couple of steps toward him, continuing to scan the surroundings, suddenly feeling uneasy as she looked out to the border land of the sprawling Tanner Farm, the quiet serenity of the property somehow appearing troubling to her under the current circumstances.

But everywhere felt troubling this morning, Allie thought. Nothing in Garmella was quite right today.

"Mr. Carson?"

Allie took another step and was now directly beside Terry Carson, but before she could reach down to give his shoulder a quick, rousing shake, from the corner of her eye, she saw a dark mask of black. Allie turned in full toward the man now, gasping as she met the burnt, shriveled face of Luke and Randy's father. He was a white man racially, but his skin was now as black as a bat's wing, the straw hat sitting atop his head like the adornment on some demented scarecrow.

"Oh my god!" Allie shrieked, covering her mouth with the back of her hand, the sting of developing tears beginning a steady burn in their respective ducts. She reached for her sidearm, but it was only an instinct, and instead she left it holstered, her fingers barely tickling the grip as she stared in wonder at the figure below her.

"What?" she asked breathlessly, staring up at the house now, her head swiveling in all directions trying to find an answer to the impossible scene that had just unfolded.

As her eyes passed over the house a second time, her gaze caught the back door of the Carson house, and she could now see that the glass door dividing the porch from the kitchen was wide open, leaving only a closed beige curtain as the barrier.

Allie's heart raced in a frantic patter, and this time she pulled her pistol and stepped toward the house, climbing the porch in three quick bursting steps. At the top, she closed her eyes and took a prayerful breath, and then she pushed aside the curtain.

Immediately, she saw the body of Luke Carson. His corpse was seated at the breakfast table, his mouth agape in a scream, his crisped head matching that of his father's outside. He was unrecognizable; the only way Allie could distinguish Luke from his brother was by the metal nameplate on his chest.

Randy was in the kitchen as well, on his knees, his torso resting up against one of the kitchen cabinets, his right cheek pressed against the side paneling, just as black and destroyed as his brother's.

"No!" Allie cried. "No, God!" Tears were streaming from her eyes now. "What in God's name is happening?"

But Allie didn't have time to figure it out; a scream exploded from somewhere in the distance, piercing the stale, rotted air of the kitchen. Allie turned and pulled the curtain wide and then ducked back out to the back porch, peering down the row of yards in the direction of the scream. She knew instantly, based on the pitch of the wail, the scream had come from the Suarez place.

Allie sprinted to the fence that divided the Carson yard from the one next door—a home that was currently vacant, having been abandoned by the Green family several months ago after going into foreclosure—and she climbed the low, chain-link fence and hopped down into the abandoned yard. She then jogged quickly to the opposite side where the fence bordered the Suarez yard and stood still beside the barrier, her chest just above the rail of the fence as she tilted her head toward the house, listening. She could hear crying now, the sound of twelve-year-old Maria Suarez, no doubt, and Allie quickly climbed the fence and dropped down onto the damp ground of the Suarez yard.

Allie stood watching the back of the house, instinctively sensing the magnitude of the danger inside, knowing that to give the scene a moment to develop was the proper action. She could still hear Maria, but the screams had turned to whimpers now, pleas, and as Allie began to move slowly toward the home, Maria finally appeared through the rear door that led from the kitchen, stepping backward out of her house and onto the patio.

As the girl backed her way outside, Allie studied her movements; Maria's stare was locked on the interior of her home, and though Allie couldn't see the girl's eyes, she knew they were wide and terrified.

Allie moved another step closer, squinting to see into the Suarez house, but with the glare of the morning and her distance from the house, she couldn't see a thing.

"Maria!" Allie called, low and stifling. "Maria, what's going on?"

Maria's head tilted slightly toward Allie's voice, signaling that she had heard the call but couldn't bring herself to turn in full, so enraptured was she by whatever was lurking inside her home.

Allie moved toward the patio now, slowly at first but then with purpose, feeling an increased sense of urgency with each step.

And then she stopped, frozen in stride by the sight in the doorway, hypnotized by the thing that had seized the mind and attention of Maria Suarez as well.

Emerging from the open back portal, thin black shafts twisted forward from the space like branches from a tree, six of them in all that Allie could see, each crooked and long, coming through the entrance in the form of floating snakes, chest-high through the doorway, slowly searching the air like frozen black serpents tracking their prey.

Allie attempted to move her legs, but they felt heavy now, as if sandbags had been strapped to her thighs. Instead, she brought her full attention to the shapes, her jaw hanging wide as she absorbed the sight, her mouth as dry as hardened clay. She had stopped breathing entirely now, and though Allie wanted desperately to run toward Maria and protect her, she was simply incapable of moving.

Seconds later, a larger form appeared, the form to which the black snakes were attached. It was as horrific and shocking a sight as Allie could have imagined, and yet it was a form that was recognizable, reconcilable with the forms of the snakes.

The creature displayed the general shape of a human, with definition at the neck and head, as well as at the shoulders and arms and throughout its torso. It was taller than the frame of the door—taller than most men Allie had ever seen—yet it was thin enough that another of the beasts could have stood beside it in the doorway. And Allie saw now that the thin snakes which had first appeared were, in fact, extensions of the creature's arms. They were finger-like in shape, though there was nothing that could be called a hand to which they were attached; they were simply three long stems sprouting from the forearm of the creature like talons.

But there was some quality in the thing that made it not quite alive, and it was a feature Allie couldn't get her mind to process. The figure seemed to be drifting in and out form, as if it were made of a thick black smoke, or perhaps a heavy ink that couldn't quite hold its shape, blurring all semblance of definition beyond just the nature and color of the creature.

But as Allie's mind was searching for answers to the thing's form, her mind suddenly shifted, as if some frequency in her brain had been changed. In an instant, she was a small girl again on her family's farm in South Dakota. Then in college—during her first and only semester—sleeping through the alarm, hungover from the night before.

And then on the boat in Mexico.

"No!" she shouted, and the outburst quickly shifted her attention back to the porch and Maria, just at the moment the figure's outstretched hands reached forward for the girl. The appendages were so black against the bright morning as to be impossible in color, not reflecting a single drop of the sun's rays, and as it stretched toward Maria with a crooked grip of death, with this imminent threat on the young girl's life, Allie came fully back to life.

She clipped open her holster and pulled the Smith & Wesson with agility, purpose, and before she could utter a word of warning to either Maria or the creature, she fired off four rounds into various parts of the beast's shape.

No sound came from the monster, but its reaction was one that indicated distress, pain, and the creature immediately dropped its long arms to its body, the thin branches bleeding into the rest of the form, configuring it into something less than human now. No blood appeared, nothing that would indicate injury or trauma, but there was no question the shots had affected it in some way.

"Maria, run!" Allie called.

Maria didn't react at first, instead continuing to stare at the creature like a rodent frozen by the sway of a cobra; but then, after a pause of five seconds or so, she turned to Allie, her eyes desperate, unsure.

Allie lowered her voice now, trying to sound calm, her eyes staying fixed on the black form that was now lingering in place, standing straight and still, the smoky outline of the creature continuing to blur in and out of focus.

"Listen to me, Maria. My car is parked on the street next door, in front of Luke and Randy's house. Get to it; get inside and wait for me."

Maria stared at Allie as if the officer were speaking gibberish, slowly shaking her head in uncertainty.

"Maria!"

Maria blinked to awareness.

"Go! Now!"

Maria nodded and broke into the sprint of a greyhound, off the patio and around to the front of the house.

Allie was now alone with the murky monster, her breaths like those of a winded bison; she was approaching the point of hyperventilation. Her eyes were static on the form, waiting for it to act before making a countermove. "What the fuck are you?" she asked rhetorically.

The beast appeared to lift its chin and turn slightly, and now appeared to be facing Allie; but she could only see the blur of a form, a countenance of spent charcoal.

Then something in the creature began to change, and the shady mug of black at the top of its body began to show something that resembled definition. At first, Allie didn't know if it was simply her eyes adjusting to the figure, or if it was the figure morphing into something recognizable, but the blank blackness at the bottom of its face became a large empty mouth, gaping wide and hungry, and above it appeared tiny circles of yellow, five or more, which Allie could only assume were eyes.

"Jesus," Allie whispered. "What in the creation of Our Father...?"

The creature, which had dropped its arms after Allie's shots, lifted them once again, this time with bent elbows, the snaky fingers pointing toward Allie like a wizard casting a spell.

Allie immediately saw the boat in her mind again, bobbing on the calm waters of the Baja peninsula like a duck on a pond, Cassidy Mayes lying naked on one of the deck chairs, save for her bikini bottom and a pair of Wayfarers, her blonde hair draping perfectly across the back of the chaise like honey over wheat toast.

Allie was terrified by the vividness of the memory, and the timing of its resurgence, but she shook it off again and raised the nine once more and fired off three more rounds, each as pure as the first four.

The creature still produced no sound of pain or surprise, but this time it dropped to the ground in a heap, as if it had suddenly been turned to a pile of sand, leaving a wispy residue that lingered in the air for several seconds before dissipating.

But the creature wasn't gone, nor was it dead, and Allie let out a shriek as the thing scampered away, low and shuffling, like a scattering insect, off the patio and toward the Suarez's neighbor's house to the left, away from the Carson residence.

She watched the creature disappear behind the side of the house and waited, and when she was confident it was gone for good, she stood in the middle of the Suarez yard for several beats, her hand covering her mouth in a pose of astonishment, her mind fighting to make sense of what had just occurred.

Allie dropped her hand now and it brushed against the two-way radio on her hip. She responded to the tactile trigger and brought the radio to her mouth.

"Sheriff?" Allie's voice came out cracked and dry. She cleared her throat and spoke again. "Sheriff, it's Allie. You there?"

"I'm here. Why aren't you," Ramon replied.

"I'm...I'm on my way now. Luke and Randy are dead. So is their father. I saw it. I saw the thing that killed them. Over."

There was a pause of several seconds, and Allie knew Ramon was digesting the news of his deputies' deaths. She could almost see the expression of grief on his face. Finally, the radio clattered to life. "What you saw, did it look like something straight from the depths of Hell?"

Allie hadn't considered that, but it was exactly right. "I think you nailed it, Sheriff. What...what could it..." She couldn't manage the question, and she knew Ramon had no answers anyway. "I'm on my way now, Sheriff. I'll have Maria Suarez with me. Not sure about her parents, but I'm assuming they're dead too." She waited, measuring whether or not to add the rest of what she was thinking. She decided to go with it. "And by the end of the day, maybe everyone in Garmella will be too."

There was another long pause on Sheriff Thomas' end, and Allie quickly regretted the add-on statement.

"Sheriff?"

"Listen, Allie, I don't know what's happening, but let's not give up before we've even started."

Allie nodded to herself. "Yes, sir."

"Change of plans also. Meet me back at the station. With what you've told me about Luke and Randy, I need to see about Gloria. And I...I'd rather try to figure this out from somewhere safe."

"Roger that."

"And let Maria know I've got Josh Carter with me, so at least she'll have some company."

"I'll do that." Maria hesitated and then said, "And Sheriff, not sure if you know this or not, but that thing, I think it can be hurt. I shot it. Several times. I didn't kill it, but it definitely is no fan of bullets."

"That's good to know, Allie. Thought I might've hit it too. Definitely scared it. I'll see you at the station in ten. And Allie?"

"Yeah, Sheriff?"

"No more stops."

CHAPTER EIGHT

Six months before the rain

"DO YOU BELIEVE IN PERDITION, Mr. Bell?"

Winston let the question linger in the air for a moment as he studied the elderly woman's face, searching for some faint, playful smile to appear which would signal a lack of earnestness in her question. But the woman gave only a polite smile in return, an expression consistent with the one she'd displayed thus far during the conversation.

Winston glanced to the clock on the wall, which, amazingly, indicated the visitors had been in his study for almost a half hour now, a span of time which seemed impossibly long to him. It felt like it had been only a minute or two since he'd watched them step from the truck, their eyes scanning his property with great care as they walked towards his door.

He couldn't say for sure why he had let the group in; they had said very little from their positions on his front stoop, making only the most basic of introductions before asking if they might enter and speak with him for a moment. He'd agreed—they had arrived in one of the Grieg's audit trucks, after all, which gave them a certain authority—but the look of them was off, out of place in the environment in which they'd almost magically appeared.

Yet, despite Winston's intellectual suspicions, he had felt a certain paralysis come over him in that moment, a hypnosis even, some latent fear that told him he had no real choice in the matter but to allow them entry. And once inside, he had led them robotically through the foyer of his large estate, past the parlor room where he had received uninvited guests years ago, during a time of his life when such events still occurred on occasion. Without once looking back, Winston had continued through the main living area and past the kitchen until he reached his study, a room he had used quite a bit until four or five years ago when he had finally retired for good. That was where they met now.

"Perdition?" Winston repeated. "To mean Hell? As in, the place where evil people go when they die?" Winston recited the definition using a certain spooky lilt to his voice, wiggling his outstretched fingers as he did.

The woman shrugged and nodded, as if that wasn't quite her definition but would suffice for the time being.

Winston wrinkled his brow, his smile fading slightly, realizing the question had been asked sincerely. "I...I don't know. I've never been much of a religious man, but I suppose I'd like to think people are punished for their cruelty at some point. Somewhere. What is this about anyway?"

"The question is not one of gradation or desire; it is one of belief. Do you *believe* in Perdition? Hell, as you say?"

Winston paused, searching his true feelings on the subject. "I guess I'm agnostic on the subject then. Of both Heaven and Hell."

"Then you *don't* believe."

Winston shrugged, slightly annoyed at the re-phrasing of his position. "I'm *agnostic*, as I said. I've no proof, no reason to believe in it. Again, what are these questions ab—"

"Agnosticism is non-belief, Mr. Bell. There is no difference."

Winston was growing more annoyed by the second, but he decided to play along. "Is that so? And what does that mean exactly?"

"It means that if you need proof of something's existence to believe in it, then you don't. That is the basis of faith. I'm sure if I asked if you believed in the Loch Ness Monster or Bigfoot, you would tell me you do not. Is that right?"

Winston snickered and nodded, adding a mocking of-course-I-don't smile.

"Yet if either suddenly appeared on the Six O'clock News, with videos and witnesses and commentary by leading scientists about the authenticity of the creatures, you would rethink this non-belief. And after a while, when everything was confirmed, you would believe in full."

Winston shrugged. "I suppose that's right." There was a lull. "Okay then, no. Based on that definition, I suppose my answer is no, I don't believe in Hell."

The woman nodded and looked to the two other people with whom she'd arrived before settling back on Winston.

"And yet it exists."

This time it was one of the two men who spoke, the elder male who looked to be even older than the woman. He wore the same complexion as she, dark and weathered, and it was obvious there was Native American blood in them, though it had certainly been diluted over the years.

"Or at least a place like it," he continued, "the place from which the myth of Hell was born."

The woman turned to her associate as he spoke, and Winston detected a hint of annoyance at his interjection, perhaps irked that he had stolen her reveal.

"Though perhaps not in the way you've come to think of it," he continued, "a place where only 'evil people go', I believe you said."

Winston stared at the older pair of the trio for several beats, studying their motives, trying to understand why Grieg auditors were currently in his study asking about his beliefs in the afterlife. "What is this about? Why are you telling me any of this?"

The man ignored the question. "But there is a place beneath this world, a place where the bodies and souls of men are taken, its passageway accessible here on Earth. It is a place known to man since the birth of civilization, mentioned on the oldest of the Sumerians' cuneiform tablets and likely known about well before the earliest times of recorded history."

Winston let the words linger in the room as he stared into the old man's face, hoping now to locate the significance of this lecture somewhere in his eyes, while also searching his own mind for what he may have been missing by this inquiry. Had they not arrived in an audit truck, he would have assumed them to be Jehovah's Witnesses or Mormons, or some other door-knocking converters of the Christian faith.

In any case, Winston was in no hurry to dismiss them. He spoke with so few people in Garmella these days—and even fewer over the last year since what was once mere privacy had devolved into reclusiveness—that the company before him, as eccentric as they seemed to be, and the banter that came with them, was a welcomed surprise to his day.

"Okay," Winston replied finally. "I'll play along. I have no reason to question your beliefs on Heaven and Hell, but as I said, I've never been a religious man. I was raised by heathens, I suppose." He smiled softly, an attempt to bring levity to the conversation, but he received no indication of success on that front. He frowned and asked, "And what is this to do with anyway?" It was a question he'd asked at least three times already, and the answer was at least twenty minutes overdue. "What does my belief in any of this have to do with the Grieg?"

The woman wrinkled her brow. "The telescope?"

"This obviously has something to do with the Grieg, right?"

"What is obvious about that, Mr. Bell?"

Winston's forehead now matched that of the woman, creased in confusion, and he thought back to the introductions on the stoop and the moment when he'd answered the door, the group of three standing in a perfect line beneath his portico. As he replayed the scenario once again, he realized they had never explicitly mentioned who they were or why they were there. Or, for that matter, that they worked for the Grieg at all.

"You're driving one of the trucks, aren't you? One of the audit trucks? I assumed when you knocked on my door at ten o'clock on a Thursday morning, your visit was to do with the audits this weekend. Or about some maintenance going on, some news of the telescope. I don't know."

As he questioned the group further, Winston felt whatever enchantment had been cast by the visitors slowly wane, and he grew a bit more suspicious, aggressive.

"What *are* you doing here then?" he asked. "Specifically? And what are all these questions about Heaven and Hell?"

"They are just questions, Mr. Bell," the old man answered, a reply wholly unsatisfactory to Winston.

"Is that so? Standard operating procedure for the Grieg auditors, is it?"

No reply, and Winston suddenly felt the curiosity and camaraderie dissolve.

"Yeah, that's kind of what I thought. So, you know what I think I'll do? I think I'll give a call into the sheriff's office to see if there are any scheduled auditing rounds going on today. It *is* Thursday, right? Not typical to come during the week, is it?"

Again, he got no reply, and though Winston knew an audit beginning a day or two early wasn't completely unprecedented, his instincts told him something was amiss.

"Yeah, I think the sheriff is sure to know something about this. Or, if not, he would certainly be interested in hearing about it. Do you think?"

The woman glanced to her peer beside her on the couch, a thin glare in her eyes as if blaming him for having blown their cover. Winston noted the look, and his instincts now told him he was definitely in the throes of a scam. He stood quickly and made his way toward the phone, picking it up and putting a finger to the first digit.

"Our visit *is* tied to the telescope, Mr. Bell."

Winston's back was to the group when the words rang through the room, but he knew instantly they had come from the third member of the group, the man who had yet to speak until that moment.

Winston stopped and turned toward the visitor, who only moments earlier had been seated quietly in one of several velvet parlor chairs but who was now on his feet, strolling the perimeter of the room. The man scanned the walls and bookshelves, casually grazing the adornments with his eyes. He was the youngest of the group—by twenty years at least—but something in his demeanor, in the confidence of his posture and the tenor of his voice, let Winston know he was the person in charge.

"Though, to be truthful, Mr. Bell, it is only tangentially related."

"Tangentially?"

The man nodded once. "We are not, in fact, employees of the Grieg Radio Telescope." He raised a finger now, pointing slightly. "Though, in fairness, no one here made that claim."

"Why would you drive a truck like that if you're not a monitor? Why would you have that thing on the back like all the others. What is that for if not to monitor transmissions?"

"Let us just say, Mr. Bell, that it allows us to move amongst them. To drive the streets without being...how shall we say...speculated."

Winston hung up the phone now and turned in full toward the man. "But why?" Winston squinted and rubbed his forehead, confused by this sudden shift in the conversation, this divulgence of information. And he was beginning to feel tired, drained of energy; the visit by the trio was beginning to feel heavy on him, stressing the limits of his body, the sickness inside him beginning to echo once more. "Move amongst them? I...I don't understand what you're talking about."

"Not yet, Mr. Bell, but you will soon."

"Meaning?"

The man sighed and bowed his head slightly, a sign that he was not quite ready to divulge the full thrust of his visit, but that he had the obligation to give at least some insight to the man in whose home they had been allowed entry. "As my associates have intimated already, there is a place...a place of the dead. *For* the dead. It is a place we know to be as true as any laws of physics or mathematics or chemistry."

"So, we're back here again?" Winston mocked, trying to sound casual, slightly exasperated. He met the man's eyes for a moment and then dropped his gaze immediately, revealing his true discomfort.

"It is the place where most in this town will end up, Mr. Bell, so yes, we are here again."

The young visitor's words rang ominously in Winston's ears, and for the first time since the group's arrival, Winston felt the sting of threat and violence, danger. The man allowed his staid gaze to linger a moment, to burn into Winston's memory, and then he smiled, flashing a grin as large as a jack o' lantern's, as if he were truly infected with the joy of his answer.

Winston swallowed and returned the smile, lips only, trying to measure the sanity of the man before him. He walked back to the chair where he was sitting previously and sat. "Hell?" he said finally, his voice cracking. "As in the literal Hell?"

The visitor shrugged nonchalantly. "My personal belief is no, not exactly. I don't believe it is the Hell as defined by Christianity." He paused thoughtfully. "Though I suspect the inspiration for the religious fable did, in fact, come from this place."

Winston narrowed his eyes. "But you just called it that. Or at least your friend did only a few minutes ago."

"Yes, well, it suffices for our purposes. Though we typically use 'Perdition'; the word carries with it a bit less sensation." The man's face grew stern now, steely. "And despite its violence and finality, it has gifts to offer. Perhaps one for you even."

"Gifts? What could that...even mean?"

"How old are you, Mr. Bell," the man asked, continuing his walk around the room until he reached the fireplace, where he stopped and ran a lone finger along a brass candlestick that sat empty atop the mantle, inspecting it as if he were some appraiser of fine ornamental parlor pieces. After a long pause, he turned to Winston again. "Mr. Bell?"

"I'm not sure that's an appropriate question to ask of someone whom you've just met."

The man pursed his lips and nodded, giving the slightest of chortles at Winston's reply. "Yes, well, perhaps under most circumstances that would be true; my question would be uncouth. But my intention—our intention—is not to insult or embarrass you, Mr. Bell; it is to offer you something of

unique import. Something that perhaps one man in a millen-
nium gets the chance to accept."

The pitch, Winston thought now. Of course. He was
right all along. These folks weren't from the Grieg—they had
admitted as much—but until now, Winston couldn't peg the
true purpose of their arrival. But he could see it coming now.
They *were* con artists. Bible-pushing predators bent on turning the world toward their beliefs.

And now the priceless offer was to come—an offer
which was certain to have a very definite price attached to
it. Winston was a wealthy man, and old, the exacta for every
good confidence man; and though Winston wasn't wired into the internet the way most of the world was, he watched
enough news and read enough papers to know that, aside
from perhaps a *woman* of his same age and wealth, his demo-
graphic was the number one target for swindlers.

Winston tightened his stare now, scanning each of the
faces in the room for some signal being passed between
them, some look that would let him know the swindle was
indeed afoot. But if it was there, he was blind to it, as he
saw only solemnness from the older members of the group,
and the younger man was still standing by the fireplace with
a look that was fixed, assured and waiting for Winston's answer.

"Okay, enough!" Winston exclaimed instead, avoiding
the question of his age and getting back to the original thesis
of the conversation. What is this really about?!"

The leader of the group turned the full frame of his body
toward Winston now, his eyes focused, his arms by his side
like a soldier at attention. "We are here with an offer. One

that has been written about in various forms for centuries." The man spoke calmly and confidently but with the speed and passion of a Baptist preacher. "And though our offer does not require the Faustian price of your soul, it does require effort on your part. Some risk."

"Faustian price?" Winston smiled. "Are you really trying to sell me Hell? Is that *really* what this is about?" Winston chortled, bemused. "What...what does that even mean? I've never heard of this before. Most people in your field, that is to say, those who spend their days knocking on peoples' doors, are attempting to sell Heaven. Peace and Jesus. You've heard of him, right?"

The younger man nodded earnestly, indicating he had, in fact, heard of the Christ.

Winston calmed himself and shook his head slowly, feeling bewildered that he was still in the middle of this conversation. "Hell," he repeated to himself, incredulously. "Even if I did believe in...that place—which I've already stated I do not, despite your assurances that it exists—why would I be interested in an offer from there? I'm not a Satan worshipper. Do you see pentagrams or goat's blood or anything like that in my house?" Winston lifted his arms high and waved them frantically in the air, inviting a full inspection of his residence for satanic memorabilia.

Suddenly the fatigue was almost unbearable, and he felt light-headed, on the verge of fainting. He leaned back in his chair and took a deep breath. "I'm an old man," he whispered. "And sick. If I have another year on this earth, it will be a gift. Nobody sells his soul to the devil at eighty. And especially not when they are terminally ill."

The man dropped his smile and glared toward Winston now, all humor and playfulness now drained from his face. He tilted his head and nodded ever so slightly. "Are you aware of the Egyptian versions of Hell, Mr. Bell? Or of those from Ancient Greece and Turkey? How about that of the Mayans?"

Winston shrugged, his energy nearly exhausted; he wanted nothing more than to lie down and begin his late-morning nap. His face felt flush, his mind dizzy.

"Each of the civilizations I have just named has a place similar to the Judeo-Christian version; that is, a place beneath the ground—the ground of this very Earth—where the souls of men descend when they die. It is why corpses have been interred for over a hundred-thousand years. Burial of the dead is the oldest known tradition of our species. That is not by accident. Man has known about this place beneath the ground for as long as he has walked on two legs."

Winston listened to the words without registering them fully; his breathing was now shallow, his head foggy.

"But religion, as it is wont to do, has distorted this place, claimed it for its own purposes so that it might elevate certain men while diminishing others. In the Christian version, this world is a place of suffering and torture for sinners, of eternal damnation where a horned figure called Satan rules like a deity, jealous and bitter of God above him. You've read your Milton, I'm sure?"

Winston's eyes were half-open now, weary, and he saw the stranger slightly out of focus now, fuzzy. "What is your name?" he asked.

"I am called Zander."

"Zander," Winston repeated dreamily, the name sounding foreign on his tongue. "Is that with an X or a Z."

"Z. My acquaintances are Tehya and Ouray."

Winston nodded, satisfied that this information had been offered without hesitation. "Those are Indian names, yes? Hopi? Apache, maybe?"

"The Stuwix tribe from which we descended has been on the brink of extinction for more than a century. We are perhaps the remaining three."

"Stuwix? I've...I've never heard of them."

"Few have, Mr. Bell. Perhaps a handful of scholars know anything at all about the tribe. Even at the height of their time in the eighteenth century, they occupied only a small territory of British Columbia."

"British Columbia? You're a long way from home?"

"Home is here now."

Winston shook his head. "I would have seen you before today if you were a resident."

"We've come to Garmella recently."

Winston closed his eyes and quivered his head, unable to process the reasoning for such a migration. "Why?"

"Why what, Mr. Bell?"

Winston felt cold now, depleted, as if the very presence of these visitors had begun to suck the power from his body, to drain him of what still remained of his life force.

But it wasn't the visitors who were to blame, at least not directly. His depletion came mainly from the scarring on his lungs, and the fact that he'd lived in isolation for too long now and was simply unconditioned to engage in extended social interaction anymore. The life of semi-hermitage—combined with the main culprit of pulmonary fibrosis—had both taken their toll.

"Why are you here? Today? Why have you come to Garmella?"

The man gave a sad grin now as he sat back in the parlor chair. But it was only for an instant before he sat up and shifted his body forward, quickly, until he was seated at the edge of the chair, his eyes burning with knowledge and secrecy. With both of his hands, he grabbed one of Winston's, and then he leaned in, his nose nearly clipping that of his host.

"That is the question, isn't it, Winston? Why are we in Garmella?"

CHAPTER NINE

"SHIT!"

Ramon stood and slammed the phone into the receiver and then glanced up at Josh, who was studying him intensely from across the desk.

"Sorry, Josh, the...the phone is dead. For some reason. It was...it was working fine this morning but—"

"It's to do with those things, right?"

Ramon gave a defeated shrug. "I don't know."

Josh nodded, appreciating the honesty of Ramon's uncertainty. He then looked to his lap. "I...I can tell you now. If you still want to know."

"About what you told the thing in the woods?"

Josh nodded.

Ramon sat down slowly and nodded, trying not to show the eagerness he was feeling inside. "Okay. Yes, of course I want to know. If you feel comfortable about it."

Josh took a deep breath and closed his eyes, nodding. When he opened his eyes, he stared toward the ceiling, gathering his thoughts. "I didn't want to do it at first, Sheriff," he began. "I swear to God I didn't. I said so at the time."

Ramon felt the urge to follow up on the 'It' of the sentence, but now that Josh was talking, he decided it best to keep quiet and let him get to the nub.

"It was Mark's idea. Right from the start. He was the one who said we should take his mom's jewelry."

The nub.

Josh sat straight in the oversized leather chair in front of Ramon's desk, his hands across his lap, shoulders slumped as his eyes pled for understanding from the authority figure looming before him.

Finally, Ramon spoke. "What exactly are you talking about, Josh? What does this have to do with what you told that thing back at the Grieg?"

"That's what it wanted to know. That's what it wanted me to tell it. It wanted to know the bad that was in me. But not just anything bad. It wanted me to know the *worst* thing in me. The worst thing I've ever done."

Ramon swallowed, haunted by the certainty of this middle-schooler's words. He nodded. "I see. But how...how did you know what it was? How did you know it wanted *that* particular bad thing? The thing about the jewelry?"

Josh shrugged. "It's the only *really* bad thing I've ever done."

He wasn't bragging, just being honest, and Ramon couldn't help but grin at the earnestness of the boy.

"Okay, tell me about this jewelry. What you took from your friend's mother. You said his name was Mark?"

Josh gave another sheepish, suspicious glance, knowing that there was no going back once the confession began.

"You won't be punished for it, Josh. I promise. I'm just trying to understand what's happening, and maybe you telling the story can help. Someone is dead today because of this thing, and maybe with your help we can stop it from killing anyone else."

At least four people were dead for certain, and likely more, including Jerry Kellerman, Derrick Zamora and Amber Godwin, and God only knew how many more people in the town. To this point, however, Ramon had only told Josh about Riley.

"Mark Yun, do you know him?"

At the mention of the Yun name, combined with the detail of stolen jewelry, the pieces fell quickly into place, and it took no more than a few seconds for Ramon to know precisely where Josh's story was going. But he only nodded at the question and said, "Of course."

"My stepdad used to be a plumber. And he did other handyman work also. Painting. Electrical repair. Stuff like that. And sometimes he did stuff for Mark's family."

"Your stepdad Ray, right?"

Josh nodded. "And Mark was my friend at the time—I guess even my best friend, even though he wasn't all that nice to me—and he knew I that I didn't really like Ray. But it wasn't even that I didn't like him, I guess, it was just that I wanted my dad and mom to get back together. And then..."

At this pause, the tears seemed destined to fall again, and Ramon had to keep from showing his frustration, the burn in his face and grit of his teeth.

Josh rallied though and continued the tale, moving forward to the point. "He said his mom had a really expensive necklace. It was worth like a thousand dollars."

The white South Sea pearl necklace had been appraised conservatively at $64,550 and was a nearly-century-old heirloom that had been passed on to Janet Yun by her mother and her mother's mother before. The family's history of the keepsake was a relevant point in Ray Bronigan's plea deal; if the case had gone to trial and he lost, he was looking at six years minimum.

"He knew where she kept it. Even though she didn't know he knew. And Mark knew that Ray was coming over that day to fix a pipe or something, and he...we planned that he would get the necklace from his mom's room and then he'd give it to me, and then I would take it and put it in one of Ray's pockets or a drawer or something."

"Jesus, Josh."

Having no other explanation than the presence of Ray Bronigan for her missing necklace—as he had been the only person outside of her family who had been in the Yun household for several days during the stretch when the item disappeared—a search warrant was issued of the Carter residence. Ramon had found the stunning item in less than three minutes, tucked neatly at the bottom of Ray's sock drawer, a place even at the time Ramon thought a bit convenient and obvious. Ray hadn't been home at the time of the search, and the look of shock on DeeDee's face had always stuck with Ramon, and it was matched only by the expression on Ray's face when told he was under arrest for burglary.

The evidence had been overwhelming and a plea was entered within a day or two. Ray was sentenced a few days after that and sent off to prison for the next twenty-two months.

"I said we should tell what happened! I told Mark that! But he said he would...he said that his father would kill him. That his father would kill us both. And not like in a kidding way."

Ramon felt little sympathy for Josh Carter at that moment, especially considering Ramon's own involvement in the incident that had robbed Ray Bronigan of two years of his freedom. His life.

But that was years ago now—Josh couldn't have been older than seven at the time—and Ramon and the rest of this town had much bigger obstacles to clear today. If life ever returned to normal again, and Ray Bronigan was still alive in that world, Ramon would do everything he could to make sure the ex-felon's record and reputation were returned to clean.

To make that happen, though, he had to stop whatever was killing the citizens of Garmella.

"That was a bad thing you did, Josh, I'm not going to say it wasn't. I know you know that now, but your stepfather lost a piece of his life because of what you and your friend did."

Josh's eyes welled up once more.

"But you were also very young when that happened, unaware of how severe the consequences of your actions would be. It doesn't excuse what you did, but don't ever think you're a bad person because of it. You're not bad, and you're certainly not evil."

Josh stared at Ramon now, considering his words. Finally, he shrugged and wiped his eyes. "Not anymore. I got it out."

Ramon narrowed his eyes, feeling compelled to ask the meaning of the boy's words, but instead he kept the story moving. "What happened next? With that thing? After you told it the story about the necklace?"

Josh's breathing became short and accelerated as he prepared to relive the event. "It...it held onto me for a little bit longer. And the whole time the burning inside me was getting worse. In my neck and throat and chest. I thought I was going to die. Or catch on fire. But then..." Josh closed his eyes and a single tear streamed down his cheek. "I could feel this...I don't know...calmness come over me, like a tingling inside. It was like the fire inside...it didn't go out, but it had been turned down until it was at the perfect temperature. It was still warm, but, like, in nice way." He shrugged. "I don't know how else to explain it. It's hard to tell it in words. But I...I knew I was going to be okay then. I knew I wasn't going to die."

Ramon swallowed, riveted by the boy's account. "How did you know that?"

Josh shook his head and frowned. "I don't know. I just did."

Ramon let these final words settle for a moment and then, despite the optics of panic it was likely to cause in the boy, he put his hand to his forehead and stared down at his desk, trying helplessly to wrap his mind around all that was happening this morning. It was all impossible. And yet he believed every word Josh Carter had said. Ramon had watched Riley in the grasp of the creature and had heard him cry out, and now he wondered if Riley too had been asked about the worst of his sins. He would never know now, but he believed it to be the case.

"Are you okay, Sheriff?"

Ramon looked up and nodded, smiling. "I'm fine."

"Sheriff!"

The door to the station burst open and Allie Nyler rushed in, turning first toward her own desk and then back to Ramon's office. Behind her was Maria Suarez.

Ramon met her at the threshold of his office. "Is everyone okay?"

Allie scoffed. "No, Sheriff, not quite." The deputy was calm in her speech, but her face was pale, and Ramon could see the fear in Maria's face behind her.

"Hi, Maria," he said, forcing a smile. The girl only stared back.

"Can I talk to you for a minute?" Allie nodded toward the far end of the station, near the rear exit, and she led the sheriff in that direction until they were outside of Maria's earshot.

"What the hell did I see today, Sheriff?" she asked, her voice cracking slightly, trying to maintain control. "What the hell was that thing I saw today?" She put her hands to her face, covering her nose and mouth, and then took a deep breath. "And Luke and Randy are...Jesus God it was like a scene from Pompeii." Allie staggered, as if ready to faint, and Ramon moved quickly toward her, easing her down into Gloria's desk chair.

"Easy, Allie. Easy. I know, I know. Just take a second. Sit here and focus on your breathing. Have you eaten anything today?"

Allie shook her head. "Not really."

"Alright, I've got stuff for sandwiches and a couple of cans of soup. Let's get some food in everyone first. No matter what's happening, we won't be able to face it without fuel."

"What was it, Sheriff?"

Ramon stared his deputy down, his face stern, controlling. "Food first."

Allie nodded and headed back to Gloria's desk, while Ramon walked to the kitchenette and found a half-loaf of bread and a jar of Peter Pan. He quickly began slapping slices of bread down on the counter and spreading peanut butter.

"What's going on, Sheriff?" Allie asked, her voice containing a tiny lilt of hope, as if they were the butts of some practical joke that she'd yet to uncover. She waved Maria toward her, patting the desktop, encouraging her to sit there beside her. She attempted a smile, but it fell flat.

"I don't know. Nothing I've ever seen before, that I know." Ramon brought the first sandwich over to Allie, who handed it to Maria, and then he walked back to the kitchenette. "But it is happening, and the sooner we accept that the better off we'll be."

Allie gave the answer a moment to sink in, and then she answered, "So, we need to get out of Garmella, right? We need to get in the car and just go."

"We can't just leave, Allie. Not yet. We have to see who needs help first. We have to canvass the town."

Allie narrowed her gaze, confused. "Canvass the town? You and me? We need help from State, Sheriff. We need—"

"Allie!" Ramon snapped, turning toward his deputy. He lowered his voice. "We can't just leave."

Allie shook her head in denial. "You didn't see it, Sheriff. You didn't see—"

"I did see it. In broad daylight, just like you. I saw it fold a grown man like an omelet and then burn him to a crisp." Ramon glanced to Maria and then dropped his eyes shamefully. "I don't know what it is, Allie, but I know what it's capable of. And we can't just run away."

"Why not?"

"Because it's my job, Allie. And it's your job too. I don't know what's happening, but I know there are people who may need help still."

"But you did call State, right. You told them what happened?"

Ramon frowned and looked away.

"What's wrong?"

"I tried calling out but there's no line."

"What?"

Ramon shrugged and shook his head, signaling he understood the likely connection, but he didn't know what it was. "And even if we wanted to, we couldn't leave anyway. You saw the sinkhole. Until that's fixed, there's no driving out. And no one is coming in. So until we figure that part out, we need to keep those things away from whoever is still...from the rest of the town."

Allie's eyes flashed wide. "Those things? Plural?"

Ramon shrugged. "Well, there have to be at least two of them. The one you saw at Maria's house can't be the same one I saw at the Grieg. The time and distance don't work."

"Jesus."

Ramon took a deep breath, nodding. "I know, but...we may have learned something. Something about why they're here."

"We?"

Ramon carried a plate of sandwiches back to Gloria's desk, giving a nod toward his office entrance along the way. Josh stood at the threshold, and the boy lifted a hand in a meek wave.

"Hi, Josh. Sheriff told me he found you. You okay?"

Josh nodded.

Allie turned to Ramon. "So, what did you learn? What are they?"

Ramon frowned and quivered his head. "I don't know that part exactly—the *what* part—but we might have figured out *why*.

"What? What does that mean?"

"Why they're here. What they want."

"What they *want*? Really? I figured that was the one part we already knew. There are what, eight people dead from those things now. And God knows how many more. Based on the number of people I've seen in this town today, I'd say it's probably a whole lot more than that."

Ramon looked to Josh now, trying to gauge his reaction to Allie's dramatic report about the number of killings; but the boy seemed unaffected by this new body count, and Ramon assumed it was because he already suspected there were more deaths than just Riley Tackard. Ramon, himself, knew about his other deputies and their father, and he had told Allie about Riley, so she would have included him in the count as well. And then there was Derrick Zamora and Amber Godwin. All those numbers came to six dead, not eight.

"Eight?"

Allie tilted her head slightly back to Maria, who had taken a seat behind her at one of the desks. She then gave a quick tremor of her head and frowned. "Maria's parents. I didn't...see them, but she said it was...just like Luke and Randy."

Ramon gave a somber nod and then bowed his head respectfully for a few beats. "I see. I'm so sorry Maria."

Maria closed her eyes and matched Ramon's head bow.

"What in God's name is going on here?"

Allie let the question hang for a moment, allowing it its proper gravity, but then she returned quickly to the matter at hand. "So, what does it want?"

"Well, we don't know for sure, of course, but it...this...creature..." Ramon paused after uttering the word and then looked to Allie for agreement on the term. She nodded.

"It spoke to Josh." Ramon paused and then flipped his hands up and frowned in a believe-it-or-not gesture. "Or maybe 'communicated' is the better word, I guess."

Allie stared at Ramon for several beats, waiting for the catch. "What?" She turned in full to Josh, her face creased with questions.

"But not with its voice," Josh added. "It was more like with its...thoughts."

Allie snickered and a wry smile replaced the quizzical look that had been draped across her face for the last few minutes. She then spun back toward Ramon, seeking clarification, and when Ramon only nodded back, asserting what Josh had said, she started to laugh.

"I believe him, Allie."

Ramon's words were drowned out by Allie's laughter, a cynical eruption which came from deep in her belly, one obviously born out of hysterics, lacking any humor at all.

"Allie!"

Allie let the last of the chuckling die naturally, and when her chest was finally empty of any more sound, she said, "You've got to be kidding me, Sheriff. Telepathy? Is that what you're saying? You don't believe that, right? That these things are what...aliens? Is that what you're saying?"

"I don't know, Allie. I just know what I saw. The same thing you and Josh and Allie saw. And even if it was some new species of animal, something that's been here all along, hiding or hibernating or something, there were things it did that were not of this world."

Allie shook her head and whispered, "No."

"Do you have an answer? You must have given it some thought. What have you come up with?" And then he added, "Did something happen to you out there? Did it get into your mind?"

Allie looked away quickly as if she'd been slapped, and then she straightened her expression and looked back to Ramon, her look now stern and focused. "No, Sheriff, nothing happened. And just because I don't accept that these things are some kind of poisonous Martians, that doesn't exactly make me the crazy one here?"

"I never said—"

"It's true."

The chirp came from Maria, her words barely audible even to Allie who was sitting not four feet away.

All eyes turned to the girl.

"It talked to me too."

Josh exited the office and walked to the desk, and then he hopped up and sat next to Maria. He pressed his hands on the edge of the desk and stretched his arms straight, matching the pose of his peer, and both children sat that way, legs dangling as if they were sitting on the pier of a country lake on a summer afternoon.

"Hey, Maria."

"Hi, Josh."

"I'm really sorry about your parents."

She dropped her eyes and stared at the floor. "Thanks." She looked at Josh now and asked, "Do you know where yours are?"

Josh shook his head. "Did you...see it happen?"

Ramon thought it a bold question, one only a child could ask another.

Maria shook her head. "But I know why it happened. I know what it wanted."

A silence fell across the room, and Ramon had to bite his bottom lip to keep from breaking it. He was a cop, used to asking questions and following up quickly on the responses, trying to find the lie if one existed. But Josh was doing great, and any input from Ramon was likely to kill the momentum.

Finally, when Ramon was on the verge of bursting, Josh asked, "Why?"

CHAPTER TEN

Six months before the rain

"JUST AFTER THE TURN of the last century, and for many decades forward, they all but disappeared from the earth."

Winston now lay on a long divan that backed to the fireplace, a wet cloth folded atop his forehead. The fatigue of his condition had forced him to this supine position, his breathing labored as he listened to the young visitor who stood somewhere above him, only a few feet away. Winston had no recollection of how he'd come to be on the sofa or who had placed the towel on his brow, but the position felt soothing, and he made no question of the new arrangement.

The other two guests, the older man and woman who had led off this discussion but had said little else since, were now gathered closely around Winston, each sitting in a separate chair as they listened to their leader recall the history of this netherworld, a world in which Winston was still reluctant to believe.

"But before 1900, the stories of them are abundant. In North America and throughout the world."

Even in his groggy state, Winston noted the soberness of Zander's speech, the measurement and focus of each word of the tale that, presumably, was leading to the reason for their presence in Garmella. But there was something more in the man's voice, something other than just an earnestness of purpose and drive. Beneath the surface of his words, Winston could detect a thrill.

"What stories?" Winston asked, repositioning the cloth across his eyes, the words coming languorously, as if he were a child on the verge of sleep, dreamily following up on some detail of a bedtime story.

"Stories of the *Arali*."

"*Arali*," Winston repeated, liking the breathy sound of the word in his ears. "What is an *Arali*?"

"*They*," the man corrected. "They are the reason why we have come to this place."

Winston nodded once, his head barely moving on the pillow. He yearned to speak, to object and question all that he was hearing, but he was drifting now, and Zander's words now floated into his mind as if he were in a delusion. But he fought through the fog, managing to get his senses beneath him for a moment longer. "What are they? *Arali?* What are they exactly?"

There was a lengthy pause, and Winston could imagine Zander collecting his thoughts, trying to arrange his explanation properly.

"I suppose they are what you would think of as demons, though it is not a precisely apt definition."

Winston removed the cloth now, feeling a rush in his chest at the mention of this evil of biblical scripture. He shook the cobwebs of sleep from his head and sat up slowly, though with a movement suggesting purpose. He was an old man, sick and dying, and his energy wasn't half what it was even a year ago when the illness began to take a steady hold; but his mind was still a razor, functioning every bit as well as it did when he was forty.

"I don't believe any of this," he said, erupting into a coughing bout that took him nearly a half-minute to work out. Finally, he gathered himself and stared coldly at Zander. He was fully conscious again—thanks in part to the strain of his hacking—and his skepticism was properly aligned, particularly considering the magnitude of the revelation. "Demons? As in devil's helpers from the ground sent forth to capture souls? Is that what you mean?"

Zander stayed quiet.

"I've lived in many places during my lifetime, Mr. Zander, and in each one of those places, there were always at least a few folks after my humanity. So, if you're telling me there are demons in Garmella, I already know that to be true."

Zander grinned, appreciating Winston's tenacity, and then he moved in beside Winston and sat. "My tribe was always sensitive to stories of a certain leaning, where the details of the tale matched those in the ancient writings of my ancestors." Zander was excited again, gesturing and speaking with the energy of a man reciting the details of a thing about which he has expertise. "There were patterns to the stories, and though there is no way to be certain that all the accounts were the *Arali*, there are simply too many similarities."

Winston nodded silently for several seconds, quietly absorbing Zander's explanation. "But let me guess: no one ever *saw* these *Arali*, right? Quick to blame them for every famine and pestilence, no doubt, but never catching a glimpse, I'm sure."

Zander shook his head slowly. "That isn't right at all. There are recorded sightings for nearly all the accounts. Visuals are an important part of the matrix; they are crucial in placing the *Arali* at the scenes of the massacres."

Winston swallowed at the word 'massacres,' but he quickly shook off the discomfort, not yet ready to move beyond the fact that the *Arali* existed at all, let alone that they were responsible for a string of calamities around the globe. "But no proof, correct? No 8-millimeters? No iPhone recordings?"

"As I said, after the turn of the century, the narrative of the *Arali* was almost completely lost."

"That's convenient."

"Yes, it might seem, but not entirely. Photography had been invented well before 1900, and there do exist pictures of the *Arali; y*ou can find most of them on the internet with very little effort."

"I'm sure those are of premium quality."

Zander shrugged. "No, it's true, no one can say for certain what the pictures show. They are certainly fuzzy. Blurry and black."

Winston frowned and rolled his eyes.

But," Zander added, "that is how they appear to the naked eye. In the light of day. So our research would suggest."

This addendum sent a chill down Winston's spine, forcing a cough to emerge in his diseased chest once more. He brought the face cloth to his mouth to stifle it. Finally, he said, "What about the massacres? How many...how many died?"

"Disappeared, in fact."

"What?"

"It is the one consistent piece of the story that has stood the test of time. Wherever the *Arali* arrive, the people of that town vanish."

Winston waited for Zander to elaborate, and when he didn't, Winston asked, "People *disappeared*? How could that be? How is it no one noticed that little detail?"

Zander shrugged. "I never made that claim."

"Really? A bunch of neighbors in the village disappeared and everyone just went about their business?"

"People disappear every day, Mr. Bell, all over the world. Children, the elderly, men and women in the prime ages of their lives. They vanish from the largest of skyscraped cities to the most barren of jungles."

Winston immediately shook his head, challenging the implied frequency of such a phenomenon. "No, no, no. People don't disappear that often. Not like that. Not without a trace. Not without some evidence or clue as to where they've gone."

Zander shrugged. "As I've said, the *Arali* always appeared in places where there were very few people. This is the type of place to which they are drawn. So—"

"So, you're saying that no one noticed these disappearances because they don't happen in the middle of Paris?"

"I am simply saying that in the more remote places of the world—many of which were in nations where mere survival was the goal of each day—verified, corroborated testimony is difficult to obtain. I referenced the Loch Ness Monster earlier. Do you know there have been over 1,100 sightings of the Loch Ness Monster? How many of them do you believe?"

"I'd probably believe a hell of a lot more of them if every time somebody saw the thing a couple of toddlers disappeared!"

Zander grinned. "Don't think yourself wiser than the people of centuries past, Mr. Bell. The mind will go to great lengths to explain the unexplainable."

Winston chortled, hesitant to continue with such an outrageous conversation. Yet he was held tightly by the story, and the burn of intrigue hovered in his chest. "Why are you telling me this? If all of what you're telling me is true, why would you have you come to me with this information. Me of all people?"

Zander nodded solemnly, signaling that this was the correct question at this stage in the conversation. And then he began the story. "In 1973, in a town called Munstereifel, West Germany, three families—seventeen people in all—disappeared without a trace. Their homes had been entered from the outside, that was evident, but aside from that detail, there were few leads to follow, and subsequent investigations turned up nothing. They were never found."

The fifty-year old account was innocuous on its face and proved nothing as it related to Zander's earlier tale, but Winston's throat tightened just the same.

"In the summer of 1985, in the Crimean Peninsula, another mass disappearance occurred, this time involving a total of forty-one people. And, just as in Munstereifel, no bodies were ever found, no cases ever solved."

This time Winston frowned and squinted. "That can't be right. Forty-one people? That story would be known."

Zander cocked his head. "Your unfamiliarity of it would suggest otherwise. The Iron Curtain was a heavy shade. And when Chernobyl happened a year later, the incident in Crimea became a pebble in the Soviet Union's mountain of secrets. And that mountain grew higher decades later, in 2009. One sunny morning during that year, one-hundred-and-ninety-three people disappeared from a town called Galenki on the east coast of Siberia."

"That's impossible."

"The Curtain is down, Mr. Bell, but Russia still controls the land with the same iron fist. Just as China does. In 1997, in the Ghizou province, approximately one-hundred-and-twelve people vanished, though the exact number there is still unknown and likely never will be."

Winston swallowed nervously, his eyes narrowing to slits now, trying to will his mind to disbelieve these unreported events. "How can this be true? Especially these last few accounts? That's too many people."

"A combination of prideful nations and fearful citizens, I suppose. That blend of sin has kept truth from the world for centuries. Millennia."

Winston blinked several times and looked to the wall, searching for the next correct question. "But *you* know. How could *you* know? And why do you think the *Arali* are responsible?"

Zander smiled softly. "It has been my life's work, Mr. Bell. Since I was a boy. I know the design of these disappearances."

Winston gave a reluctant nod at the reasoning, suddenly feeling a mixture of fright and hope, though the latter sense he couldn't explain. "Okay. Then why are you here?"

Zander nodded at Winston, his face grim and focused, indicating that a pact was being signed in that moment, that whatever was said from that point forward would bind the four of them forever. "You may have noticed a pattern in the years I mentioned: 1973. 1985. 1997. 2009."

"Twelve-years, Winston whispered immediately, realizing the relationship of the numbers at just that moment.

Zander nodded. "That's correct."

"That means they'll be back this year." The statement were words of discovery.

Zander flinched his eyebrows. "Yes."

Winston let this possibility swirl in his mind for a moment and then asked, "They're coming here to Garmella? Is that what you're saying?"

Zander nodded. "That is what we believe."

The desire to laugh at the absurdity of such a notion flooded Winston, but instead he asked, "Why?"

"All of the places I named—in Germany, Russia, and China—they all have something in common. One very big, unique thing."

Winston was silent for several seconds as he searched his mind, and then the answer came to him in a burst. "A telescope."

"A *radio* telescope, to be precise."

Winston was confused by the connection, at least as it concerned the telescope and the arrival of ground demons;

but the audit truck, as well as Zander's reasoning 'to move amongst them', now made more sense.

"The telescope tracks sounds from space," Winston said, shaking his head. "You said these beings come from the ground. What is the connection?"

Zander sighed and nodded, acknowledging the complexity of Winston's question. "It is an interesting inquiry, Mr. Bell. And one to which we don't know the answer exactly. Some combination of the signals coming from above, perhaps, the way they are received by the dish and then re-transmitted through the ground. That is what we can assume, but we really don't know. It is something that is simply beyond our science at present—and perhaps always will be, much like God Himself."

Winston appreciated the idea that everything in the universe couldn't be answered by science, and though he found himself believing in Zander's *Arali*, he was struggling with the explanation as it related to the telescope. "Maybe it's a coincidence."

Zander's face sank hearing the rebuttal, and it was clear to Winston that this possibility had kept the man up many a night. "No. In all four of the occurrences I've described, there was a radio telescope within fifty miles of the town. And in most instances, twenty. It can't be an accident."

Winston agreed that would have been quite a fluke, but still, knowing what he did about the giant antennae—which wasn't doctorate-level knowledge, but was still ample—he was skeptical about the explanation. "What about before? What about all the stories from before 1900. There were no radio telescopes then."

"As I said, Mr. Bell, we don't know all the answers, just where the next occurrence will be."

Winston glared at Zander now, doubting the man's science even more, and then he let his eyes drift around the room to the other two members of the trio, wondering if they had any different hypotheses on the pattern. But Tehya and Ouray sat silently, obediently. "How do you know it will happen here?" he asked. "There must be dozens of other telescopes around the world."

Zander scanned the study, as if he'd anticipated the question, and he quickly locked on an antique-looking globe sitting on a bookshelf at the far corner of the room. The spherical model was the kind one might find in a nineteenth-century British library, where the Earth—land and sea—was represented in various shades of sepia rather than the colorful blues and reds of modern day globes, with a decorative wooden base that tilted the sphere on its axis. "There."

Zander walked to the bookshelf and grabbed the globe, and then he carried it to Winston, placing it on the table in front of the elderly man.

"If you look at the places I've named and line them up with the years, you can see the pattern. 1973, Germany." He put the tip of his index finger on the European country. "1985, Ukraine." He moved his finger down and to the right until it was on the southern peninsula of the Eastern European nation, and then he continued in that direction—west to east—passing through China and then finally to the far edge of the Asian continent in the Russian town of Galenki. He looked up at Winston, his eyes questioning.

"What? I...I don't get it."

Zander was bemused. "They move from west to east. The *Arali*, they travel...through the earth I suppose, the world below the world."

Perdition, Winston thought.

"Whatever their way, the pattern is indisputable. The *distances* between the pre-1900 events are very different from those of the last fifty years, but the directional pattern is the same. West to east."

Winston shrugged. "Okay. I guess. But Garmella? How do you know Garmella is next? I don't see it."

"The Grieg Radio Telescope is the largest in America, which makes it a likely place for the *Arali* to visit. But more than that, the Grieg is the next major receiver in line as you travel East."

Zander slid the tip of his finger southeast across the khaki-colored Pacific Ocean to the west coast of the United States, then across the expanse of California until his finger landed on the disfigured trapezoid of Arizona.

"They're coming here, Mr. Bell. We know it with some confidence. But more than that, we know when. With some precision."

Winston hesitated and then asked, "Precision? You know *exactly* when they're coming? To the day?" Winston's voice was almost a whisper, now enchanted by the story and the possibility of what he was hearing.

"Within a few days, yes."

Winston waited for the unveiling of the mysterious date, but Zander said nothing. "When?" he asked.

Zander grinned. "June. As we get closer to the day, we will give you the details."

Winston's head was spinning now, both from the enormity of the story he was being sold, and from the fact that he now believed every word of it. The only thing left now was to review the offer that had yet to be made. But he knew that whatever proposition was forthcoming, he would never be able to decline it. "What do you want from me?" he asked finally. "And don't tell me nothing. I was in sales for many years, and I know an overture when I hear one. What are you selling exactly, Mr. Zander, and, more importantly, what is the price?"

Zander gave a weary smile, as if relieved to have finally reached the point at which they were now. "The offer is a life that will not see an end for many decades."

A well of tears filled the inside corners of Winston's eyes, and then a single drop rolled down the left side of his nose to his chin, where it hovered there impossibly.

"And the price? Well, Mr. Bell, let us just say it is something you can quite easily afford."

CHAPTER ELEVEN

"MY BROTHER WAS BORN almost eight months ago."

Maria's words came with volume and clarity now, spoken as if the girl were reading them from a teleprompter that had been hung on the wall in front of her.

"My parents didn't tell anyone when my mom got pregnant though, and they made me swear not to either."

Josh gave a sheepish look to the girl next to him and then asked, "Why not?"

Maria closed her eyes and sighed. "They tried for so long to have another baby. I'm almost thirteen, and I know they wanted me to have a brother or sister that was close to me in age. So, they had been trying for that long, I guess." She raised her eyebrows and frowned. "But every time my mom got pregnant, the baby died. It never lived past the third month." She paused and took a gulping breath. "They kept trying though."

Ramon and Allie sat at separate desks listening to Maria, while Josh retained his seat on the desk next to his classmate, staring at the floor as he listened to the tale.

"But then it happened. I don't even know if they were trying or not, but my mom got pregnant again. Last year. But instead of telling everyone, this time they kept it a secret—from everyone, even my abuelos and abuelas. They said they didn't want to jinx it, but I know it was because everyone was getting tired of hearing about it. The pregnancies, I mean. Everyone got so happy at first when they heard the news, and then later my mom would have a miscarriage and have to tell everyone. It was...I don't know...weird for them. For everyone. Sometimes we'd see people on the street that we hadn't seen for a couple weeks, and they would ask how the baby was doing, and my mom would just start crying. After, like, the third time, people would just avoid us. They would cross the street or look away when they walked by. They didn't know how to ask about the baby anymore, so they just stayed away."

Maria paused, appearing to reflect on the number of losses over the years.

"But the last time was different. My *mom* was different. Right from the beginning. She was so excited. I never saw her like that before. She had that glow that people always talk about. And she was right. The baby was still alive inside her after four months. We even went out and had a celebration dinner. I mean, it was still possible that something would go wrong, and my mom and dad tried not to get too happy, but you could see it in their faces. They really thought it was going to live. And the doctors did too."

Maria swallowed and her face grew suddenly grim. She closed her eyes, holding back tears.

"And then my mom went for a checkup one day and found out the baby was...sick."

Josh turned slowly toward Maria. "What was wrong with it?" he asked, his words soft, delicate.

Maria swallowed and took a deep breath. "It's called anencephaly."

"What's that?"

"It's a birth defect. A bad one. Most babies die before they're ever born."

Josh shook his head. "I never heard of it."

"I didn't either. And my parents were..." Maria shook her head slowly, her eyes distant and distraught. "I can't even explain how sad they were. My mom was like, crippled. She cried every night. For hours. Every night it was like she was hearing the news for the first time. And my dad...my dad just stopped talking completely."

"There was no chance it could get better?" Josh asked. "Or that the doctors were wrong?"

Maria shook her head. "No. They were sure. I saw the sonogram. His head was..." She closed her eyes, clearing the memory. "They all said the same thing. There's no cure for anencephaly. There's no way to fix it. The baby was going to die. Either before it was born or right after. So, my mom and dad decided they were going to stop seeing doctors. There was nothing they could do anyway, so what was the point of getting the checkups?"

"To make sure *your mom* was healthy, I would think." It was Allie now, and the feminine pitch of her voice sent a refreshing sound through the room.

Maria shrugged. "I guess, but she stopped caring about herself too. She just figured when the time came, she would just go to the hospital and be done with it. And if she went the full term and the baby was born alive, my aunt is a CNM who was going to deliver the baby anyway—just like she did me—so nothing was going to change with that." Maria's voice had become defiant now, supportive of her parents' decision. "The doctors said there was no way of saving it past a few hours anyway—a day at the most—so she decided just to let it die in the house instead of in some plastic bin hooked up to a bunch of tubes."

"But he didn't die," Allie muttered, suddenly realizing the twist of the story that had already been revealed in the beginning.

Maria shook her head. "No."

"Why not?"

Maria swallowed and stared back at Allie with a look that was both challenging and tortured, and then her face melted into something closer to sadness. "I don't know. I still don't know what happened that day. His birthday. I came home from school and my mom was in the kitchen making dinner. I had barely seen her for months since she stopped going to the doctor. And the last time she cooked? All I ate was soup and sandwiches that I made myself for, like, months." She hesitated. "But she wasn't pregnant anymore—that was obvious—so I asked her about...it...about the baby...and she just said it was 'fine.' 'It's over,' she told me." Maria shrugged. "I thought she meant it was dead. I didn't ask for any details. I mean, I was sad for her, but I was also glad to have my mom back."

There was a pause and then Josh blurted, "Wait, you said your brother was born eight months ago. That means there was a baby in your house for eight months? And you didn't know about it? You never heard it cry?"

Maria glared at Josh, unappreciative of the challenging tone. "I didn't say I didn't know about it, did I?"

Josh instantly dropped Maria's stare, eyes now locked to the ground. "Sorry. It just...it sounded kind of crazy to me."

Maria kept her laser glare on the side of Josh's face and then added, "And besides, even if I didn't know about him, it wouldn't have been impossible. He never cried."

There was silence again throughout the station, another awkward pause as this latest detail settled in. Finally, Ramon spoke, verifying the remark. "The baby never cried, Maria?"

Maria's eyes thinned and stared forward as she shook her head, as if the memory she was recalling was of a thing not quite real, an event that was in question as to whether it had happened at all. She shrugged. "I don't know why. I guess it had to do with his condition. But he didn't. At least I never heard him." She looked at Josh again, more sympathetically now. "And you were right, I *didn't* know about him at first. Not for a month or two. After that first day, my mom went back to being in her room almost all day. And my dad stayed at work as long as he could. And then when work was over, he would go somewhere else. I don't know where, but I'm sure it was someplace my mother wouldn't have liked too much. But I was used to living like that, alone most of the time, so I just thought everything was back to the way it was. I assumed my parents were still grieving or something. And that they were going to get a divorce at some point." She stopped and hung her head. "But he was alive. My brother was alive and in that room the whole time."

The tears came in a sudden wave from Maria Suarez now, and Josh quickly put his arm around her shoulder and pulled her toward him. Ramon expected the girl to shove the boy's grip away, an instinct to protect herself, but instead she leaned into Josh and rested her head against his thin bicep.

Ramon let the girl cry, allowing the tears their organic flow until they finally waned to a sniffle, at which point he decided to get to the core question. "What does this have to do with your parents, Maria? With what happened at your house today?" His voice was deep now, authoritative, the tone he used when pressing a witness for information. It was a gamble to take on this firm persona, but he didn't have the time to coax Maria back to an even temperament.

The girl gave a series of rapid blinks, a bit stung by the question, the paths of her tears still bright against her copper skin. "Because she rejected him. He was her son and she rejected him. She never wanted him in the womb or when he was born. She never took it to the doctor. She never took him outside or to meet his family." She hesitated. "And my father..." Maria shook her head, choked from speaking, the tears threatening to come again.

"What about your father?"

She swallowed and closed her eyes. "He wouldn't even go in the room. Not even to see my mother. He didn't want to look at either of them. He just...he just wanted the baby to die."

Silence fell on the room for several seconds, and then Josh asked, "But why?"

"He was so...deformed. You wouldn't think a baby could look like that." Maria hesitated, considering her own answer. "But I don't think it was just that. My dad heard for so many months how the baby was going to die, that he would never get a chance to raise him or...anyway, he just thought it was over. And then when he was born alive—and he kept living—my dad wasn't...I don't know...he never learned how to love it. Or to have any feelings at all for him."

"Maybe he was just in shock," Josh said doubtfully. "Maybe he just needed time."

Maria shook her head. "I thought so too. At first. And then I heard him praying one night, in the living room after I'd gone to bed. And I knew he would never change how he felt. He was crying and praying, pleading to God for my brother to die."

"Jesus," Allie whispered.

"But it wasn't just him," Maria added quickly, defensively. "My mother felt that way too. At least at first. I mean, he had been born for two months before I even knew he was alive. And during that time, I never heard her say a word to him. Or sing to him or anything. If she had, I would have heard. At least once."

Ramon felt a wave of sympathy for the Suarez family come over him. Not just for Maria and the baby, but for Maria's parents too. Ramon had no children himself, and thus he was in no position to judge the couple on their reaction to the heartbreak their daughter was now explaining. He assumed they were decent people—he needed only talk to Maria for a few minutes to realize the job they had done raising their daughter, the love and strength they had instilled in her—but they had been unable to handle the tragic news of their unborn baby. They'd been dealt a shitty hand by the universe, and it was one they were simply unprepared to play.

"How did you find out?" Allie asked. "About your brother?"

"It was a Sunday, when my dad was at work like always, and I snuck into my parent's room when I knew my mom was napping. There were bottles everywhere. Cans of formula scattered around the room. The smell was..." She closed her eyes and shivered off the memory. "And then I saw him. He was lying in the bed next to my mom. His face and head were wrapped in a blanket, and I could only see his bulging eyes staring back at me."

Allie nodded, allowing Maria to get back to that place in her mind, to see the memory of that day. She then continued Ramon's line of questioning from a moment ago. "You said you knew why it happened, Maria," she said flatly, steering the girl back to the point. "You said you knew why that thing killed your parents. Why?"

Maria took a deep breath, gathering her words into their proper order. "It wanted to hear their sins. From their owns mouths. It wanted them to say it out loud. Like a confession."

Allie swallowed and felt a burn in her chest, unable to believe the eloquence of the girl sitting before her.

"But they wouldn't do it," Maria continued. "They couldn't. They couldn't bring themselves to say it."

"What was it? What was the sin your parents couldn't speak?"

Maria thought a moment and then said, "Hate. Hate for Antonio. And worse, hate for God. For the curse He put on their son."

"But she grew to love him, right?" Allie asked, her voice that of a wondrous child now. "Or at least to accept him.

Why else would she have kept feeding him and taking care of him if she hated him? If she wanted him to die?"

Maria smiled and nodded, blinking back new tears, these of happiness. "By the third month, when he was still living, he became the *only* thing she loved. She loved him more than she ever loved me, and she loved me a lot."

"Why wouldn't they have just confessed?" Ramon asked. "Just admitted their feelings? Their sins?"

"My mother would have rather died than admit it, and my father..."

"What is it?"

"My father wanted to die. Those things just made it easy for him."

Josh rubbed the top of Maria's back now as he wiped away a tear from his own face with his other hand.

"We have to go there then," Allie said suddenly, her voice laced with something bordering on frenzy, as if she'd just realized the answer to some long-puzzling question.

"What are you talking about?" Ramon asked. "Go where?"

"To Maria's house. We have to go back to Maria's house. There's a baby there, for Christ's sake! All alone!"

"Allie, it—"

"No!" Allie shook her head defiantly, not wanting to hear the litany of reasons why they shouldn't go. "I don't care. I don't care if he might be dead or if he's probably dead or whatever. We came from there less than an hour ago, so he might still be okay. If I had known there was a baby..."

She broke off the sentence, not wanting to make Maria feel guilty for keeping the secret of her brother from Allie.

After all, the girl had been conditioned to keeping the secret of her brother for the first eight months of his life—and for somewhere around nine months before that—so mentioning him to Allie, especially under the circumstances, wouldn't have come naturally to her.

"Listen to me, Ramon, we have to check on the town anyway. We have to see who is still...alive, who we can help. Maria's house will give us something to focus on. A direction."

Ramon took a breath, pondering the suggestion. "Fine," he said, "okay." He could hear the headstrong commitment of his deputy and knew it meant she would refuse to accept any other answer. "We'll go, but we'll do it this way: you head back to the house, to Maria's, see if you can find the baby. If he's there, alive, try to gather as many supplies as you can—diapers, formula and bottles, whatever—and then bring him back to the station. We'll do our best for as long as we can." Ramon frowned, indicating he wasn't hopeful. "I'm going to head to Gloria's house. Her car is gone, so I'm hoping she went home for some reason. Maybe she had an...encounter, I don't know. And I'll canvass some of the homes on my way back." Ramon looked at the kids. "You two are staying here."

Both children shook their heads in unison. "No way," Josh said, his eyes electric with fear.

"I'm sorry, you are. It's too dangerous. We don't know what is happen—"

"Sheriff," Allie interrupted.

"What?"

Allie shrugged, frowning. "What's the point of leaving them here? We don't know what we're dealing with exactly—at all, really—so just leaving them here alone and locking the doors isn't going to protect them. Not necessarily. Even if we locked them in one of the cells, we don't know what this thing is capable of. And how will they protect themselves. Are you going to give them shotguns? They're children."

Ramon sighed through his nose and gritted his teeth. "Fine. We'll keep it divided equally then. I'll take Josh and you—"

"I want to go with Ms. Allie," Josh asserted. He gave a quick nod following his request, eyes wide and hopeful.

Ramon frowned, returning to the boy a look indicative of betrayal.

"I just want to help get Antonio. And I want to make sure Maria is safe too."

Maria shot a twisted look toward Josh and leaned her shoulder back, staring down her nose at the boy from her perch on the desk. "I'll keep *you* safe, you mean."

Josh smiled and nodded. "We'll keep each other safe."

There was a beat of silence as the tacit agreement between everyone settled into the room.

"Allie," Ramon said, his voice subdued. "Don't stop for it."

"For what?"

Ramon nodded, indicating she knew what he meant. "If you see it, don't stop. Don't be brave."

Ramon wanted to say explicitly that if she saw one of the creatures at Maria's house, she was under explicit orders not to enter. But he didn't want to upset Maria any further and was hoping the meaning of his words was obvious.

"I need you back here, okay. No chances. Not yet. Not until we know what's happening."

Allie nodded. "Same with you then, Sheriff."

Allie and Ramon locked eyes for several beats, and in that moment a feeling passed between them that had not previously been felt, certainly not from Ramon. He'd always found Allie attractive, but there was an age gap—eleven years—that was wide enough that he'd never thought of his deputy in that way. And he wasn't feeling that now exactly. What he was feeling was even more primal than sex or romance, a sensation that perhaps only blossoms during existential circumstances like the one in which they found themselves now.

Allie turned and walked toward the door, leading the kids behind her, and as she grabbed the doorknob, she stopped in her tracks and turned back to Ramon. "Hey, Sheriff?"

Ramon clicked his head up. "Hmm?"

"Do you think that sinkhole has anything to do with what's going on?"

Ramon gave a thoughtful nod, his eyebrows raising just a tic. "At this point Allie, I think anything is possible."

CHAPTER TWELVE

Two months before the rain

WINSTON BELL STARED at the phone as if it were a screaming baby in a crib, watching it with a look of both annoyance and concern. He slowly closed the book he was reading and placed it on the sofa cushion beside him, and then he closed his eyes in thought, considering whether to answer.

He decided to let it ring out this time, but he knew that would only delay the inevitable; there was little doubt the next call would come within the hour.

The weekend of the monitors was a stressful one for Winston now, and though the mysterious infiltrators of the Grieg Radio Telescope had yet to visit him again since that one strange morning four months earlier, Zander had advised him—warned him—of a follow-up call that would come well before the day of the event. There had been no specifics as to the time frame of the call, but to Winston, four months removed seemed about right. He couldn't be certain it was they who were calling now, but to the core of his soul, he knew it was.

And there was another thing he knew as well: although Zander and his associates hadn't returned since that first visit, they—or someone connected to them—had been monitoring him the whole time.

He hadn't seen any trucks near his estate, nor pedestrians stalking around the perimeter of his property, but there was little doubt he was being surveilled. More cars than usual passed on the road now, makes and models that Winston had never seen in the area before, several of which slowed to a crawl before finally moving on. This rolling scrutiny happened at least once a week now, as if the driver were attempting to locate an address on a mailbox or on the façade by the door. But Winston knew that somewhere in the back seat there was a man snaking an antennae through a crack in the window or trunk, pointing it toward his home, ensuring he was interrupting the frequencies with the proper consistency and signal levels, keeping in compliance with the arrangement that had been made months ago in his parlor.

Winston was fine with the monitoring though; over these last four months, he had performed his duties with absolute vigilance, despite his doubts about the effectiveness of the signals, which wasn't for him to argue. Zander had stressed the importance of daily transmissions—several times a day for hours at a time was his preference—enough that the analysts at headquarters would question their own readings and then ultimately dismiss them as useless, ruined by the noncompliant citizens of Garmella. It was an absurd plan as far as Winston was concerned, one that seemed to overestimate the impact his scrambling device would have on the Grieg's readings, and underestimate the scientists who analyzed them. But that was the deal he had made, and for the last four months, a day hadn't passed without him upholding his end of it. It was a fact Winston had become quite proud of, frivolous though his actions may have been.

But there was also a catch to these new spikes in electromagnetic activity. Because the signals had to be sent with such regularity, there was simply no way to avoid being caught by the actual monitors, those legitimate inspectors who were sanctioned by the Grieg and drove the streets of Garmella every month in search of violators.

For all the years he'd lived in Garmella, Winston had stayed off the radar of these auditors—quite literally—but over these last four months, they had discovered him as a new source of interference, and Winston now received a visit from the sheriff every thirty days or so. To this point, Sheriff Thomas had been lenient—giving Winston only a verbal warning on each of his visits—but it was only a matter of time before the man's patience expired. The pressure Ramon Thomas was undoubtedly getting from the Grieg would trickle down to Winston, and at some point, the verbal warnings would become written citations.

Of course, Winston wasn't concerned about paying whatever pittance of a fine came that with the violations—he would have paid a fortune just to keep the monitors away—it was the fear that on the next visit a warrant would be issued, and if the subsequent search of his home revealed the cause of the interference—which it most certainly would—his deal may be broken, and the promise of his future would be extinguished like the flame from a match dropped in the ocean.

And that result simply would not stand. Winston had invested too much of himself now, both in time and emotion. He could taste the possibility of life again, the potential for a future. It was a sensation which, despite his successes over the last several decades, he'd not felt since he was in his thirties, when the future seemed like a never-ending tunnel of hope. All of the money he'd made in life, all of the wins he'd captured in his professional career—as well as in other aspects of his life, including romance and friendships (though those were long past)—all amounted to a thin residue on his memory now, a sheen on his soul that he could barely detect anymore. Death was too heavy an idea, too overshadowing a concept to allow the light of more pleasant notions to shine through.

And Death had loomed over Winston for a year now, watching him like a dragon over its prey, helpless in the confines of its lair, the fiery creature waiting for the precise moment to take him in its jaws. And though the pain and sickness which had led to that first diagnosis had mostly passed, Winston could always detect the illness flowing beneath his skin, sense it in his belly and taste it in his mouth, as if his blood had been infected with some thin, poisonous element.

So, when the auburn man of the extinct American Northeast tribe finally made his offer, giving Winston the price he would have to pay for the reward of Life, the elderly millionaire could barely restrain his enthusiasm. A manic pleasure had grown steadily in Winston's belly and loins as he listened to the bargain; it was the feeling he'd thought gone forever, but it had resurfaced in that moment, recalling in him some lost moment from a day in his teens, when the smile from a pretty girl had flashed his way, her eyes sparkling and suggestive, locking with his.

But Zander's offer had been more marvelous than any tingle sparked by a flirtation. It was a proposal that offered more than just the religious notion of afterlife, of golden streets or awaiting heavenly virgins. Beyond just a cure to

Winston's sickness and the hope of living out his natural, earthly form, Zander had suggested a life that went beyond any normal span, decades perhaps. Centuries?

But why him?

Winston had assumed his proximity to the telescope was the most reasonable explanation, and for several weeks following the visit, he thought nothing more of the question. But as the weeks grew to months, he meditated more on the matter, and although he suspected his home's location certainly played some part in the selection process, he now believed there was more to it than that.

It was his age. His age and the fear of death that resounds—to varying degrees—in all men.

And perhaps his wealth played a part as well, money suggesting the qualities of greed and opportunism. Winston never cared as much about money as much as most in his tax bracket—his net worth was somewhere north of thirty million—and 'materialistic' wasn't a character trait to which he would have ascribed to himself. But there was desire in him just the same, and only those at the brink of death could ever understand such avarice for life, such avidity to continue beyond one's natural cycle.

And there was no doubt the visitors had done their research on Winston, beyond just an inspection of his years in retirement in Garmella, Arizona. He was the CEO of Demornay Labs for just under twenty years, and though that certainly was no position of celebrity, it was one public enough that anybody looking could have discovered certain personal beliefs about Winston, beliefs that would have made him a qualified candidate. He was no man of god, for instance—they would have learned that much—and, based on the handful of interviews he had done over the years for various trade publications, he probably came off like a burgeoning atheist. That would have played into Zander's evaluation, Winston figured, as such a stance would eliminate any karmic barrier that might interfere with his decision-making, any fear that his soul would burn forever in the place which, to that point, he doubted existed at all.

But Winston was no fool either, not the kind of man who would have willed his assets over to strangers for some secret elixir or be taken in by a low-rent pyramid scheme while his fortune dwindled. Thus, his reaction to the grandeur the visitors had touted should have been one of extreme pessimism or amusement even. And as he recited the story in his mind now for the thousandth time, he recalled how much the offer had sounded like that of a Jehovah's Witness or some other religious peddler, pledging the eternal while offering nothing other than a story as proof.

But Winston had listened with zeal and anticipation to this potential for an extended life, and in that moment, he could feel nothing but hope and elation. Euphoria. He was convinced the *Arali* were real despite a lack of even a shred of actual evidence. But there was something about Zander that had captured Winston's fascination in a way no one ever had before. It wasn't just charisma or passion, nor was it just the man's own true belief in the beings that he was describing. There was something physical about Zander that was different, a shine in his eyes and a depth to his voice. It was a glow—that was the only word that came close—an all-encompassing radiance that had filled the room when he spoke.

So, the threshold of belief had been crossed that day, the belief that the *Arali* had the ability to grant Winston a life that hinted at immortality, and once he found himself on that side of faith, his mind was open to anything. Everything.

And if the price for such a prize was simply to interrupt signals coming into the Grieg Telescope from some unknown satellite or star or sentient being on the edges of space, that was a minor effort for the payday that was to come. And as the visit had drawn to an end that day and the two men and one woman left his home almost ten hours later, Winston Bell was all in, a full-fledged servant to their cause.

He shook off the memory and focused on the vehicle approaching him now. It wasn't an audit truck, but it was an unwanted visitor just the same.

Garmella police.

Winston had always considered Sheriff Ramon Thomas a rather pleasant fellow, at least as people went generally, and under most social or professional circumstances, he would have welcomed the young man's company.

But the sheriff's phone calls and visits, despite the mostly pleasant tone of them up to that point, now came to Winston soaked in dread and tension. And the fact that the Sheriff was making his visit so early in the month this time, Winston took as a bad sign.

Winston stood and shuffled down to the foyer where he waited for Sheriff Thomas by the door, watching as the dark blue cruiser pulled into the driveway. As the sheriff made his way up to the front porch, Winston absently practiced his look of despair and confusion, the look an old man might give to a police officer after being apprehended for walking naked along a residential street at nine in the morning. Sheriff Thomas knew Winston wasn't senile, though—far from it—but he also wouldn't discount the troubles of an old man living alone in a modern world. Perhaps Ramon himself struggled with the battles of technology, so why wouldn't the old hermit who lives down the lane?

Winston opened the door before Ramon knocked and immediately hung his head, no trace of humor on his face, selling the act of shame. After a few beats, he looked up at the sheriff. "I've done it again, I guess. Is that right?"

Ramon frowned. "Afraid so, Mr. Bell." All former deference was gone from the sheriff's voice this time, his pitch laced now with a dusting of annoyance. "This is getting to be a monthly thing. Not sure they're gonna let this continue with just a warning. You know the arrangement."

Winston said nothing, allowing the silence to be his apology, even showing a glisten of moisture at the corner of his right eye.

Ramon closed his eyes and frowned, and then he slowly began to swivel his head. He looked back at Winston and smiled weakly. "You gotta keep the radio off, Mr. Bell, that's all there is to it. What's so intoxicating anyway that you can't find it on one of the cable music channels? There's gotta be fifty of those channels on the TV."

Winston brushed a knuckle against the corner of his eye and then waved the hand dismissively. "Those stations are all rap and robot music. They don't cater to people my age."

"I'm pretty sure they have a fifties format on one of those channels. That's probably around your generation, right? And, come to think of it, I don't know of any terrestrial radio stations around here that play that anyway. Not anymore."

Winston raised a finger and waved it in mock accusation. "Ah, but that's where you're off, Sheriff Thomas. I'm no fan of Elvis Presley or Buddy Holly; that's what those channels on television play and that's not my style. Sinatra and Dean Martin. Those are my guys. And there's a wonderful station out of Mesa that plays them all day long."

The sheriff smiled and nodded, and Ramon knew by the look that he had made distant enough inroads for today, at least far enough that the next time he violated the transmission agreement, he could start his latest explanation from a place of good will. Sheriff Thomas wasn't fed up with him—not yet—and perhaps he could make it a couple more months without him ever getting to that point. After that, if Zander had been honest and accurate with his timeline, none of what happened after that would make much difference.

"All right, Mr. Bell, I'm not going to cite you this time, but the next time I'll have to. And worse, I may have to come inside and look around. And definitely take the radio away. It won't take but a minute for a judge to give me that authority."

Winston let his smile fade and then he nodded solemnly. "I understand."

The sheriff nodded back, a trace of a smile still lingering on his lips, and Winston thought absently that the man had a naturally good temperament, perfect for the job to which he'd been elected.

"I'm going to let the folks at the Grieg know that I talked to you, okay? So, I don't expect you'll hear from anyone else this month. But if you do, do me a favor and don't mention all the warnings I've given you. They're gonna think I'm soft over there. Fair?"

Winston Bell flashed a soft smile and nodded lightly. "That is well beyond fair, Sheriff. Thank you."

"Okay then. And maybe invest in a CD player. They still make them, you know? I'll bet Ol' Blue Eyes sounds wonderful on digital."

Winston's eyes and lips narrowed now as he studied the sheriff, suddenly rueful that the polite lawman of Garmella would have to die along with everyone else in the town. "I shall look into it then, Sheriff. Thank you again."

CHAPTER THIRTEEN

ALLIE PULLED THE CRUISER from the station slowly, her palms already sweating at the idea of entering Maria's house and confronting the creature up close.

Creatures, she reminded herself. *At least two of them. Maybe more.*

The idea that there existed more than one of the dusky monsters from Maria's kitchen, and that they were somewhere in Garmella at that very moment, probably turning another innocent citizen into a statue of granite, was almost too much to conceive.

Or was it already over? Was everyone in town already dead? And how many outside of Garmella were gone?

Allie let her mind explore the latter thought further, and she soon realized she hadn't had contact with anyone outside of Garmella since early yesterday.

Was the world destroyed?

"Stop," she whispered, instinctively flashing her eyes up to the rearview mirror, checking to see if the kids had heard the command to herself. But Josh and Maria were engaged in their own narrative, one in which, based on the looks on their faces, was almost certainly to do with the calamity of Maria's mother and father.

Allie returned to the moment, encouraging herself to keep her mind from spiraling into disaster.

Just focus on what your eyes see. What your ears hear. Everything else is just your mind. Just pictures.

She eased the cruiser onto Courthouse Road and then crept along the deserted street, letting the car roll along on its own momentum, propelling at a speed just above a walking pace.

It's hard to focus on what your eyes see when there's no one left in town, she thought.

Of course, Allie couldn't be sure about the truth of that notion, but if it were the case that the town was gone, exterminated, then that was the only thing there was to deal with. What other choice did she have but to accept reality for what it was?

She peeked again to Maria and Josh in the backseat where the children now seem focused on something lighter. A whisper and giggle soon erupted, and Maria caught Allie's eyes in the mirror and instantly dropped them, embarrassed. The girl's loss was catastrophic, unimaginable, and yet the power of a single friend's kind words and attention had already given her—if only temporarily—the sweet relief of distraction.

Allie considered again the tale from Maria and the haunting impossibility of what she had described. Allie still held firmly to a grain of skepticism, just as any rational adult would; but in the silence of her mind, with the pride of her intellect and experience now stripped away, she knew every word of it was true.

The silence of her mind.

If she was committing herself to honesty now, to reality, and she believed in Maria's story, then Allie had to examine what she, herself, had experienced in the Suarez' backyard. The images she had seen in her own mind. Ramon had picked up on it, and there was no point in Allie denying it to herself.

Cassidy Mayes.

Allie had consciously approached the full memory of that day on the boat only once in her life, and that moment had come during a therapy session several years after the incident, when she had committed herself to getting sober yet again. She knew it was the pain of Cassidy that was at the root of her drinking—and occasionally heavy drug use—and that exorcising the pain of her friend's assault would be the most important step to getting clean.

Allie had shown up on time that day and with the true intention of clearing her conscience and starting on the road to recovery; but despite her willingness to sit with the therapist, she couldn't muster the strength to actually talk about the experience. It was a naïve idea to have considered in the first place, she realized, to be able to unload all of her troubles out during that first session; the single event that had plummeted her into depression and substance abuse was probably years away and thousands of dollars down the road.

Allie's cynicism toward psychology grew exponentially that day as she walked from the therapist's office—twenty minutes early and feigning a sickness that felt real in her gut but was almost certainly brought on by psychosomatic guilt—but even then, Allie knew it was she who was unwilling to talk about the event, and she vowed never to return or think of Cassidy Mayes again.

And true to her promise, since the day of that failed therapy session, any time the images of Cassidy—or Cody Reynolds or Brian Clark, for that matter—began to creep into her mind, Allie shooed them away like gnats, refusing to let their faces come into focus.

"Ms. Allie?" Josh chirped suddenly from the backseat, the demure voice snapping Allie back to reality.

Allie blinked several times, scanning the sidewalks on either side of Cyprus Lane, taking note of the quiet of the air, the stillness in the branches of the mesquites. A few birds chirped from somewhere inside the canopy of the trees, and the echo of a dog barking in the distance filled her ears, both sounds bringing a mild, albeit faulty, sense of reassurance to Allie.

Focus!

It was an action easier intended than done, especially with her mind bent on dredging up demons from her past.

Demons.

"Ms. Allie?"

Allie locked Josh's eyes in the mirror now. "Yes, honey, what is it?"

"Can we try to find out about my mom next?"

Allie dropped her eyes instantly, reflexively, the question unsettling her. But she quickly regained her composure and brought her focus back to the road, considering the question.

Josh Carter's family.

Everyone had been so focused on Maria and her story—and for good reason—that Josh's household and the whereabouts of his parents had yet to come up. Maybe Josh had spoken to Ramon about it, Allie couldn't know for sure, but considering the circumstances and the chaos of the day, she doubted it.

"Where do you live again, Josh? Sanderling?" Allie tried to sound casual, but the squeak as she said Josh's name gave away her concern.

"Desert Squall. But my mom is supposed to be at work now. At Carla's."

Carla's Diner was in the opposite direction of where they were headed currently, but in a town as small as Garmella, nothing was very far from anywhere else.

"Sure, Josh, of course. We'll check the diner. It's probably a good idea anyway. Maybe everyone decided to have an early lunch today."

Allie smiled broadly and checked the mirror again, where she saw both kids' faces plastered with stoicism.

Allie frowned and nodded. "We'll head there afterwards. I promise." And then she added, "Have you spoken with your mom since this happened? I never quite heard the story of how you ended up with the sheriff."

Josh told the tale of his evening, how the rain had drawn him to his backyard, and there he had seen the creature and was drawn in by the oddity before following it up to the telescope. He also told the story of the necklace, of his lie, and about how the creature had allowed him to live after hearing his confession.

But he had no knowledge of his mother or stepfather, and though he sounded hopeful, especially about his mom who had work in the morning and wouldn't have been at home if the creatures had invaded them, Allie knew that wasn't an entirely sound belief. After all, Riley Tackard and Jerry Kellerman were both killed at work, so being out was not a magic shield.

But Josh hadn't yet reached the same point as Allie, which, if not in the actual neighborhood of hopelessness, was certainly in the vicinity.

"What do *you* think it was, Josh?" Allie ventured. "What do you think the thing was that grabbed you? That spoke to you?"

"I don't know exactly. It was...a monster. There's no other word I can think of to describe it."

Allie gave his response a moment of consideration. "Do you think—?"

Allie suddenly stifled her question, her eyes now locked on the tail end of a white pickup that emerged like a mirage at the intersection of Idaho and 91 and then turned slowly onto the main interstate.

"Oh my god!" Allie whispered.

"What is it, Ms. Allie?" Maria asked.

"Look! Do you see that? It's a Grieg truck. Right there!"

"Yeah, I see it. It must be their weekend to be here."

Obviously, Maria hadn't recognized the unusual emptiness of the town either, the presence of the truck unsurprising to her.

"Maybe *they* know what's happening," Josh added. "Maybe they know about those things."

Allie had the same thought, and not giving herself a moment to deliberate, she pressed the accelerator to the floor and gave chase to the truck.

She was on the bumper of the pickup in seconds, nearly tapping the tailgate as she pulled up to the rear of the vehicle. She quickly flicked a switch on the console, sending the blue lights spinning as she gave a whoop of the siren.

There was no evidence of resistance from the white truck, and it slowed almost immediately and turned on its hazards before pulling to the right shoulder. Allie followed it, leaving less than a yard or two gap between the two bumpers, and when the truck came to a full stop, she threw the cruiser into park and spun around, facing the children.

"I want you two to stay here, obviously, but I also need you to pay attention. Approaching a stopped vehicle, especially under these circumstances, should be done with two people. But there's only me right now, so I need your eyes. Both of yours. If you see anything unusual happening, like someone coming out on the other side of the truck, for example, I want you to honk the horn. Do you understand? Just lean on it. Let me know."

"You want us to cover you," Josh said, grinning.

Allie smiled back. "That's it. Cover me."

Allie was beyond caring about violating protocol at this stage in the day, and she snatched her sidearm from her holster and then checked it for readiness before opening the door and stepping from the cruiser. She walked quickly to the truck, her pistol pointed at the driver's window as she approached.

"Roll down your window and put your hands outside! Now!"

She kept her pace steady, and by the time she reached the truck, the window to the vehicle was fully down and a pair of empty hands was dangling outside.

Allie arced around the side of the truck until she was facing the driver from about ten feet away. She lowered the gun and stared at the man, who looked to be in his late sixties;

his eyes stared forward, his face expressionless. A woman sat next to him on the passenger side of the bench seat, another man in the back.

"Put your hands on the steering wheel," Allie ordered. "You two," she nodded to the passengers, "hands flat on your laps where I can see them. Slowly." When everyone was in compliance, she asked the driver, "Who are you?"

The man's expression didn't change as he answered. "I work as a monitor for the telescope." He looked over his shoulder to the man in the back. "What have I done wrong, Mr. Filemon?"

The man in the back seat, who looked as if he could have been the driver's son, wrinkled his brow and stared at Allie. "Hello, officer, my name is Zander Filemon."

Allie said nothing, studying the interactions, looking for a signal between the two that might tip her off to danger. Thus far, however, there was nothing unusual.

"I am a senior analyst at our Headquarters. My associate, Mr. Jari, is new to the company. This is his first assignment as an auditor. I've come as an observer. On-the-job training, yes? What is the problem exactly?"

Allie had met many of the employees from the Grieg over the years, but never this person, and she disliked him instantly. "I've never seen any of you before."

"As I've said, this is my associate's first assignment. And I am only here today as a trainer." The man's words were flat, stoical, which Allie inferred as something of a challenge, if not a threat.

"And who is this?" Allie nodded to the woman sitting next to the driver, who was also much older than Zander Filemon.

"She is my boss."

The woman met Allie's eyes with the same lifeless stare and nodded.

"That's a lot of muscle for a simple observation."

No replies.

"When did you get here? I was told you wouldn't make it this weekend due to the giant hole in the middle of the interstate." This was a lie, but Allie thought it the perfect item for which to set a trap.

There was a pause in the man's response, a slight thinning of his eyes. "We arrived a few days early."

"Why?"

"This is not anomalous. Our trucks often conduct audits off their normal schedule. If everyone knew the exact day and time of our arrival, it would negate the quality of our auditing."

This was correct, of course, in terms of both activity and rationale. Off-the-books audits were, if not common, not entirely abnormal either, and had been conducted as long as Allie had been on the force. She frowned. Can I see some ID, please? From all of you?"

Zander and his cohorts handed their credentials to Allie, and after perusing them for several seconds, she handed them back and asked, "Have you noticed anything unusual today? Any of you?"

"Unusual?" Zander replied.

The question was clear, and Allie kept silent.

Zander squinted and frowned in thought, and then he stared forward through the windshield. "If you're referring to the absence of citizens on the streets today, yes, we noticed. Is that unusual?"

Allie chortled. "Uh, yes."

Zander shrugged and looked toward the empty street again. "As I said, Mr. Jani is new to the town, and I've not been here in years. My superior has never been. We didn't notice."

Allie measured the reply, mentally examining it for logic. "Do any of you have a cell phone?"

Zander looked up at Allie curiously, the first sign of true expression that she'd seen in the man's face. "Of course not! They are forbidden here! We wouldn't risk polluting our own data."

Allie frowned and turned back to her cruiser, checking on the kids inside. She could see Maria through the windshield, her eyes desperate and worried. She began waving Allie back to them, encouraging her to hurry. Allie nodded and held up a finger, and then she turned and looked down the empty street ahead. "Where are you headed now?"

"To the telescope."

"Oh yeah? Why's that?"

"As I said, my associates are here for the first time, and we at the Grieg believe it important everyone become acquainted to the foundation of our work. The tele—"

"It's not safe," Allie suddenly announced, now feeling the pressure of the task ahead and the children waiting for her in the car. "You can't be out here."

Zander's eyes didn't move, but the corners of his mouth turned up just slightly, as if he didn't quite trust Allie's warning and was studying her for the tell of a prank."

"Did you hear me?"

Zander finally blinked several times and asked, "Not safe? What does that mean?"

Allie studied Zander for a few extra beats, trying to find the physical characteristic in his face that was provoking her suspicion. But she couldn't place it, and after a few more seconds, she decided there was no point keeping secrets. Whoever these people were—whether auditors or burglars or missionaries—they were trapped in Garmella too and had a right to know the danger. "There have been...people have been killed here today. Several people. At least six." She then added, "And likely more than that."

Zander blinked back at Allie, his face a blank slate, as if he were hearing some off-color joke and was now waiting for the punchline. When none came, he whispered, "My goodness."

"It's not safe to be here. On the road or in this town at all. But for now, there's not much we can do about the latter."

"Are you sure? We haven't seen anything that—"

"Do you think I would make that up!" Allie regretted the shout immediately, but she didn't apologize. "There's someone—something—in this town that is killing people. So, I'll say it again so it's clear: you are not safe on the road and you have to find shelter. And even then, protect yourself."

"Who is aware of this killer? Aside from you?"

Allie thought the question an odd one; not the content but rather the timing of it. It seemed an inquiry for further down the road.

"The sheriff," she answered. "He's out now trying to find anyone else in town who might have been...affected."

"What about the state police? The FBI?"

Allie shook her head. "The phone lines are down. And you already know about the cell phones. And with the sinkhole, we don't have a way out of town right now. We're locked in as far as communication goes. And I guess literally too."

Zander let the information settle and then said, "You said 'something.'"

"What?"

"You said, 'Something in the town is killing people.' What does that mean? It's not a man? Is it an animal or something?"

Allie averted her eyes and swallowed. "Yeah, something."

Zander waited for Allie to elaborate, but he quickly understood her brevity was no accident. "Then we will heed your warning, officer. We shall retreat to our residence."

"Where is that? Where are you staying?"

"We usually stay at a hotel in Simonson—as you probably know—but the company rents a house by the lake in the summer when activity is heavier. It allows us more flexibility with the off-schedule audits. The summer tourists have not yet arrived, but the house is paid for, so that's where we are."

"What house? Where? Who owns it?"

Zander shook his head. "I don't handle the accommodations, so I don't know the owner. But it's across from a seafood market. Kelly's, I believe is the name of the store."

Brian Brandt's house. He was recently divorced and weighing his options on what to do with the lake house. "Okay, listen very closely. Go back to the house and stay there until I come and get you. I would escort you there if I could, but I have somewhere else I need to be right now. I will be back though, so don't leave."

Zander nodded, the hint of a grin still upon his face, and Allie now considered it was simply his resting expression. "Of course," he said.

"And if you do see something, something that you've never seen before, don't go near it. Don't open the door for it or even look at it. There's danger in this town right now. Real danger."

Zander's lips turned up just a twitch higher. "What exactly is it we should be looking for, deputy?"

Allie wasted no time in answering. "It's a monster, Mr. Filemon. There's no other word I can use to describe it."

CHAPTER FOURTEEN

RAMON KEPT HIS HEAD moving at a steady pivot as he crawled his cruiser up the incline of Tecumsah Canyon Road. He reached the corner at Wicomico where the large green space that acted as the town's only real park was situated. Normally, on a weekday in late spring and early summer, the area swarmed with young mothers and children, retirees and college kids. But today it was empty.

He passed houses that looked exactly as they did on any other day, except, in the context of the situation, they now looked more like props on a movie set, lifeless structures of siding and wood and metal, uninhabitable. He said a silent prayer that a car would start in one of the driveways, or that the light from a lamp would flash or a curtain would open. But with each house he passed on his way to Gloria Reynolds' residence, there was only stillness.

He reached the end of Tecumsah Canyon and then turned right onto the gravel driveway that led to Gloria's house.

Ramon parked the car and took a quick, heavy breath before exiting and striding with purpose toward the house, taking three jogging steps up to the front porch to the front door. He knocked once, waited a beat, and then turned the knob and entered.

And with the first scent of the interior air, Ramon knew Gloria was dead.

There was no obvious evidence of a break-in, no over-turned tables or broken glass that he could see from the stoop; but the smell hit him immediately, the odor of demise and catastrophe, a smell that he'd experienced more than once over his lifetime, almost always in the home of some elderly person who had passed several days earlier and who had no one in their lives to notice.

"Gloria?" He called in, his voice barely above a whimper, hopeless. He cleared his throat. "Gloria, it's Ramon."

There was no reply, and Ramon stepped across the threshold and directly into the living room of the small rambler. He closed the door behind him and, despite the bright sun shining in the sky above, the house became a dungeon.

Boxes of all designs and sizes blocked each of the grimy windows, eclipsing any light trying to force its way in. Ramon felt his heart begin to race, the early signs of claustrophobia setting in.

"Stay cool, Ray."

He stalked through the living room and into the hall that led to the kitchen, squeezing through the maze of cardboard cubes that had been arranged for just that purpose. He left his gun holstered, but he kept his hand parallel with his hip, his fingers dangling, expecting to find the crisped corpse of his deputy with every step, her mouth wide and desperate as she screamed in frozen fear, her body wrecked in a way that resembled the young guard at the Grieg.

But as Ramon stood on the sticky linoleum of the kitchen floor, staring at the cascading overflow of glass and ceramic, plastic and metal, coming from the kitchen sink, he realized the smell and mayhem inside Gloria's home had nothing to do with any mysterious creature. It came as a result of his deputy's lifestyle.

She was a hoarder.

Ramon had missed something in Gloria, obviously, some sadness or trauma that had led her to a life of solitude and despair, filth and misery. Her outward personality, at least as far as Ramon could see, displayed nothing that would have led him to believe she lived this way. He hadn't been inside Gloria's house for several years, but on the previous occasions when he had, it had been pristine, austere.

But there was no time now to reflect on Gloria's personal life; his town was under attack, under siege. And he still had the rest of Gloria's house to clear. There were still rooms to check.

Ramon moved across the kitchen and into a narrow hallway that contained four doors, two on each side of the hall. The far door on the right was to a bedroom, a fact Ramon knew based on the window that looked out to the front of the house. But the other doors were a mystery, though one was obviously a bathroom.

He took two paces forward and quickly opened the first door on the left and instantly turned away at the stench that erupted.

The bathroom.

He inhaled and held his breath and then turned back, looking for any sign of his deputy inside; but the room was barely big enough for the toilet and bathtub it held, and the latter fixture was curtainless, exposing the only place in the room where Gloria could have been. It was empty.

On the opposite side of the hall was the first door on the right, which Ramon opened without hesitation. The pressure of time—a feeling that every passing second was drifting him further away from surviving the day—was beginning to weigh down on him now. He prepared for an attack as he swung the door wide, turning his body slightly and stiffening his core; but the door led to a tiny coat closet, and Ramon was met there by a wall of boxes stuffed so tightly inside he was unable to close the door again.

Ramon walked down the hall to the bedroom door next and opened it slowly, more conservatively than the closet, and inside he found exactly the dishevelment and chaos he'd expected. The smell of rot was even more pungent than in the kitchen, and though it likely came from old food and deceased rodents and not from the decomposing body of Gloria (if she was dead, he reasoned, it would have been too soon for her body to take on that odor), he couldn't hold off that feeling of dread, that sense that she was inside the house somewhere, dead and literally petrified.

Ramon did a quiet scan of the bedroom, covering his mouth and nose like someone who's just learned of an astonishing secret, searching for any movement beneath the piles of blankets and papers, or behind the thick musty drapes that had been hung across the entire length of the far wall.

But there was only stillness in the room, staleness, so Ramon closed the door and turned finally to the fourth door behind him, the last door on the left. He stepped to it and eased the door open as if he were entering a nursery, careful not to make a sound, and though he could sense an openness in the room that was nonexistent anywhere else in the house, he could see nothing in the darkness.

But there was a smell there as well, not the stench of decay or mildew, but just as revealing. It was the smell of chemicals, ammonia and urine.

He knew it instantly.

Meth.

Ramon flicked the switch on the wall beside him, and as the room illuminated in a swell of dull orange, Ramon scoffed in disbelief at the sight of the long, wooden L-shaped table that ran along the right and rear walls of the room. On top of the surfaces, spaced a few feet apart, were six single-burner electric plates, each of which held a 12-quart stock pot. On the floor, in addition to the filth and disorder present in the other rooms, was a litter of propane tanks, as well as an army of 10-gallon Home Depot buckets, each stained and coated with the powdery residue of the product that had brought so much misery to his home state, though, at least until that moment, had largely circumvented Garmella.

"Oh no, Gloria. No, no, no."

Ramon closed the door slowly and hung his head for a moment, the scene of the lab still surreal in his mind, impossible. But he didn't linger long there, knowing the larger concern was still lurking in his town somewhere, and as he headed back to the cruiser, his mind began to spin with possibility, ideas that maybe Gloria was somehow involved with the rest of what was happening in Garmella, that maybe she'd found a way to narcotize the town by mixing the drug in the water supply, or through the release of toxic fumes, vapors that caused visions, hallucinations. Maybe what he and Allie and the kids had seen hadn't actually happened at all, at least not in the way it appeared to their eyes and brains.

These thoughts—that everything had been imagined—were ones of lunacy, of course, but Ramon also knew meth was a different kind of drug, one capable of producing vivid delusions, images like the one he had experienced. Of course, people were still being killed—that part wasn't a mirage—but perhaps the meth had somehow made them believe a man was a monster and was being used as a cover-up for some other purpose.

None of what was ricocheting through Ramon's head made any sense, and he quickly considered that if he were, in fact, high on crystal meth in that moment, he wouldn't have been able to entertain the very ideas and conspiracies which blamed the drug for the visions. It would have all seemed normal and natural. But that was the way the human mind worked, always grasping for logic, continually searching for an answer that fit into what was known about the universe.

Still, though, he left the meth explanation open as a possibility.

Ramon reached the cruiser and clicked the radio button, intending to call out for Allie but instead saying, "Gloria? Gloria, it's Ramon, do you copy?" He waited, and when he received no reply, he added, "Listen, Gloria, whatever you've done, whatever troubled you're in, it's okay. We'll work it out. Just please answer me if you can hear this."

He waited with anticipation, and for a moment, his intuition told him that Gloria's voice was about to blare through the handheld, that she was alive, in hiding likely, perhaps from whatever Mexican drug lord she'd crossed who had now made the short journey to Garmella to exact his revenge. Maybe he was responsible for the day's events, the one who had orchestrated the intoxication of the town and had somehow coerced Gloria into the plot.

"Sheriff?" It was Allie.

"Allie." Ramon took a breath. "What...what do you got on your end?"

"We're outside of Maria's now, about to head in. What was that all about? With Gloria? Did you find something? What did you mean, 'Whatever you've done?'"

Ramon paused, not sure how much to get into. He decided the drugs could be important, so he would reveal that much, wanting to get Allie's opinion on his far-fetched theory. "I checked her house, Allie. Jesus, I still can't believe what I saw."

"What is it?"

"In a sentence: Gloria was cooking meth."

"What!?"

"Yep. No question about it. The smell, the hot plates, the pots and filters, it's all there. And she's been living like a hoarder. A complete basket case. I think it was to cover up the smell maybe, all the trash and shit, but I really don't know. I...I still can't believe it."

"Oh my God." Allie's words were a whisper on the other end of the radio. "I can't believe it either. I wouldn't have pegged Gloria for a drug dealer if I had a thousand years to guess it."

"I know, me either. She wasn't there though, which is good, I suppose." Ramon paused. "Allie, I had a crazy thought."

"No such thing today."

"Do you think we were drugged?"

"Drugged? What do you mean? When?"

"Last night. Or this morning. I don't know. But what if we were drugged somehow? What if what I saw up by the telescope, and what you and Maria saw at her house and Josh in his yard, what if none of it was real? What if it had to do with the meth and...whatever Gloria was in to."

There were several beats of silence on the opposite end of the radio, and then the receiver came alive in the form of Allie chuckling. She settled her light laughter and said, "Listen, sheriff, I never made the leap to meth, thank god. Way too freaked out to ever try it. But—and I guess I shouldn't be saying this to my boss right now, but job security's not at the top of my concerns at the moment—I've taken enough drugs in my life to know that what I saw on that porch—and what you and Josh and Maria saw—that didn't come from meth or acid or PCP. It was too isolated. Too specific. That was real, Sheriff. That shit happened."

Ramon took a breath and closed his eyes, frowning. He accepted Allie's experienced opinion on the matter, but he was also rattled by the significance of it. Intoxication was the only explanation he could imagine, so if the drugs weren't responsible for what he had witnessed this morning, it meant the creatures were real. The murders were real. And Ramon's view of the world was now changed forever. The world itself was changed, no matter what happened to them in the end.

"Sheriff, you there?"

"I'm here. I just had to throw it out there. My brain is like scrambled eggs right now."

"Well, let me scramble them some more. I've got some news on this end too."

"What is it?"

Ramon listened to Allie's recital of her encounter with the Grieg monitors, about the van and the trio of auditors and her instruction for them to head back to the Brandt house. He was suspicious of their presence, as Allie was, but he couldn't connect them to anything that was happening.

"Did you ask about a phone?"

"Yep. They don't have one." Allie paused. "There was something wrong though, Sheriff. Beyond them just being out on the road."

"What do you mean?"

"I don't know. They didn't seem as worried as I would have thought they'd be. I mean, I told them there was something loose in the town murdering people, and that they were trapped here for the foreseeable future. And, oh by the way, everyone who lives here has decided either to barricade themselves in their homes for the rest of the day or has disappeared entirely. I don't know, if that was me, I'd a had a few more questions and a little less blind compliance."

Ramon let Allie's concern resonate for a beat and then said, "Okay then, trust that instinct then. I don't like the sound of it either. Any of it." And then he added. "But, if those auditors are still alive, there might be others too. I think it's time to start kicking in a few doors."

"Well, I agree about the doors part anyway."

Ramon paused, chilled by Allie's words. "I hope you're wrong, Allie, I really do. And I wouldn't get my hopes up too high about that baby. Can't be much chance he's still alive."

Ramon could hear Allie swallow on the opposite end of the receiver before she spoke. "I gotta keep hope alive, Sheriff. In something. What else if not that?"

"Fair enough, deputy. I hope you're right."

"I'll let you know how it goes and call you back asap."

Ramon frowned at the enormity of what Allie was preparing to see, of the deformed baby who was likely dead in its crib, either from starvation, its condition, or, more than likely, the black creatures who had invaded his town at some point during the night, bringing what appeared to be Garmella's mass extinction.

And then there was Maria, the sister and daughter who had been left behind to deal with yet another death in her family.

"Be careful, Allie," Ramon ordered with authority. "I want to hear from you in ten minutes. No more."

"Roger that, Sheriff. Over and out."

Ramon replaced the receiver and started up the cruiser immediately, and then he sped from Gloria's house as if he were chasing down a Camaro on a desert interstate. In minutes, he was back in the center of town, ready to discover the true magnitude of Garmella's desolation.

He parked the car diagonally in the middle of the street at the corner of Quarry Hill and Oak, the informal hub of Garmella and the place that was as diverse as any in the town, made up of several blocks that contained a mix of private residences, businesses, and a pair of local government buildings—a small firehouse and a library.

Ramon stepped out quickly and stood in front of the cruiser, scanning the blocks in each direction, deciding which area to investigate first.

St. Patrick's Catholic Church stood directly in front of him, a beautiful structure that had been renovated within the last ten years and was now one of the more modern buildings in Garmella. He considered starting his investigation there, but it was Thursday, and if the church had been empty, that wouldn't have been unusual under even the most typical of weekdays.

Instead, Ramon decided to start with a brown and sienna rambler that sat atop a low hill which looked over Quarry Hill. Up until a month ago, the house had been rented by a young family who had since moved to Vegas, and a new retired couple now lived there, having moved in just a week or so earlier. Ramon had yet to meet them, but he decided there was as good a place as any to start.

He scaled the concrete staircase that led from the street to the property, taking the steps two at a time, and within seconds, Ramon was through the unlocked door and standing on the stone tile of the foyer.

As expected, the main area of the house was empty, but there was evidence that it had been abandoned in a hurry. A blanket hung from a couch cushion and draped halfway to the floor, and the television was on, though there was no reception coming through it, only a message informing the viewer that something had gone wrong with their cable reception and to try again later.

Ramon did a cursory check of the house, giving half the effort he had given at Gloria's place, and then, finding nothing extraordinary, he exited and made his way back down to the street. He walked to the front of the locked gate that led to the grounds of St. Patrick's church and gripped the bars like a prisoner, rattling them a few times in a test of their integrity before beginning his descent down Quarry Hill, his sights set now on the Baker residence about a hundred yards in the distance.

He passed the Market Café and the Garmella lodge beside it, both of which, at least based on Ramon's view from the street, appeared as empty as St Patrick's. Several cars were parked along the road, and, despite Ramon's expectations to see stone-faced citizens sitting like statues in their respective drivers' seats, they were empty as well, a few with their doors swung wide.

The last business on Quarry Hill, before the commercial zoning ended and the street became a long ascending row of residences, was KD's Gas and Convenience, one of two fueling stations in Garmella proper. Ramon glanced toward the station casually, prepared to pass it without perusing, but he was instantly captivated by the brightly lit interior of the store, the fluorescence of the mart drawing him like a moth. Additionally, there was a late-model sedan parked along one side of the only pump at the station, so Ramon decided to alter his path toward the Baker house slightly and veer onto the property of the station as he went.

He walked first to the car at the pump and slowly put his face to the passenger's side window, cupping his hands around his eyes. Empty.

He then set his sights on the interior of the store twenty yards to his left, and as he began his brisk walk toward the front of the market, he suddenly downshifted his gait to a slow walk and pulled his Glock, loading the chamber. Ramon hadn't seen anything specific that called for the firearm, but something about the glow of the store, the flicker of the lights inside, indicated life, action.

He pulled open the door with his free hand and waited, and when nothing appeared in his sight line, he stepped inside, stopping on the welcome mat as the door closed automatically behind him.

Ramon took stock of the food along the cashier's counter and in each of the four or five rows that lined the tiny store, as well as in what appeared to be a functioning refrigerator along the back wall. He doubted he and his group would be stuck in Garmella long enough to die of starvation—it was far more likely they would be killed by the creatures, or perhaps by whatever thing had brought them there in the first place—but his instincts noted the food anyway.

Ramon moved around to the cashier's side of the counter and stooped down, and then he pulled a small shotgun from a makeshift shelf that had been installed thigh-high to the cashier. He scanned the remaining area of the cubicle for any more weaponry and then placed the shotgun on the counter and stepped back into the customer area of the store.

He moved past the coffee maker that anchored the market and then pushed through the swinging door that led to the storeroom. The dim space at the rear of the store was empty except for several stacks of empty milk crates and cardboard boxes, but the back door that led to the outside was open, and Ramon could see what looked to be a white delivery truck parked along the rear exterior wall.

"Hello," he called, walking slowly through the back of the store toward the open door.

Ramon stepped just outside so that he was now facing the side of the truck, which was only a few steps in front of him. He leaned to his right, trying to get a peek inside the cab, but, having no clear view, he decided to head in the other direction, moving cautiously around to the truck's rear cargo hold.

He reached the back of the truck and saw the roll-up door to the vehicle open about a quarter of the way. At the base of the elevating tailgate, which had been lowered all the way to the street, was a dolly stacked to the height of the handles with cardboard boxes. Ramon moved in closer to the dark gap between the truck's roll door and the rail at the base of the bed, and then he stooped down, trying to get a view of what was happening inside the cargo space.

Too dark.

"This is probably a bad idea," Ramon said aloud, and then he holstered his gun and placed his palms on the bottom of the door, fingers pointed back toward him as if he were power lifting a barbell. He then shoved upward, driving with his legs and shoulders, heaving the door up as if he were helping to push a sofa over the railing of a second-story deck.

The roll-up door clattered open to about three-quarters, and Ramon immediately stepped back and pulled his sidearm free, aiming it at the center of the truck's cargo space. But the body of the truck was empty save for a few boxes stacked near the refrigeration unit at the back of the space nearest the cab.

Ramon set the gun on the surface of the dolly's top box and placed his foot on the bumper. He then grabbed the side rail of the truck and climbed up into the cargo space and walked back to the remaining arrangement of undelivered boxes. He cracked the seal on the first cardboard container, and inside he found a variety of dairy items, butter and margarine, cream and non-dairy creamer. Beside that box was a white container holding a case of dozen-packaged eggs, the contents of which had been written in red on the outside of the box.

Ramon turned back to the open door of the truck again, trying to piece together what had happened in this scene exactly. There were items still undelivered, and the driver, based on the full dolly parked by the truck, was clearly in the process of bringing in another round of supplies. But where was he? If he had been killed, where was the body?

Then again, Ramon thought, *where was anybody?*

If everyone in the town was dead, which was the hypothesis toward which his mind was steadily heading, then the streets and homes should have been littered with corpses, similar to those of Luke and Randy and their father at the Carson residence. As of now, however, those were the only bodies that that had been left behind, not including Riley Tackard's, who Ramon suspected would have disappeared as well if he hadn't been at the scene at the time of his death.

Ramon turned back to study the contents of the remaining boxes, opening two more quickly, noting they were full of more perishable items—yogurt, cream cheese, individual servings of milk—nothing that was going to last long if they were stranded for any length of time, especially if and when the power decided to go.

He pulled the two open boxes from the top of the stacks and placed them on the truck floor, and then he gripped the sealed flap of the next box in the left stack and wedged his fingers between the small opening, preparing to rip it open. But before he began the tug of his hand, the lightest of sounds drifted into the truck, hovering just barely in the air before fading to silence.

On any other day, Ramon would have dismissed the noise, irrelevant shouts from a ballgame in the park, or the call of a bird in season. But today was different, obviously, and Ramon focused on the noise, keeping his eyes to the floor in concentration as the sound rang through the truck again. It was the voice of a human—there was little doubt about that—and it sounded distressed.

Ramon stood tall and turned back to the open cargo door, taking a step toward the opening to move closer to the voice, to find the general direction of where the sound had originated.

"Hey!"

Ramon heard the word clearly now, and he remained like a pillar in the body of the truck as he stared and listened, not wanting the footfalls on the aluminum floor to drown out the call if it came again. He gazed off to the area where he suspected the call had originated, in the direction of the low, stone retaining wall that ran along Palmetto Street perhaps a hundred yards in the distance.

Ramon squinted and cupped his hands around his eyes, staring toward Palmetto like a sailor searching for land, but as his gaze moved along the deserted crumbling road toward the wall, his eyes stopped and froze on a chocolate-brown dumpster sitting in the foreground about halfway between the box truck and the wall.

And he saw it again.

The fuzzy shadow of absolute blackness from the forest appeared beside the receptacle as if materializing from the dust below. It stood tall and malformed, a barely human-like figure that was both thin and hulking, and as it stepped forward, separating itself from the camouflage of the dumpster, Ramon could sense only evil and malevolence in its shape.

"Fuck me," Ramon whispered. "Oh, my Jesus."

Ramon held his breath, stunned for the moment but for his eyelids, which were shuttering up and down in a steady tempo, a reflex brought on by the hope that the continual visual interference would protect him from the creature's lure, its ability to mesmerize.

But as quickly as his eyes were moving, Ramon's feet had already failed him, and the delay in moving to the edge of the cargo bed had cost him dearly. The creature was moving toward him now, only twenty yards from the truck and advancing quickly.

Ramon focused on the opening of the truck now, but it was too late, he would never make it to the edge in time. And even if he did, it would be by a hair, leaving him no time to hop down and create the necessary distance to get up the pace to escape.

"Fine, come on then," Ramon said with resolve, knowing the day would be settled for at least one of them in a matter of seconds.

He licked his lips lightly and reached for his sidearm, and in an instant, the air of confidence in Ramon's gut turned to sickness. His stomach seized and his throat turned to sandpaper.

The holster was empty.

Ramon's eyes quickly shifted to the box at the top of the dolly, and there his Glock lay sleeping like a sunning cat, adorning the stack of boxes like the topper on a wedding cake.

"Dammit!"

Ramon considered again bolting for the opening, but it was far too late now, suicide at this point, so he retreated, pacing only four or five steps in reverse before his back hit the rear wall that housed the refrigeration unit.

He turned toward the wall in desperation, beginning a frantic search of the gaps between the boxes, hoping to find some door that led from the cargo space to the cab, or perhaps to the ground below, a secret trap door that certain trucks installed for special deliveries perhaps. Instead, he found only the cruel flatness of bolted metal. There was nowhere else to go now. He was trapped.

"Come on, Ray!" he barked at himself. "No!"

The black figure reached the edge of truck's cargo space, looming now in the opening like a silhouette, the bright sun providing an intense backlight. The tops of the creature's legs were nearly even with the height of the cargo bed's door rails as it continued to fade in and out of focus, always seeming to be on the verge of dissipating into the ether before reforming to a more distinct mass of horror. Something resembling a face appeared for just a moment and then shimmered to blurriness. Then nothingness.

Ramon searched the truck for a weapon, and though there was nothing that fit that proper description, there was an empty pallet leaning against the side of the truck, old and blackened, slightly molded. Ramon was in full emergency mode now, no longer spellbound by the monster, and he wasted little time in lifting his foot karate-style and smashing the sole of his boot into the center of three of the wooden planks. Two of the long thin boards broke almost perfectly in half, and Ramon quickly gripped one of the pieces and pulled it toward him, tearing it free from the rest of the supporting structure.

The creature was oblivious to Ramon's actions and had now placed its massive hands on the surface of the cargo floor, the long appendages stretching forward like lava, extensive and searching, climbing toward him like black ivy. Its movements were impossible, dreamy and fluid, as if the creature were made of ink, or molasses that had been heated and diluted with water. Within seconds, the beast was inside the truck and standing tall, its menacing shape casting a shadow over Ramon like the moon eclipsing the sun.

Ramon lifted the broken board and held it wide with his trembling right hand, poised like a nervous tennis player about to volley a return at the net, trying to gauge the perfect timing for the swing.

The beast moved forward another pace, its advancement a hair slower now, proceeding with what Ramon considered might be caution, perhaps recognizing the potential threat of the board in his hand.

Or maybe it was the final slow measurement a snake makes just before its fatal strike on the mouse, and with that image in his mind, Ramon suddenly considered this was likely the last moment of his life, the last few seconds of breath on earth. He said a silent prayer, a request to the universe that whatever was to come wouldn't be too painful, and then a brief sense of peace fell over him as he considered the afterlife.

"Come on, demon," he said softly, "let's see what you got."

Demon! That's what it is!

But Ramon had barely a second to explore the discovery further before the thought was replaced aggressively by another presence in his mind, a voice so powerful it was as if the Devil himself had spoken it into his brain.

Tell me your ev—

But as quickly as the voice arrived, it was broken by the sound of another one, the voice of a person, the man who had been shouting to him moments ago.

"Hey!" the man repeated once more.

Ramon's transfixion was broken, the wicked voice in his head now drowned by the new audible call from the street.

He shot his eyes from the demon, which was now less than five feet from him, to the road outside, and there, just a few steps past the dumpster, was a man running toward the truck, a shotgun in his hands, the weapon held low by his waist but pointed toward the opening of the truck.

The man stopped a few yards from the cargo opening and raised the gun, measuring the beast in his sights. "Hey!" he called again, and Ramon now recognized Tony Radowski, the owner of Tony's Guns and Tackle. Tony repeated the command once more, louder now, demanding of attention.

The creature's face, blank and absent a second earlier, suddenly wrinkled into something resembling form, an expression even, some primitive look that Ramon interpreted as a combination of fear and anger, though it was impossible to tell for sure, like trying to construe the look of a jellyfish.

The monster twisted its full body back toward the opening and took a stride forward, an aggressive, unstructured lunge that seemed to leave its body in pieces before reorganizing again, like a magnet pulling together lead pellets.

But the creature made it no further than its first step before the blast of the shotgun exploded into the truck, the detonation of metal projectiles appearing to strike the center of the form's torso, sending the beast hurtling backwards toward Ramon.

Ramon covered his ears and head with his forearms and dropped to the floor, cowering by the rear wall as the smoky monster careened in his direction, smashing against the metal barrier just to his right and nearly landing on top of him.

Except it didn't 'smash,' Ramon thought, *not exactly, not the way any animal of flesh and bone would have struck the wall. It was more of a dull thud, the way a sock filled with sand would have struck the barrier.*

The black monster was down for only a beat before rising quickly and dashing forward toward the opening of the cargo area again, this time seeming to move on instinct, under-standing that the only available escape was in that direction.

In seconds, the creature leapt from the edge of the truck and was on the street, flattening itself along the ground the instant it landed, in the same way it had back at the forest by the Grieg. It then scuttered in a panic toward safety, moving with the galloping fear of every animal on earth that hears the sound of exploding gunpowder.

Tony rotated calmly to his left, tracking the retreating demon with his weapon, and then he shot again, this time appearing to miss it, that assessment based on the powder of concrete that exploded just off the creature's left shoulder.

Ramon and Tony watched the creature disappear around the corner onto Palmetto, neither taking their gaze away until it was out of sight for at least ten seconds. Finally, Ramon stood and walked to the edge of the truck, staring down at the man who had just saved his life.

"Tony Radowski," he said, his breathing heavy with adrenaline. "Thank you, sir."

Tony ignored Ramon and walked over to the base of the truck where the creature had retreated seconds earlier, and then he followed its fleeing path for several yards away from the truck, studying the traversed ground like a detective. He then walked back to the truck and climbed inside, passing Ramon without a look, exploring the metal floor with the same intensity as the street. Finally, he sighed and shook his head. "That's not a good sign," he said, speaking as much to himself as to Ramon.

"What's not?" Ramon asked.

Tony looked at Ramon now for the first time. "No blood. No skin, no bones. No nothing."

Ramon didn't need to ask what the significance of that meant, and he immediately looked to the ground to verify Tony's assessment of the scene. It was impossible. Tony had hit the beast squarely, there was no doubt about that, which meant there should have been blood not only on the floor of the truck and on the street, but all over the sides of the truck as well. Yet there was no fluid of any kind, no body parts, and this, Ramon concurred, was, indeed, not good. If the thing couldn't be injured, it couldn't be killed. At least not by something as crude as a wad of metal pellets.

"How do you figure that, Sheriff? No blood from a thing I just sent soaring through the air with a twelve-gauge?"

Ramon stared Tony in the eye and shook his head. "I can't, Tony. Can't figure that or about a thousand other things today."

Tony nodded. "It didn't like something about what just happened though. You think it was the sound?"

Ramon thought back to the scene in the forest when the creature had fled with the same panic. He was certain he had struck the beast as well, but there was no indication he had hurt it. At least not physically. "You know what, Tony? I think you might be on to something."

CHAPTER FIFTEEN

Two months before the rain

"WHEN WE PHONE YOU, Mr. Bell, it is imperative that you answer."

Winston rotated quickly toward the voice, his torso moving faster than his feet, causing him to stumble forward, only remaining upright by clutching the handle of the full grocery cart in front of him. Today was the first of his bi-monthly trips to Carson's, the local grocery store, to stock up on supplies that would last him for the next two weeks.

Tehya stood like a mannequin between two vehicles in the store's lot—one a tall black van, the other a white truck—the latter of which was the imposter audit vehicle that had appeared like a wraith at Winston's house two months earlier. The vehicles had hidden the mysterious woman until just that moment, when Winston was parallel with her, and as he met her eyes now, he felt the threat of her presence immediately, the gravity of her stare pulling at his nerves like the vacuum of a black hole.

"Our mutual success depends largely on communication, which we don't have when you ignore us."

"I'm...I'm sorry," Winston replied. "I wasn't ignoring, I was napping when you phoned earlier. I've not been feeling—"

"Please don't lie to us either, Mr. Bell. Even more important than communication is trust."

The fact that Tehya knew Winston was lying meant she had been watching him the day before—they had been watching him—spying when he answered the door to speak with Sheriff Thomas.

"Of course, I didn't mean to say—"

Tehya held up a hand and gave an annoyed shake of her head, instantly stifling Winston's attempted qualifier. She then cocked her raised hand toward the van beside her, bringing Winston's eyes to it like a showroom model. "If you please."

Winston balked. "Well...I've got groceries. Perhaps, I—"

"Ouray will take care of your bags. This will take only a few moments." On cue, Ouray appeared from the opposite side of the van, and despite his age and relatively small stature, the man's appearance intimidated Winston. Tehya nodded toward the van again, a more insistent motion this time. "Please."

The woman slid the van door wide, and Winston reluctantly stepped to the vehicle and through the opening. At the back of the van, Zander sat in the middle of a bench seat, his back stiff, hands folded across his lap like a nervous schoolgirl's. But his face was stern, confident, and when the door closed behind Winston a second later, the full threat of the man was realized.

"Please, Mr. Bell," Zander said softly, extending a hand toward a sole captain's chair that had been modified so that it faced backward in the van, toward the bench seat on which Zander sat.

Winston swallowed and gave a deferential nod before following the order.

"I will get right to the point of our visit today, Mr. Bell," Zander started. "Your time is as valuable as ours, I'm sure."

Winston nodded, his face tense, anticipatory, indifferent as to whether there was any sarcasm in Zander's remark.

"They're coming, Mr. Bell. The *Arali* will be here soon."

The nervous lump in Winston's throat turned to one of surprise, eagerness, and he forced it down quickly, trying to contain his emotions. "When?"

"Two months. Perhaps to the day."

"Two months?" Winston's words were a recital, non-judgmental, testing the sound of the time frame as it flowed from his own lips.

"We wanted to make you aware. Allow you time to prepare."

Winston slowly raised a hand to his mouth and gazed absently toward the floor, considering the news in silence, digesting it fully. After several beats, a smile sprouted across his face and he lifted his gaze back to Zander, his eyes broad, glimmering. "Thank god."

Zander nodded, the suggestion of a grin on his face as well.

Winston held his smile for several seconds, unmoving, and then he began to laugh. "I can't believe it! I thought...I thought you might not return."

"You ignored our call."

Winston swallowed nervously, but his smile remained. "I know, I...I think I was afraid if I answered that...that it would end. That I would find out everything you told me before was just a myth, an elaborate hoax maybe. Maybe some sophisticated psychological experiment."

Zander was dubious. "Did you really believe that?"

Winston didn't, not truly, but he didn't entirely dismiss the possibility either. He shrugged and his face became somber. "It's just that it's...it's becoming quite taxing, honestly. More difficult than I'd been led to believe frankly. To keep up the constant interference, I mean. You must be aware of the warnings? The police visits? They know it's me now. The sheriff, he—"

"We are aware of the challenges," Zander interrupted. "Rest assured, we do. But your work has not been in vain. There is frustration amongst the analysts. Perhaps not enough to dismiss the Grieg's readings, but, I suspect, enough to concern them about the reliability of the data. The unusually high frequencies coming from the residents of Garmella have been a topic of priority lately."

"But it's not *the residents* who are interfering. "It's *me*. And they *know* it's me."

"We are obviously aware of this, Mr. Bell, but there was little we could do about the attention. There was no way to prevent the auditors from discovering you." Zander clicked his chin up curiously. "They are putting pressure on the town to fine you. Are you aware of this?"

Winston flipped his hands up and shrugged. "Of course! I mean, I didn't know for sure, but I suspected as much. The sheriff certainly gives that impression, if not explicitly says so." He settled. "But does it really matter? I mean, they'll just issue a fine, right? And I don't care about the money."

"Fines will lead to inspections. Or, perhaps, they will bypass the fines altogether. And that is very much a concern."

"Then I have to stop," Winston said hopefully, wanting to add that he doubted his activities were having any real impact on the Grieg's data anyway. When the quiet zone was imposed on Garmella, it was done to keep a whole town of people from interfering with signals from the cosmos. The interference of a single resident, on the other hand, though perhaps a minor nuisance to the analysts, wasn't going to negate the data of a multi-billion-dollar telescope. If there was some special signal emanating from space, some once in a decade beacon from the gods calling to the *Arali*, the scientists would have known about it by now and detected it. Nothing Winston did was going to affect that.

"Not entirely, no," Zander answered. "But you will need to reduce the rate. Two days a week from now on." He paused and added, "And perhaps a generous endowment to the town's library might be in order, as well. Or the police or firefighter fund, if such a thing exists here. It might create a bit of space for you."

Winston nodded as he took in the instruction, and after a moment he verified Zander's declaration from earlier. "Two months? Is that really true? They're arriving two months from today?"

Zander nodded; there was a shine in his eyes that Winston now remembered from his first visit. "Our calculations are sound. Perfect. They're coming; they should arrive between June 10th and June 12th."

Winston took a breath and stared distantly past Zander, toward the back wall of the van, weighing this enormous revelation and the implications of what such news meant to him, ignoring as best he could the consequences to the town at large.

"And then what?" Winston asked, his eyes wild with eagerness.

Zander looked at Winston curiously. "What do you mean?"

"I mean, what happens on those days in June? What will it...what will it look like when they finally arrive? And what should I do to prepare for them?"

Zander nodded at the practicality of the question, as if he'd temporarily forgotten that Winston wasn't privy to all the information he and his colleagues had collected over the years, to the millennia of data he and his compatriots had amassed. "There is not much you'll have to do to prepare, but there is some. Your home is the last residence before the telescope—you must have figured out that your proximity to the device was one of the criterion upon which we based your selection—so you will be amongst the last of their collections."

The collections.

Winston recalled Zander's description of the process from his first visit, but the details were vague, and Winston had been spellbound by his promised prize of eternity, or something close to it. He knew the *Arali* were bringing with them death—death to the townsfolk, some of whom were his friends—and then the collections of their corpses would follow. And perhaps their souls. This last part Winston was never quite clear on, as Zander had been nothing short of coy on the subject, but he assumed once the bodies were

dragged away, something to the effect of soul swallowing occurred in the depths of Perdition.

"Two of the *Arali* will begin the collections, beginning
at the town's entry, and they will continue inward until the
reach the highest point in town. In this case, that is the location of the telescope. They will begin at dawn—this we're
almost certain of—and once they begin, the process will go
quickly."

Winston recalled Zander's revelation of the process, his
description of how the creatures would go from house to
house making their collections. The image Winston had
conjured at the time was one of swooping black phantoms
moving through the streets like dusky shadows, and as he recalled this memory now, so close to the day of their arrival,
he shuddered at the picture.

At each residence, the *Arali* would attempt to compel
confessions, continuing through the district until the small
town was entirely canvassed and each resident addressed.

It was the detail of these confessions that had allowed
Winston to sleep at night, rationalizing that since evil existed in all men, his role in the upcoming catastrophe was justi-
fied. Still, though, the impending slaughter weighed heavily
on his conscience, exacerbating his sickness whenever he ex-
plored the future carnage too deeply. He could only imagine
the terror his town would face on that morning, how most
of the victims—many of whom would be children—would
be incapable of processing the monsters in their presence.

And the pain. He assumed that was inevitable as well;
this piece of the image he kept tucked away in the furthest
reaches of his mind.

Winston swallowed and gave a long, shameful blink, unable to keep the casualties from his mind. "Will...everyone be visited? Every home?"

Zander stared hard at Winston and tilted his head slightly forward. "A town this size, that is our belief. And within each residence, if there is evil in a person's heart, a collection will be sought." He leaned back now and lowered his voice. "And there is evil in everyone's heart."

Winston closed his eyes and took a deep breath and then rubbed his forehead, exhausted. He stared back at Zander, his eyes half-mast. "But not everyone *dies*? Not everyone is...collected? These towns you mentioned before, only a sample of people died in those cases."

Zander shrugged and nodded lightly. "Some will survive the collections." He then added, "At first."

"At first?"

"It will depend on the day. On the people and their habits. There are those who will leave home at the perfect hour and not recognize what is happening until well after the collections are under way. Some may even recognize the danger and retreat to a bunker or safe room beneath their home and remain undetected by the *Arali*."

Winston doubted there were any such bunkers in Garmella, and though he hadn't one either, his sprawling property had more than a few spaces that could serve his purposes.

"But most will succumb on the first pass. Once the mind has been set upon, it is very difficult to extricate it from the *Arali*. They can sense the thoughts of anyone within a radius of many miles. And they will hunt the mind for as long as they can."

"As long as they can?"

"Historically, the collections have ended by solar noon, when the sun reaches its highest point in the sky. We believe that is the reason so many survived previously. The *Arali* simply ran out of time." Zander moved forward on the seat now and leaned in, trying to get as close to Winston as possible. "But we...I am hoping that will change this time, Mr. Bell."

Winston swallowed nervously as his eyes welled, and something in his heart told him not to explore this wish of Zander's. Instead he asked, "What can *I* do to avoid them?"

Zander looked away for a beat and then quickly back to Winston, as if slightly annoyed by the question. "You cannot avoid them, Mr. Bell. Not if you intend to collect on your end of the deal. There will come a point in the day when you must meet them face to face."

Winston had anticipated there would be some risk in the arrangement, some potential for punishment beyond what might come from interfering with the Grieg and its data. But until now, the physical consequences from the *Arali* hadn't been discussed, and the potential for his own pain and death. "But what am I to say?"

"You will have the same opportunity as everyone who confronts them: the chance to confess the evil of your heart. This is the only group who will ultimately survive, that small faction of people who confess their gravest sins." Zander paused, ensuring Winston understood the magnitude of this instruction. "The way to prepare for their arrival then, Mr.

Bell, is to search your heart. To find the cruelty that lives there."

Cruelty. There was plenty to choose from on that front, Winston knew, and he digested this new instruction with dread. His life story was littered with a long list of sinful deeds. How would he choose the right trespass? The one which registered highest on the scale of malevolence? It seemed an impossible task to even catalog all of his transgressions, let alone to rank them.

"In the meantime," Zander continued, "on the day of their arrival, take whatever precaution necessary. Knowledge of their coming is its own prophylaxis. And perhaps loud noises."

"What?"

Zander shrugged. "It is a possibility. Still, before your time comes to repent, you must make an effort to avoid them. That is a solution you must find on your own. But make no mistake: your payoff can only come in their presence. There is no alternative to that part of this deal. Your extension on this earth will only come once you have professed your sin."

The stifling air of the van suddenly felt thick in Winston's throat and nostrils, and the disease that had ravaged his lungs over the past year now raged in his chest like magma in the mantle of the earth. He stifled a cough and managed to croak, "I understand." He then tugged at his collar and cleared his throat, "Where will I go to find them? When my time comes?"

"Before the *Arali* descend, they will congregate at their arrival point. That is where we will meet them."

"Arrival point?"

"The gorge will form a day early. It is from there that they will emerge, and there that they will descend."

"Gorge?"

Zander nodded. "Keep your ear to the town. You will know."

Zander was tiring of the questions, that was obvious, but Winston's head was swimming with the details of the arrival, facts that he knew would be important and that he was bound to forget over the next sixty days. And this would be the last time he would see Zander and his partners before the arrival, about that he was almost certain.

"How will we get out? Once it's...done?"

"We'll need to walk to a car we've prepared about a mile down from the sinkhole. It's parked at one of the overlooks along the roadway. When we reach Simonson, you'll be driven to the state line of your choice. Bring money and a passport, in case that choice is Mexico."

"Will I be able to come back? Ever, I mean?"

Zander shrugged. "That will be up to you, Mr. Bell; a risk you'll have to assume. If you have a reliable alibi, you might indeed wish to return. I'm sure there are affairs you'll need to clear, valuables to retrieve. But you will never see us again. The moment we drop you and drive away, that will be the end of our relationship forever."

Winston nodded, agreeing to the fairness of the arrangement, and then another question occurred to him, one that had been only partially answered the last time they spoke. "How can this be explained, Zander? To the rest of the world, I mean. This isn't China or Soviet Russia; this is the

United States. How will all these murders be explained? Especially if there are survivors? Witnesses?"

"I understand your concern, Mr. Bell, but rest assured, we have thought this part through, and it is not your worry. Just remember the dates and your own preparation. And, as we discussed, from this day forward, reduce the interference. Two days per week."

Winston took a deep breath and nodded. "I understand."

With the message conveyed, Winston rose from the chair and turned back to the van door. As he gripped the handle, he turned back to Zander. "One more thing," he said.

Zander looked up and nodded.

"How will I know when the day is here? How will I know exactly?"

"Because it will rain, Mr. Bell. The *Arali*, they always come with the rain."

CHAPTER SIXTEEN

ALLIE PARKED THE CRUISER in front of Maria Suarez' home and slammed the gearshift into park. She left the car running and took a deep breath and then looked to the front porch, studying the cluttered containment of patio chairs and decorative pots, all of which combined to make the tiny home appear even smaller.

She shifted her gaze to the yard now, a rather wide area of dirt and disorganized stone remnants with random patches of grass and shrubbery popping from everywhere, including at every crease in the broken sidewalk. The front gate was open wide, and Allie automatically scanned the other fences on the street, noting the similar open barriers at each of the houses as far down the road as she could see. It was almost systematic, she thought, as if the creatures had gone door to door, entering each home like salesmen before radiating their destruction appropriately.

Allie turned and faced the backseat once again, deciding to replace her stern demeanor from earlier with one of compassion and teamwork.

"Listen, I'm going in alone, okay?"

"But I'm—," Maria began.

"Maria?" Allie's voice was calm, and the deputy simply stared at Maria, ensuring that the girl understood she was to listen now, not speak. "I'm going in alone because I need someone out here to watch the street. Remember how you covered me earlier? I need that again. It's even more important this time."

"Josh can cover you. It's my house; I know where my brother is."

"Maria, it's a small house. I think you can describe how to get to him."

"Why can't I go with you?"

"Because it's dangerous, Maria. That's why you can't go with me. I think you know that."

Maria looked down, sullen. "I don't care."

"And that's why you're with me, because I *do* care." She paused. "And, to be honest, I move faster alone. And in there, I might need to move really fast." Allie smirked. "Hey, did you guys know that I still hold the Grand Forks County girls' record for the 2000-meter steeplechase?"

The kids looked at each other and then back to Allie, foreheads furrowed. "What's that?" Josh asked.

Allie put her hand to her heart as if she'd just been shot there. "*What's that*? The 2000-meter steeplechase?" She raised her hands to shoulder height, palms up, and then quivered her head, bemused, as if the kids had simply forgotten the event and needed to search their brains further.

Both kids shrugged.

Allie frowned. "It's a very prestigious event, as a matter of fact. Ugh. It doesn't matter, except that my holding that record proves that I'm fast—faster than both of you for sure—and nimble, and if I need to hustle out of there with a baby in one hand and a gun in the other and some tall, smoky bastard on my tail..."

Josh and Maria giggled at this image.

"...then I'm not going to want to spend a second searching around in the kitchen or the bathroom or wherever you two might end up." Allie let her eyes linger on both children for several seconds until both Josh and Maria nodded in agreement. "But keep your sights on the neighborhood, just like you did before with the truck. And honk that horn if you see anything." Allie hesitated and then disengaged the shotgun. "Either of you know how to use this?"

Josh nodded instantly. "I do. My dad used to take me hunting all the time. And I've gone with Ray a couple of times too."

"Good. Take it." Allie handed the gun to Josh as if he were a professional. "And keep it on safety unless...well, I guess you'll know when to take it off." Josh nodded and Allie looked to Maria. "So where am I'm going once I get inside this palace of yours?"

"My parent's bedroom is to the left when you walk through the door. Just past the stairs that lead to the basement. Antonio will be in the bed if...if he's still alive."

Allie sighed and gave a nod of her own now. "Okay then."

She gave a final wink to the frightened girl and exited the car without another word. She paused and took in the full setting of the house and yard in front once more, and then she strode toward the Suarez house, keeping her mind as clear as possible, not allowing herself even a glance in either direction as she approached the porch, climbing it quickly and then entering through the front door.

Allie braced herself for the sight of Maria's parents, black and twisted on the living room sofa perhaps, or crumpled across the kitchen floor like Luke and Randy. But inside was only the stale emptiness of the house, remarkably tidy compared to the porch from where she had just come.

As directed, Allie turned left, clearing the staircase that led to the basement, and then she made a beeline for the bedroom where she stood and stared at the closed door, feeling an instinct to politely announce her arrival with a knock. Instead, she turned the handle and pushed the door in slowly, and then she snapped her head around briskly, instantly hit by the odor that Maria had been unable to articulate earlier at the station. Allie immediately felt the wrenching of her belly and throat, but she recovered quickly, placing her nose and mouth into the crook of her left arm as she walked into the room.

Allie's focus went to the queen bed, and there she saw the movement almost instantly. It was just the lightest swirl of linen in the middle of the mattress where a puddle of thick blankets had been nested together in such a way as to act as a cradle for its contents.

Allie froze a moment, preparing herself for what she might see, and then she took the four paces between her and the bed and pulled one of the blankets to the side, exposing the deformed face and head of Antonio Suarez.

Allie's breath seized in her chest, and she instinctually closed her eyes, trying to process the image of the baby in her mind. After a second, she opened her eyes again and locked them on the baby beneath her.

"Oh my," she whispered.

A combination of shock and shame flowed through Allie now, shock at the sight of the baby's head—the top of which didn't exist in any normal way—and shame for feeling that shock.

But it wasn't repulsion she felt—not really—she had simply never seen a baby with the condition before. In fact, Allie didn't truly even know such a condition existed, and at the sight of the infant, it seemed impossible that he could be alive.

But he *was* alive, and Antonio's large eyes stared up from the top of his head like a pleading bird's, wide and searching, the lightest tint of pain in them, desperation and longing.

"Okay, kid, just hang tight."

Allie left the baby lying in his makeshift crib and immediately scanned the room for supplies, scrambling beside and under the bed, searching for the things that would keep Maria's brother alive for as long as its natural life would allow, which, based on the look of him, couldn't be very long. She found a used bottle and a large, nearly full, can of formula on the nightstand, and she quickly shoved them and a handful of clothes and washcloths into a drawstring nylon backpack which she found hanging in the closet.

Allie went back for the baby now, but as she went to scoop him, she paused, suddenly fearful that any wrong movement, any abrupt shake or jerk, harmless to any other infant, would hurt him permanently. She took a breath and set the backpack down on the floor, and then she leaned in carefully, her hands outstretched, fingers apart as if she were preparing to diffuse a bomb. And as she wedged her fingertips behind the baby's tiny back, an explosion like dynamite rang from outside.

Allie bolted upright, staring at the ceiling, trying to decipher the sound, and then a second blast rang, and this time there was no doubt what it was.

A shotgun.

Allie scooped the baby quickly now and headed for the door, turning back on a dime to retrieve the bag, and by the time she made it into the hallway and back to the front door, she heard another sound ring through the air, and she knew there was trouble.

"I'M GOING IN."

Maria grabbed the handle of the cruiser door and unlatched the door, pushing it wide and putting her foot to the street, purposeful and defiant.

"Wait, what?" Josh asked, perplexed.

Maria paused and looked in the boy's eyes. "What I said. I'm going inside." And with that, less than sixty seconds following Allie's entry into the Suarez residence, Maria was outside and strolling defiantly toward the open gate that led to her home.

Josh reacted quickly and was outside just a step behind Maria, on the opposite side of the cruiser, and, unlike Maria who was walking quickly, he broke into a trot toward the house, reaching the gate a half-second ahead of Maria.

Maria was prepared to go through Josh, but at the last moment she stopped inches away from her friend, her eyes still focused on the house ahead. "Move, Josh. I mean it."

She shifted her gaze down to Josh's hands. "Are you going to shoot me?"

Josh followed Maria's eyes to the shotgun in his hands, and then, realizing the implication, exclaimed, "What? No! Of course not!"

"Then move."

"But...I am going to stop you from going inside. Or at least try." He rolled his eyes and threw his head back. "Come on, Maria; you heard Ms. Allie. She needs us to watch the street for her. Can we just do that?"

"You watch. I'm going inside to see my parents."

Josh averted his eyes and looked down nervously, and then finally he met Maria's eyes again, his gaze soft now, sympathetic. "Maria, they're...your parents...you saw what happen—"

"Yes, Josh, I get it! I know. I know they're dead! But I—" Maria stopped mid-sentence, caught by the drift of Josh's stare from her face to some point in the distance over her shoulder, his gaze slowly blooming like sunflowers. "What? Josh, what...?"

Josh swallowed and gave several rapid blinks, and then he frowned and looked back to Maria. "Move," he whispered, his lips barely twitching. "Move to the side."

The inside of Maria's mouth shriveled dry, and she fought the urge to turn and see the threat behind her, though there was little doubt in her mind what it was. "Which...which way?"

Josh barely tilted his head to his left, Maria's right, and the girl gave an even subtler nod in return and then quickly followed the instruction, taking a single step to her right.

When she was clear of Josh's path, she rotated slowly toward the street, and as she turned, from the corner of her eye, she saw Josh lift the shotgun to hip-level, and then a second later the towering sight of the monster entered her sightline.

Maria opened her mouth to scream, but nothing sounded there. The creature was maybe ten yards away, which seemed an impossible distance considering neither she nor Josh had noticed its approach. But as she studied the monster further, its clandestine approach seemed less improbable. The shapelessness of the monster was something she'd never seen before in a living thing; it was as if the monster existed as part of the atmosphere, like a blot on the air itself, the remnants of some dust devil that had sprung to life in the middle of the desert, picking up a slick of oil as it raged through the town before stopping to hover only paces from them.

"Shoot it," Maria said flatly.

Josh fumbled his index finger around the trigger guard, searching for the safety pin, eventually looking down from his target to find it. He pushed the tiny cylinder in and quickly squeezed the trigger, gritting his teeth in preparation for the blast.

But still nothing happened. "What?" Josh was in a panic now, his eyes welling and his legs so shaky he could barely stand.

"Is it loaded?" Maria asked, her voice like cracking ice.

Josh swallowed and took a breath, and then he nodded in renewed confidence and slid the pump toward him and released it, chambering the round with a satisfying click. He squeezed the trigger again, finally releasing the wad of shot wildly into the air like the blast from a drunken cowboy. He missed badly, but the creature reacted in what seemed to be an expression of fear, its movements twitchy and backwards, spilling away from the kids, increasing the distance between them by double.

But it wasn't a true retreat; the monster remained in the vicinity, watching Josh and Maria like a giant owl on a perch, appearing to measure them from its new position.

"Again," Maria said with a bark.

Josh gave a blank look at Maria, shaking his head. "It's too far."

Maria gave an encouraging nod. "Do it. Quick."

Josh emptied the shell and reloaded with a slide of the pump, and this time he brought the gun to his eye and aimed properly, keeping his head still, just like his father had taught him. And then he squeezed the trigger.

Again, it was a miss, but it was a better shot than the first, and the creature retreated another yard or two, again crouching and twisting as the gunshot rang through the air. The monster was agitated by the barrage, as before, but the reaction was diminished compared to the first blast, despite the improved accuracy. Maria and Josh looked at each other, uneased by this new resilience.

Maria looked to the creature first and then glanced quickly to the cruiser. "Cover me," she said, not looking at Josh as she spoke, and without another thought, she dashed toward the car.

CHAPTER SEVENTEEN

TONY RADOWSKI WAS IN his late fifties with a head of buzzed grey hair and a body as solid as the face of a stone cliff. Ramon had always assumed he was ex-military, though he'd never had a long enough conversation with the man to find out for sure. And that was just fine with Tony—at least it seemed so from Ramon's perspective—as the man was as coarse and off-putting as any in Garmella.

Despite the rough reputation and manner, however, Tony was, by all measures, successful, owning and operating one of the most profitable stores in the small town, a result that came from an intimate knowledge of his products and prices that were unyieldingly fair. That, and that he sold hunting and fishing gear, by far the two most popular pastimes in Garmella.

Tony and Ramon sat at a small metal picnic table outside the front entrance of KD's, Tony with a pre-packaged cold cut sandwich spread out before him, dissected on the thin sheen of plastic in which it had been wrapped. He squeezed the contents of a mustard packet on a slice of rye bread and then looked up at Ramon, cutting right to the chase.

"They're aliens, right?" Tony asked, his tone indicating the answer was as obvious as the sun in the sky above. "I mean, what else if not?"

Ramon hadn't settled on an answer to Tony's question, though he had his own ideas, ones he wasn't yet ready to share with the store owner. "Could be."

Tony frowned and looked away, unsatisfied with Ramon's lack of opinion on such an existential matter as the one currently before them.

"But we can't just sit here and wait for it to come back. We need to get moving."

Tony popped the top slice of bread on to the deli meat and took a bite of his sandwich, never looking at Ramon or acknowledging his command. He stared up the long empty stretch of Quarry Hill, chewing his lunch as if he had nothing but time. "Well, whatever they are, I knew they was coming," he said casually. "Or that something was?"

The words landed like a punch to Ramon's gut. He cleared his throat. "Knew they were coming?"

Tony nodded. "Oh yeah. For five months or so. Maybe a little more."

Ramon squinted and shook his head, disbelieving. "How?"

"Signals have been different. Scrambled or something."

"Signals? What are you talking about?"

Tony clicked his chin toward the sky and then looked at Ramon. He shrugged his shoulder sheepishly. "I figure I'm gonna live in a town quieter than the surface of the moon, I might as well make a hobby out of it. 'Course, I don't get the same signals as that monstrosity up on the hill, but I wasn't really looking for Martians anyway. At least not to start."

"I'm not following. What are you talking about?"

"Space signals. The telescope. You've seen it. That big dish-shaped leviathan that sits up the road?"

"What about it?"

"I got my own little receiver at home. Built it myself. Like I said, little hobby of mine."

Ramon hadn't figured Tony for a man of science, though he conceded that was probably just his own bias and stereotyping at work. "So what *were* you looking for?"

"Hmm?"

"You said you weren't looking for Martians. What were you looking for?"

"Nothing in particular, I guess. Just browsing the airwaves, really. And I get some crazy shit from time to time too." Tony smiled. "Mexican radio—that's always interesting—and even a few broadcasts from Canada. Shit, I think I even heard a traffic report from Hawaii one morning." He paused, a quizzical look replacing the smile. "But these last six months, it's been a whole lot...cloudier. Lots of blips and pings and crackles. Like goddam Rice Krispies. Total fucking Space Invaders shit. Pissed me off at first, thought my receiver had gone to shit. But then I figured it was something...I don't know, something to pay attention to maybe. Like maybe it had to do with whatever that behemoth of a telescope has been lookin' for for the last thirty years."

"Signals were from space."

Tony nodded matter-of-factly. "Exactly."

"But how? How do you know?"

Tony shrugged. "Cuz what I said before, Sheriff. You been listening? I been catching airwaves on and off for over eight years now. I know everyone here thinks I'm some redneck good ol' boy that doesn't know nothing past Merle Haggard and bass fishing. But I got a college degree, Sheriff Thomas. Did you know that?"

Ramon pursed his lips and shook his head, generally surprised at this addition to Tony's resume. "I did not."

Tony let this news of his education set in fully before continuing, making sure appropriate consideration would be paid to him going forward. "Anyway, after these blippy noises kept on—and getting louder and more frequent—I started doing a little research. Library. Online. Trying to find out what it all meant."

Ramon waited for the reveal, and when it didn't come, he asked, "So, what is it? What causes them?"

"Well, shit, Sheriff, they don't know that. But it ain't all that typical. These sounds, I mean. Maybe if it was an isolated night it wouldn't be nothin' to think twice about, but not when they go on for months at a time."

Ramon processed this revelation carefully, trying to piece together whatever connection there was to be made between Tony Radowski's pings and pops and the murky murderers from Hell. "So, you think they're aliens?"

Tony shrugged. "Didn't at first. But after this morning? Can't think of nothin' else."

Suddenly, Winston Bell popped into Ramon's head.

"Wait a minute!" he blurted, his eyes wide with recollection. "Mr. Bell! Winston Bell! He's been...interfering these last few months. Blocking up the airwaves like a road full of boulders. Way over the ordinance limit."

"Winston Bell?"

Ramon nodded, his eyes wide and eager. "He's been...into his music lately. His radio. That's what he told me last time I was there anyway."

Tony unleashed a staccato burst of laughter and nodded his head sardonically. "Yeah, I'm sure that's it. His *music*. What's he been listening too, China's top 40? The greatest hits of Zimbabwe? No sir, the kind of interference I been hearing ain't the result of no ham radio trying to pick up Golden Oldies from Palm Springs."

"Well, whatever he's been up to, it's been giving the monitors fits for the last several months. HQ's been on my ass to fine him. They've laid off the last couple months, but it started about the same time your Rice Krispies started."

Tony pondered the new information in silence, trying to place the meaning of it and how it related to his theory. Finally, he looked at Ramon and asked, "So you think Winston Bell is purposely trying to mess up the signals. Why?"

"They don't give me the details," Ramon answered, "just the orders."

Tony considered the answer for a few beats and then asked, "How did he know?"

"Know what?"

"How did he know they were coming? How did he know to disrupt the signals? To throw the analysts off track?"

"Maybe it's just coincidence," Ramon offered, unconvincingly.

Tony grimaced at the suggestion. "Old man Bell doesn't make a peep during his entire residence here in Garmella. Which is what? A decade now? And then suddenly he starts buzzing like a chainsaw these last six months or so. I don't think so?"

Ramon frowned and shook his head. "So he *was* purposely interfering with the Grieg to provide cover for these creatures to arrive? Is that what you're saying?"

"Yes, I guess I am saying that."

"But...why? If that's true, why would he want...aliens to come? Or whatever they are?"

"Don't know that part, but I do know if that kind of commotion came from anyone else other than the man in the high castle there, they'd a been served, searched and seized three months ago." He gave a pragmatic shrug of his shoulders. "But, I guess, what, fifty grand in property tax revenue a year gets you a little distance from the man in this town. Most towns, I suspect."

Ramon doubted Winston Bell paid quite that much in property taxes, but still, he got Tony's point, and Ramon released his stare on the man, understanding that the jab about leniency was mainly directed at him. And he was right, of course; anyone else in town would have been penalized after the second violation, and after a third, his deputies would have served the warrant and begun traipsing around the suspect's living room looking for contraband. "Well, Mr. Radowski, if you're about done here, how about we go pay Mr. Bell a visit."

"Thought you'd never ask."

"HAVE YOU SEEN ANYBODY else in town today?" Ramon eased the cruiser up Quarry Hill and merged on to 91, headed north.

"Nope," Tony answered, "but I get to my shop at 5 am. Every morning. Nobody out at that time in this town—present company excluded, of course. And the rest of our brave police force."

Ramon ignored the gibe. "5 am, huh? Your shop doesn't open until what, eight o'clock?"

"Seven-thirty. But I ain't like most of the pansies in this town. Soft and lazy, that is. Army slapped that pussy shit out of me forty years ago. And thankfully, it stayed out."

"So, anyone who sleeps past 4 a.m. is a pansy?"

Tony frowned and shrugged. "I just know that I don't. And I definitely wasn't gonna start today. Not with all that beautiful rain falling from the sky last night. That was a nice surprise, wasn't it? I forgot what that smelled like."

Ramon conceded the feeling. "It was."

"But no, to answer your question, I ain't seen a soul 'sides you all day. 'Cept for that alien I blasted back at the truck." Tony then added, "I'd been tracking that son of a bitch for hours."

Ramon flashed a quick glance toward Tony, locking in on him for several seconds before focusing back on the road. "Tracking it? What...what does that even mean?"

"Means what I said. Saw it not long after I opened today. I usually got a couple of boys out front waitin' for me to open. And almost always on Thursday. Fishermen usually. But not today. I went out around seven and wasn't nobody there. So, I stepped out, taking in the moist air or whatever. And that's when I saw it."

Tony's cocky persona, on full display since he'd arrived behind the delivery truck, waned, and he gave a noticeable swallow as he recounted the sighting.

"Yeah, I was scared. Shit yeah, I was. No shame in admitting that. I didn't know what I was seeing—still don't, I guess—but I knew whatever it was, it wasn't there to bring me flowers."

"Where when you saw it?"

"Just come out of that house 'side Meredith Looney's—don't know who lives there now—but the way it moved was like nothing I'd ever seen. My mind tried to make sense of it, to fit it into some kind of box that worked with what I knew about people and animals; but...I don't know, my brain wouldn't allow it."

Ramon understood the feeling and nodded knowingly.

"And then it went to Meredith's house next—just glided there like...like it was part of the air itself, but still solid, you know? It was..." Tony couldn't come up with the words, so he shook off the sentence and took a breath. "And then it pushed in the door like it was made of paper. Easy."

Ramon thought back on the strength of the creature, how it had crumpled Riley Tackard's torso effortlessly.

"I was frozen, Sheriff; I'm telling you, I couldn't move. And when that thing disappeared inside Meredith's, all I could do was just stare at the open door. For the first time in my life, I really thought I was dreaming, even though I knew I was awake. I never believed that shit when it happened in movies—where people think they're sleeping when something bizarre happens—but I actually thought that exact thing. You know what I mean?"

Ramon did and nodded. "I think I do."

"I just kept standing and staring, waiting for the thing to come back outside or for me to wake up, whichever was gonna happen first. And not a full minute later it appeared in the doorway and bled out to the yard, and then it was on to the next house, moving there like a shadow."

Ramon pictured the movement of the creature in his mind, remembering how it almost melted into the forest, fleeing from the explosion of his gunshots.

"And that was when I finally snapped back to life. When my military training finally reignited. It's been a long time since them days, you know, and sharp as I try to stay, physically and mentally, sometimes it takes a while to come back."

Ramon gave a wry smile. "Understandable. I would think the appearance of a demon moving through town might delay your reflexes a bit."

Tony smiled back, but the look faded quickly. "It's always there though, you know. Even after a few decades pass. You're a cop. Relatively young still. One day you'll know what I'm talking about."

Ramon grinned, but his eyes were sad, doubtful, and the two men flashed knowing looks to each other, understanding that Ramon's retirement party was unlikely ever to happen.

"Anyway, I got my shit together and went back inside and grabbed this boy here." Tony ran a hand over the shotgun on his lap as if it were a sleeping Pekingese. "But by the time I came back out, the thing had already moved on and was four houses past Meredith's. It was like a fire was spreading." He paused. "And when I went to check on Meredith,

I didn't realize how appropriate my metaphor was. She was burnt to a crisp. But hard like stone. Like she'd been dipped in liquid iron or something."

Ramon nodded, and he could see that Tony had expected a different reaction from him.

"You've seen it then? The bodies?"

Ramon swallowed and nodded. "Not only a body, Tony. The whole thing soup to nuts."

Tony chewed on this for a while, staring toward the roof, attempting to fathom the transformation. "Damn, Sheriff. Jesus Christ."

Ramon pulled the cruiser to the shoulder about a hundred yards from the driveway that led to Winston Bell's estate. He shifted the car into park and stared hard at Tony. "Oh no, Tony. It was much worse than anything He could have done."

CHAPTER EIGHTEEN

ALLIE'S HEART SANK at the noise of the car horn, and she stood frozen for just a beat before dashing through the hallway to the front of the house. She opened the door and pulled her Glock from its holster as she pattered down the porch stairs, Antonio in her left arm as silent as a mouse.

Josh stood beside the cruiser with the shotgun, the barrel of which he held low at his hips, aiming. Maria was beside him, and both were both transfixed on the street ahead.

Allie followed the children's stares down the empty street which was still and quiet. She could see only cars and streetlamps and the low roofs of the ramblers that lined the street like giant steppingstones. It was an eerily beautiful sight, with the sky as blue as topaz, the sun illuminating the backdrop of the mountains rising miles in the distance. "What's happening?" she whispered, anxiously surveying the road.

"It...it went behind the house. Over there. The house with the red car in the drive." Josh pointed to a small brown rambler, third house on the left of Hermosa about a hundred yards down.

"Did it see you?"

Both children nodded in unison.

"It was coming for me," Maria whispered.

Josh turned to Maria and shook his head slowly. "It was coming for both of us."

"No. I could feel it. It wanted me. Only me."

"Why?"

"I...I think because you already gave it what it wanted." Maria looked to the ground, as if exploring a thread that was developing in her mind in real time. "But it never got anything from me. In the backyard. Ms. Allie came before it could...ask me."

Josh pondered Maria's theory, and though there was little evidence to support it fully, he trusted his friend's instincts and nodded in agreement, accepting the truth of it.

Josh focused again on Allie. "I shot at it. Twice. Not sure I hit it, but it seemed hurt. At least at first. Then Maria got to the horn and you came outside and...that's when it ran. I don't think it liked the sound of the horn."

"Less than the sound of the shotgun?

Josh shrugged.

Allie looked at Maria for confirmation of the events, but the girl had turned her focus from the road to Allie's left shoulder and the bundle cradled there. Allie smiled weakly.

"Is he...alive?" Maria asked.

Allied sighed and nodded. "He is."

Maria moved in closer and peeked through the blanket, hesitantly. Antonio's eyes were closed; he was sleeping. "How?"

"How what?"

"How can he be alive? How is it possible?"

Allie shrugged. "I don't know. But he is. It must not have seen him before."

Maria shook her head. "That's not what I meant."

Allie squinted, confused.

"He wasn't supposed to survive birth. And then the doctors said he would only live a couple hours even if he was born alive. How...how hasn't he died yet?"

Allie swallowed, the question sending a chill through her. "I don't know, Maria."

"And he was all alone in the house." She looked to Josh and then back to Allie for answers, now becoming animated, teetering on hysterics. "Just lying on the bed, right?"

Allie nodded.

"And you're wrong about it not seeing him. It was in the room. That thing was in the room when it turned my mom..." She lowered her voice, wiping away a tear. "When it turned my mom and dad to black. It saw Antonio. It had to have seen him. But it...it just left him there. It left him and came for me instead. Why?"

The question felt philosophical to Allie, rhetorical, and she had nothing that resembled an answer anyway. And she certainly didn't have the time to concoct one that would ring true or even comforting. "I don't know, Maria, but this isn't the time to figure it out. Let's just call your brother lucky for now and ponder the questions later, okay?"

Maria looked away quickly, as if she'd been dismissed, unsatisfied with the answer.

Allie looked at Josh now. "You had good instincts. Both of you."

"Instincts about what?"

"To fight. To try to scare it. Most people would have stayed in the car and hid, and under most circumstances, that would be have been good advice. But not in this case. You did great."

Josh said nothing, his eyes still focused on the street.

"And I think you might be right about it being startled. I fired at it earlier and scared it away." Allie furrowed her brow and looked away, suddenly questioning her hypothesis.

"What is it, Ms. Allie?"

"I hit it. I know I did. Earlier, on the patio. It ran away. Like you just described. But it didn't look hurt. Not physically anyway."

"If the one hiding behind the house right now is the same one you saw earlier, it didn't look hurt to me either." Josh paused. "Maybe you just hurt its ears."

Allie glanced up as if Josh had read her mind, just at the second the thought arrived. She nodded; eyes wide, hopeful. "That's what I was thinking. I think it hates the sound of guns. Horns. Maybe anything loud."

"Why didn't it leave when I shot at it then?"

"I don't know."

Josh looked down, considering the theory. "So, does that mean we can scare it but not kill it?"

Allie gave the question the pause it warranted and then said, "I don't know that either. The noise thing is a good theory, but not one I want to test right now. We need to get out of here. We got who we came for, and now we need to get this little guy back to the station."

Allie, Josh, and Maria returned to the cruiser, with Josh taking the front passenger seat now while Maria held her brother in the back. As Allie drove in the direction of the station, she passed the house that Josh pointed out, behind which the creature had fled, but there was nothing to be seen.

The interior of the car was quiet for the next several minutes, and during the respite, Allie replayed the events of minutes earlier again in her mind, exploring Maria's questions about Antonio, as well as Josh's and her theory about loud noises being a repellent.

She thought of Maria's parents' room again, empty but for a baby. A baby that was, almost impossibly, alive.

But the room was *empty*.

Allie spun her head around now, swerving toward the shoulder of the road as she did, rolling the cruiser up on the sidewalk and nearly clipping a fire hydrant. She stopped the car and put it in park. "Maria?"

Maria looked up as if expecting a reprimand; Antonio was cradled tightly in her arms, its delicate, misshapen head covered like a monk's.

"Your parents. You said your parents were home and that the creature turned them to...whatever it turns them into, right? That's what you said?"

Maria nodded.

"Where? Where in the house did it happen?"

"In the room."

"In *their* room?"

"Yes. Why?" Maria's eyes glistened with the memory of her parents.

Allie frowned, suddenly embarrassed that she hadn't been more discreet with her questions, more considerate of the child whose family had been destroyed only hours earlier. It was too late now, however, and at this stage of the game, there was no use lying to these kids. "They weren't there, Maria. Your parents weren't there."

"What? But I...I saw them. What do you mean they weren't there?"

Allie shook her head. "They weren't. If their bodies were there before, they weren't a few minutes ago. Not in the room or in the main part of the house either."

"It took them?"

Allie had the word 'moved' in her mind, but Maria's term 'took' sounded more appropriate somehow. "I don't know, but it seemed something did. Or else they just disappeared."

She thought back to Luke and Randy, fried and frozen in their kitchen, and then to their father on the patio outside. Obviously, the bodies of those three had been present, but as Allie reflected on the scene, their deaths had likely just happened, an assumption she made based on the location of the creature when she first saw it, only two doors down from the Carson home. On any normal day, that kind of reasoning would have been close to nonsense, but in the context of this day, she thought it made reasonable sense.

"What does it mean?" Maria asked.

Allie could only shake her head. "I don't know, sweetheart. I have no idea."

Allie pulled the car off the sidewalk and then turned onto Magnolia, heading in the direction of the station.

"We're going to Carla's now, right?" Josh asked.

Allie had forgotten about the diner and her promise to look for Josh's mom. Not only had she told him they would try to find her at Carla's, but that it was also a good idea. And maybe it was. If there were others alive in Garmella, that was as good a place to look as any. And Josh needed to have closure on his mother one way or the other.

"Yes, Josh, Carla's Diner. Absolutely."

There was a grim silence in the car now as Allie headed toward the diner, an understanding looming now that the fate of Josh's mom would be known in minutes, and perhaps the rest of the town's as well.

But they had also found Maria's brother alive—they had accomplished their mission—so that was at least one win for the day, and Allie was going to revel in it for a moment.

Allie turned the corner on Quarry Hill and drove until she saw the top of Carla's sign rising above the hilltop at the corner of Coralbean and Sweetclover. It was lit up like on any other day, the red lettering on the canary yellow background giving the sign a certain carnival feel, a contrast to the rather dull, underlit interior of the place.

Ahead, at the end of Quarry Hill, Allie could see the back of KD's neon green banner, its letters seeming to beckon still, advertising its promise of fuel and convenience despite the catastrophe that had descended on the town. Those were two nouns Allie thought might be useful right now, and she made a mental note to hit KD's next.

She pulled into Carla's, and her gaze focused on the lone vehicle in the lot, a Ford F-250 which was parked in the first spot to the right of the door. Allie assumed the truck didn't belong to Josh's mother, but she didn't voice the judgement, hoping maybe she was wrong and that Josh would recognize it and voice his excitement. When he said nothing several seconds after entering the lot, she had her answer.

Allie chose a spot at the rear of the lot, well away from the entrance, not wanting to box herself in too closely in the event she needed to make a quick getaway. "All right guys," she said, shifting the car into park and beginning to twist her torso to the back again, preparing to give her 'Stay here' speech once more.

But the moment the cruiser locks popped up, Josh swung the passenger door wide and started his dash to the front of the restaurant.

Allie was quick, however, stepping down to the crumbling concrete lot only a second after Josh, and before he could make it to the door she called, "Josh! Stop this second!"

Josh froze in his tracks, the authority in Allie's voice irresistible to his eleven-year-old ears and brain. He was still five steps or so from the front door, but he wasn't dissuaded from his quest, and he turned slowly back toward the officer. "I'm going in, Ms. Allie."

"Me too." It was Maria, now standing beside Allie by the cruiser, the ever-silent Antonio still in her arms, the young girl cradling her brother as naturally as if she had been caring for him for years. "I don't want to stay in the car again. It wasn't safe last time."

Allie sighed and put her hands in the air as she nodded. "Okay, that's fine. We'll all go. But I can't have you running off like that, Josh. Both of you." She paused. "You either, Antonio."

Maria looked confused for a moment, but then she found the joke and giggled in the way only pre-teen girls can.

"But I'm leading us in," Allie continued, not giving a hint of humor at the joke she'd just told. She nodded to Josh. "Can you see inside?"

Josh turned back toward the restaurant and hunched slightly, leaning forward, trying to peer in through the front windows and glass door. But the sun was too bright, and he got only his own reflection and the desert landscape behind him in return. He shook his head. "I can't see anything."

Allie strode slowly toward Josh now, Maria following closely behind her, and both joined the boy in his location a few yards from the door. "Ready?" she asked, and when both kids nodded in unison, she said, "Let's go."

The three took the final few steps toward the diner until they were standing at the front door, and there Allie cupped her hands around her eyes and peered through the glass, giving her vision several seconds to adjust.

"It looks empty," she said, "but I can't really tell for sure," and without hesitation, she pulled open the door and stepped inside, ushering in Josh and Maria behind her.

Carla's Diner was the only true breakfast place in town, and for that reason, every morning by 8 am, the place was bustling like a Bangkok street market, with a wait time of not less than fifteen minutes. Most of the clientele at that time of day were retirees, north of sixty-five, but as the day progressed, and especially at dinner time, the diner saw customers in every age range. It was a healthy business, and Carla—now retired herself—was a local celebrity in Garmella.

In that moment, however, as Allie, Josh and Maria stood in a tight circle on Carla's welcome mat, each staring to their right down the long laminate aisle that divided the diner's booths from the service counter, the place appeared as empty as a college dorm in July.

A "Please Wait to be Seated" sign stood guard in front of them—absurdly—and no one took a breath as they surveyed the scene, each waiting for the stark emptiness of the place to suddenly explode into chaos.

Finally, Maria spoke. "There's no one here."

The girl's words broke the spell, and Allie swallowed and blinked for the first time in what felt like several minutes. "Doesn't look like it, does it?"

It was certainly true that the dining room was empty—there wasn't a soul in sight—but the emptiness wasn't one of abandonment or panic, as if the people had fled in the middle of breakfast. The eating surfaces of the tables had not a single plate or utensil atop them, nor a crumb of food from what Allie could see. And but for a single cup of coffee that sat nearly full to the right of the register, the service counter was clean as well. Carla's Diner didn't look abandoned; it looked like it had yet to open for the day, the empty lot out front seeming to verify that hypothesis.

"She's not here," Josh said, his voice cracking on the word 'not.' He cleared his throat and repeated, "She's...she's not—"

"Let's go," Allie whispered sharply, interrupting the boy. "We haven't even stepped off the welcome mat yet. Sheesh. What kind of police work would that be if we left right now?" She stared at Josh, awaiting an answer to her seemingly rhetorical question.

Josh looked at Allie sheepishly and shrugged.

"It would be *bad* police work." She gave a disappointed shake of her head and then nodded in the direction of a pair of double doors behind the counter, each with a small window carved at the top. "The kitchen's back there, I guess?"

Allie had been to Carla's a thousand times and knew as well as anyone where the kitchen was, but she wanted to keep Josh involved.

Josh nodded.

"Okay, stay close then. Let's see what's going on behind the scenes."

Allie stepped off the mat and led the kids around the counter, squeezing past a cake display and a double-barreled coffee maker, both with two full pots on the burners. She noted again the organization of the place, clean and prepped and ready for business.

Allie stopped at the double-doors. "You been back here before?"

Josh nodded. "Yeah, a few times."

"What are we looking at in terms of layout?"

Josh shrugged. "It's small. I don't know. Everything goes to the right, just like the dining room. The stove and sinks and...everything. You can see everything as soon as you walk in."

Allie nodded and took a deep breath and then pulled her gun once more. "I'd really prefer if you both stayed here."

Both kids averted their eyes, neither speaking, an indication that they had heard Allie's preference and were now ready to proceed with her as planned.

Allie frowned. "Fine. But again, stay behind."

She pushed in the door on the left, the Out door, and, as Josh had described, the kitchen flowed to the right, giving an instant visual of the entire kitchen, which wasn't much bigger than the kitchen in a large house. She imagined Winston

Bell's kitchen was probably twice the size. And there was no one to be seen.

Allie took a breath. "What's that back there?" She nodded toward a large metal door at the end of the kitchen.

"It's the walk-in."

"Refrigerator, right?"

Josh chuckled. "Yeah. You haven't spent much time around a kitchen, huh?"

Allie gave a sarcastic smile. "I have my strengths, young man."

Josh smiled, but within seconds, his face turned white and tears took the place of laughter in his eyes. "She would be here," he said. "Today is her early shift. She gets in at like five-thirty on Thursdays."

"Carla's opens at six, right?"

Josh nodded.

"Well, it definitely opened today."

"How do you know that?"

"For starters, the front door was unlocked."

Josh seemed unconvinced at that piece of evidence. "I guess. But I think whoever opens for the day just leaves the door unlocked. People aren't lined up at the door at six in the morning."

Allie nodded. "Fair enough. But there was also a cup of coffee on the counter. With a used spoon beside it. Somebody—probably the first customer of the day—was served coffee this morning."

Josh compressed his lips, now intrigued. Then Allie tilted her head and added, "But your mom's car wasn't out front, was it? I assume she drives in to work."

Josh nodded and his eyes lit suddenly. "She does, but employees have to park in the back."

Allie looked at the rear exit, where a panic bar threatened to sound the fire alarm if the door was opened. "Does that thing work?"

Josh shrugged.

"All right, well, I don't want to set off any sirens just in case we're wrong about the noise and those creatures are actually drawn to that sort of thing. Maria, I'm going to need your help."

"Okay." Maria nodded eagerly.

"While we check the freezer, I—"

"Refrigerator," Josh corrected.

"Right. While we check the fridge, I need you to see if Josh's mom's car is parked in the back."

"Okay."

"You have to go out the front though, okay?"

"I get it. What kind of car does she have?"

"It's a Buick LaCrosse," Josh answered.

"What's that?"

"It's just like a regular car. Kind of long. White with four doors."

"The model of the car should be on the back," Allie instructed. "And I doubt there will be more than a couple cars parked out there."

Maria nodded. "Okay."

Allie nodded toward Maria's arms. "Are you okay? With Antonio, I mean. Do you want me to take him for a little bit?"

Maria's eyes turned steely, her lips flat. "No," she said, holding Allie's look for a few beats longer before turning and pushing through the double doors toward the front of Carla's.

Allie watched the swinging door close and then looked back at Josh. "Okay, then. Shall we?"

Josh nodded, and he and Allie strode slowly toward the walk-in cooler, a modern-looking piece of equipment that was probably ten by ten, maybe eight feet deep, and took up the entire wall at the end of the kitchen.

When they reached the refrigerator, Allie quickly placed her hand on the door handle and pushed down, but she paused for just a moment, bracing herself. She took a breath and then pulled the door open wide, and she was instantly met by a fog of condensation, the cool gush of the interior air so refreshing in the heat of the day. She stepped onto the floor of the cooler, and the moment she cleared the haze of the mist, she immediately saw a woman huddled in the corner with what looked to be a curtain draped across her back and shoulders.

"Mom." The word came whispered and coarse from behind Allie, trapped in Josh's throat as if he was about to vomit.

Allie rushed toward the woman and grabbed her face with both hands, gently turning it towards her, studying her eyes, checking for life. Allie gave her face a tender shake and the woman's eyes fluttered, her blue lips quivering, searching for warmth.

"What's your mom's name, Josh."

Josh stood motionless, not answering.

"Josh!"

"Huh?"

Allie lowered her voice. "Your mom. What is her name?"

He swallowed. "Deedee."

Allie turned back to the woman and leaned in close, her nose only a couple inches from her face. "Deedee, I'm Deputy Allie Nyler? I'm a police officer. Do you understand me?"

The woman's eyes wobbled and rolled, struggling to focus. She formed her lips in a pucker as if preparing to speak, but no sound formed in her throat.

"Mom!" Josh shouted this time, broken from his trance, and he raced from the threshold of the cooler toward his mother.

"Josh," Deedee whispered, and Allie knew this recognition of her son was a good sign.

Deedee tried to raise her arms and reach for Josh, but her limbs wouldn't quite lift, and she turned away, huddling again under the curtain as if ready to return to her slumber.

"No, no, Deedee. It's time to get up now. It's too cold to stay in here."

"No!" Deedee whipped her neck back around toward Allie, her eyes flashing open, locking on the deputy as if she'd just asked her to dive into a vat of bubbling acid. She began to shake her head violently, her blue lips and pale skin making her look like a corpse on the cusp of reanimating.

"Listen to me, Deedee, it's safe now. I promise. You're going to die if you stay here."

Deedee's eyes softened slightly, blinking in understanding.

"I'm going to lean in now, and when I do, I want you to put your arm around my neck. We're going to get up and take a walk. Okay?"

"I can't. I ca—"

"Right now, Deedee! You are going to put your arm around me and we're going to walk out of here. There's no one...there's nothing out there. It's just me, you, and Josh."

Deedee didn't reply, but her eyes reflected her earlier expression of terror as they bounced from Allie to Josh and then back to Allie. The woman had seen the creature; Allie had no doubts about that.

"Mom?"

Deedee's eyes shifted to her son again.

"Please, mom, you have to get up." He shook his head. "It's not here. If it was before, it's not anymore."

Deedee blinked several times and then forced out a short breath, an exhalation that was raspy and staggered, suggesting her lungs didn't have many gasps left.

"Come on," Allie said, "let's get you warm."

She dipped her shoulder low by Deedee's right armpit, compelling the woman to take the crutch. Deedee hesitated for a moment, but then some primal instinct kicked in, compelling her to comply, and with some effort, she hoisted her arm around the deputy's neck. Josh moved in quickly and draped his mother's left arm around his own neck, and then he and Allie lifted the nearly frozen woman to her feet.

"Good job, Deedee, you're doing perfect."

Allie and Josh walked Deedee down the length of the kitchen, through the double doors and out to the front of the restaurant. There they deposited her in the first booth by the door, and then Allie quickly returned to business side of the counter to start a fresh pot of coffee. As she filled the filter with coffee with one hand, she noticed a pile of soup crackers beside the coffeemaker and began grabbing packets and pocketing them, figuring Deedee would need some nourishing to get back to par.

Suddenly, Allie gasped and spun on her heels toward the front door.

Maria.

MARIA SPOTTED THE VEHICLE immediately in the back lot, long and white, just as Josh had described. She took it as a bad sign, that Josh's mother had shown up for work and was now in the same dark place where her own mother and father now lived.

She turned to head back to deliver the grave news, but as she pivoted toward the front of the restaurant, the vast landscape of the desert caught her eye for the first time in months. She felt drawn to it, the freedom and openness of the dirt and sand and dust that stretched for miles before finally ending at the craggy red mountains in the distance. Maria stepped slowly to the edge of the concrete back lot and stood motionless for several seconds, staring across to the world beyond the horizon.

Were they out there too?

It was the question on everyone's mind, though no one had yet asked it aloud. If the answer was 'yes,' it meant the world was ruined, and Maria now pondered that possibility, imagining what such a prospect would look like a month from now—or even a week.

As if triggered by his sister's apocalyptic thoughts, Antonio began to stir, making noises that Maria had yet to hear from her brother, whines and grunts, the sounds of a normal, fussy baby. She gazed down at him and rubbed his forehead, fighting back tears, understanding that, monsters or not, her brother's future was not to be.

She looked up to the desert again and forced an image of hope into her mind, wedging it tightly between her rogue visions of an awaiting, desolate world. She had a duty—not just to Antonio and the remaining days of his life, but to Josh and Allie and anyone else who was still alive in their town. And to the world outside, if the rest of humanity was indeed in the path of Garmella's new evil. What she could do for the world personally, a girl her age and size, Maria couldn't concretely conceive; but she was alive, breathing, and that meant she had the power to help.

Maria brought Antonio tightly into her breast and spun defiantly back toward the diner, but before she landed her first step of return, a dull scraping sound echoed from the far end of the diner. She froze with Antonio clutched to her shoulder and craned her neck slightly forward, searching the air for remnants of the sound. She wanted to run but was unable to move, despite the surge of adrenaline that was signaling for her legs to flee. And her renewed inspiration, her ideas of valor and obligation, suddenly became blurry and dark, as if an umbrella had been opened above her head, shadowing her ability to think.

"No," Maria whispered, squeezing her eyes tightly, fighting the sudden leak of cognizance. She knew it was close, it had to be, and when she opened her eyes again, she saw it immediately, or at least the outline of it, hovering like a small fog at the opposite end of the rectangular building that was Carla's Diner. Yet its approach didn't seem imminent; instead the beast lingered at the corner of the adjoining walls of the restaurant, just below a cluster of overhanging trees where an umbra shrouded the lot.

Maria could still feel her mind slipping, but it wasn't spiraling in an uncontrollable whirlwind the way Josh had described, and Maria focused again on the fight ahead, pulling her ideas toward her like the stronger of two tug-o-war participants, bracing her body so the tension in her muscles matched that of the thoughts in her mind. The thing wasn't close enough to lock her mind in fully, it was the only explanation for her mental resistance.

Why aren't you coming for me?

She didn't have the answer, but Maria knew not to force her luck, and she began to back away slowly, taking each step with meticulous care, never taking her eyes from the beast, expecting it to whoosh through the air like a dark wind at any second and consume her in a tempest.

But the monster showed no signs of movement, ensuring Maria's escape at this point, and when she reached the corner of Carla's and was out of view of the creature, she turned to run, and as she did, she nearly collided with another figure that was racing toward her from behind.

And then she screamed.

ALLIE DASHED FROM BEHIND the counter and was through the front door before Josh or Deedee could turn to see her leave. She turned right at the entrance, her throat tight, heart racing, her mind preparing itself to witness the charred, mangled body of Maria Suarez. Or, perhaps worse, not to see her at all. Maybe she had already been scalded to black and her body snatched away like her parents before her. The thought of this final vision brought a sudden splash of tears to Allie's eyes, and as she raised her hand to wipe them away, she saw a body backing its way toward her.

Allie stopped on a dime and sidestepped, just missing a head on crash with Maria and Antonio.

Maria screamed, letting the yawp explode through the air until there was no breath left in her lungs, and then she reloaded and screamed again, instinctively covering her brother's ears.

"Maria." Allie put her hands softly on Maria's forearms. "Maria, shh, shh, shh; it's okay."

The girl was stuck in her panic, and Allie continued shushing her until her breathing finally slowed enough that she could speak.

"Maria, honey, what's wrong?"

Maria looked up at Allie for just a moment and then stared down at her brother, inspecting him. He was breathing, and Maria glanced back to the deputy. "It's here," she said.

Allie flashed her eyes past Maria and scanned the back lot, and then she unholstered her weapon and walked past the girl toward the back of the restaurant. "Where?"

"No!" Maria shouted after her, but Allie was already at the corner of the restaurant, staring down the length of the wall. Nothing.

Maria moved with trepidation until she was beside Allie, not an inch away from the deputy, and then she pointed absently in the direction of where the creature had been only moments ago. "It was there. At the corner."

Allie took a few steps in the direction, to ensure whatever danger had been there was truly gone, and then she turned and looked at Maria, her eyes soft, apologetic. "I'm so sorry," she whispered.

Maria swallowed and nodded. "But it...it didn't come for me. For us. It saw me. I know it did! And Antonio, he started to fuss and make noise."

Allie could only imagine how hungry the baby must be, and she made a mental note to prepare a bottle of formula when they got back to the cruiser.

"But it never made a move toward us. Why?"

"I...I don't know."

"And now it's gone?" Maria asked rhetorically.

Allie smiled softly. "Well, we know they're no fans of loud noises, and that shriek was about as deafening as I've heard from someone in a long time."

Maria gave the explanation some thought and then nodded, acknowledging the possibility. But her scream wasn't louder than the shotgun blasts from earlier, and the creature hadn't fled then. There was something missing, and she couldn't quite place it.

CHAPTER NINETEEN

The Day of the Rain

WINSTON STOOD A PACE and a half from the window of his fifteen-foot-high deer stand and stared out at his private lake, intoxicated by the smell of the rain on the morning breeze, a signal that his prize was only hours away. The deer stand—which was actually more like an exotic hotel, one where the rooms are built in jungles and cater to the more adventurous traveler—was more equipped than Winston's first two apartments combined, and though it was his first trip to the stand in well over a year—maybe two—he wondered now why he used it so seldomly. Of course, he'd never actually shot at anything from the stand—the structure was built by the original owners and Winston wasn't much of a hunter—but since it was a feature of the property, Winston had decided years ago to invest well over fifty thousand dollars into it, thus turning it from a hunter's hideout to a luxury, on-site getaway.

He kept the power button on his boombox off, but he spun the wheel of the volume control three-quarters of the way to maximum, just in case. Should he need it, the music—a term he thought of as loosely as any combination of sounds he could have imagined—would come from a band called Belphegor's Prime, which was, as promised by the muscle-bound clerk who sold him the CD at Strutman's Entertainment Exchange in Flagstaff, "*the hardest shit he'd ever heard.*" Not Winston's cup of tea, of course, but it was a second line of defense, and one he'd chosen not to ignore.

It was already 6 am, and Winston knew by this time of day the creatures were well into their slaughter. By his own estimate, they had likely made collections of half the town by now. Perhaps more.

That hour of morning also meant that at any moment the *Arali* would reach his house—or perhaps were already there—at which point the black, amorphous shapes would continue their relentless hunt, unconcerned with any arrangements that had been made amongst a handful of their quarry living on the surface above them. And, as Zander had assured him, when the creatures found no one home at his mansion, the last site of their campaign, their initial mission would be complete, and the *Arali* would move on to the second phase of the quest, a recanvassing of the town in a search for any souls missed during the initial pass.

Winston had already been up for hours, of course, ever since the moment the first drop of rain hit his bedroom window, which, he estimated, was sometime around one in the morning. At the plunk of the droplet against the glass pane, his eyes had flashed like lightning, the noise startling him as if a boulder had crashed onto his roof, so expecting of the rainfall had Winston become.

Zander had been right; he had predicted it all correctly. From the arrival of the storm (not a single forecast of precipitation from any source Winston had seen) to the effectiveness of the interference of the telescope (though that part Winston was still leery of, unconvinced it had any effect on the Grieg's readings), the stranger from an extinct Canadian Indian tribe had navigated the months leading up to this day with precision. Even his suggestion of an endowment to the public works was spot on. Winston had sent a hand-written apology to the county council for his noise violations, along with a scholarship offer of $25,000: $5,000 each to five separate county students, to be decided on by a vote of the school board. Since that mailing, he'd not received a single visit from the sheriff's department.

This was all the evidence Winston needed, and the instant the rain began to fall, he knew the day of the *Arali* had arrived, and he quickly grabbed his bag and headed out back to his awaiting golf cart, which he drove to the lake where he would ride out the day of butchery in the safety of his tree stand.

Winston paced the floor of his hideout, trying to dredge up a distraction, something that would keep him from exiting the log structure, where he could step to the outer perch and look down past the lake, across the valley to the handful of homes visible from that position. With binoculars, he might even be able to spot one of the collections in progress, or at least catch a glimpse of one of the creatures as it strode menacingly through the streets, a cloudlike personification of death entering the residence of one of its unwary targets.

But restraint was a quality Winston carried with him proudly, and with a deep breath and a moment of mental silence, he shook free from the voyeuristic draw and walked to the main living space where he sat at a small card table and considered again the strategy for the day.

What a waste it would be if he got sloppy now. What a squandering of his time and effort if he were to let greed and curiosity lead him on this special day, revealing himself to the hunters.

His time would come. He could feel it in his body as clearly as he could the sickness that had driven him here in the first place.

Besides, he had no time for rubbernecking; it was his life he was concerned with now, and there was still a lot for which to prepare.

The sin.

Winston had gone through his memory bank dozens of times since Zander's last visit, perhaps hundreds, attempting to find that most precious of treasures, that darkest of secrets that lay hidden beneath the thick floors of his psyche, stories upon stories which had been constructed over the past eighty years in an attempt to protect his fragile ego from harm.

And demolishing the grounds had proven a trying effort indeed. Whenever it seemed he'd found the bottom, additional layers of mental sediment emerged, covering up some other lie or harmful action he'd committed in his life. Many of these moments of wickedness or immorality Winston had inflicted upon himself, and he discarded those immediately, believing nothing he had done to himself could qualify as his greatest sin. It was how he treated others that mattered, he decided, and that narrowed the candidates by half.

But what was the *worst* crime of his past? And how should it be calculated? Was it based on the net effect of his actions, the magnitude of the consequences? Or was the sin weighted more heavily by the number of people it harmed?

Winston ultimately decided it boiled down to his intent at the time, to how little regard he had felt for another when the sin was committed.

And it took a week or so before Winston finally arrived at the answer, but he eventually found it, buried deeply beneath an ancient fold of his brain, a place which he'd vowed never to explore again.

Until now.

Diana Modesto. The night of the Christmas Party. 1975.

Nikolas Barth was Diana Modesto's secretary and the second in charge at Demornay Labs at the time. He was technically Winston's superior, but Mr. Barth knew Winston was on the fast track to leadership in the company—and that he'd probably be working for Winston one day—and thus he had taken him under his wing, elevating Winston at every turn, even allowing him the services of Diana to perform routine errands, things like coffee, dry cleaning, and other not-quite-essential services.

And Winston and Diana had hit it off immediately. From the day she became unofficially assigned to Winston, they had formed an instant rapport, and within the first week or so, this connection quickly evolved into flirting.

But Winston was a dozen years older, and Diana was engaged, and thus the two had reached a certain understanding, an unspoken rule that the flirting would never pass the point of double entendre or slightly sexual wordplay in the office. And since the office was the only time Winston and Diana interacted with each other, nothing beyond that type of banter ever materialized.

Until the night in early December—Demornay's Annual Christmas Party—when, to the best of Winston's recollection, he'd attempted to rape Diana by the pool of the Pinnacle Spa and Lounge in Sedona.

Many of the details from that night had eroded permanently from Winston's mind, but as he replayed the memory of the party over and over again, events and feelings from the evening began to surface, slowly and fragmented at first, and then more quickly as certain pieces began to fall into place. Soon he could smell the sage that was in the air that night, taste the roasted tomato of the hors d'oeuvres and the smooth burn of the Don Julio. And after several weeks of this type of mental work—careful not to fill in any gaps by inventing what didn't happen—Winston could return to the scene of the incident with regularity and a good degree of clarity.

He remembered a certain shyness arising when he first saw Diana that night, a fear even, especially at that moment when she spotted him from across the room and quickly marched over wearing a panicked grin, seeking his company as refuge. And that unease he had felt stuck with him well into the first part of the evening. Winston had never seen Diana in casual clothing before, or with her hair down, and he was suddenly clueless about how to behave in her company. The quick-hitting witticisms that had passed as conversation in the office, and that were spaced out over the course of an eight-hour day, now seemed inappropriate and awkward, forced.

But then the tequila began to pour, and by the time the second or third shot had begun swirling in Winston's stomach, he started feeling relaxed—and then cocky—in the presence of his informal secretary, and the two spent much of the middle part of the evening laughing and drinking and having a fine old time.

Then, at some point, Winston asked Diana about her fiancé and why the lucky fellow hadn't joined her at the party. He had even not-so-jokingly accused her of inventing the beau to prevent men at the office from hitting on her, a fairly common technique used by single working women at the time. Diana wasn't stunning by any measure, but she was thin and young and had a great smile, and, perhaps most importantly, at Demornay Labs, she was one of only three women in an office of several dozen men.

According to Winston's recollection, Diana had laughed off the accusation at first, but he had kept the charge going for at least several minutes, until he eventually pushed it across the threshold into embarrassing and rude. At that point, Diana had excused herself for the restroom, giving a humorless smile as she departed, clearly disappointed at Winston's drunkenness and the turn the night had taken.

Winston couldn't remember the exact set of circumstances that later placed him alone with Diana by the outdoor pool, a secluded area of the spa that was situated on the first level of the Pinnacle just below the party, but he assumed he had followed her there, or had searched for her when she didn't return from the restroom, perhaps with the intent to apologize.

But the liquor—and the depravity in his heart—guided him to a much darker place.

His most vivid memory of the incident was the feel of his erection against her buttocks as he grabbed her from behind, his hands cupped across her breasts, pressing his chest against her back and shoulders. He had tried to walk her in that position toward one of the dozen or so chaises lined beside the pool, where he could then press her torso down into the long fabric cushion and force himself upon her.

But Diana had begun writhing and flailing the moment Winston touched her, and those struggles had caused them both to topple to the concrete pool deck before they ever reached the row of lounge chairs.

Diana had gotten to her knees in a flash, but as she pressed her hands to the ground to rise to her feet, Winston had grabbed her by the wrist and pulled her to him, feeling a strength throughout his core that he'd never known existed inside him. His heart was racing, his groin throbbing; it was a feeling that today he could only have compared to an insatiable hunger, a ravenous sexual famine.

His lone-hand grip was no match for Diana's desperate need to escape, however, and before Winston could find his focus and absorb the meaning of what had just occurred, Diana was through the doors of the pool deck, disappearing into the spa and out of Winston's sight.

When Winston returned to the party a few moments later, Diana was gone, and by the end of the week, she had left Demornay Labs for good. Within six months of the party, Winston was promoted to assistant vice president of operations, and he had all but erased Diana Modesto and the memory of that night from his mind.

Winston opened his eyes now, allowing the memory to end and then reset again in his mind, to be primed and ready for retelling, knowing he would need to reveal the sin again in only a few hours, and with as much vivid detail and feeling as he'd just conjured in his mind. He prayed it was the answer the *Arali* sought. In his heart he believed it was, but a sliver of doubt still nagged at his conscience. After all, in the scheme of all things, the incident didn't amount to much, at least not as far as Winston rationalized. There were true villains of the world—killers of cops and wives and children—and he, himself, had probably done greater harm to people, at least in ways that were more lasting than what Diana Modesto had endured. There were investors he'd bankrupted, or at least had been partially responsible for doing so, and woman and children he'd walked by without a second glance as they begged for a few coins on the street. Surely those financial iniquities had had a more lasting effect than what Diana had incurred.

But it wasn't the outcome that mattered, Winston decided; it was the feeling in his heart at the time. If Diana hadn't escaped, he would have raped her. There was no doubt in his mind about that. And in his most honest and unforgiving recollections, which was where he had finally arrived, whenever he replayed the moments of the attack, his body still longed, ached for the effort to be complete. The sin was still present, even in his imagination, unbiased in its animal desire.

So that was the answer. That was the fare of Winston's heart that he would feed to the *Arali*. And in exchange, the elimination of his sickness and decades more life would be given.

That was the promise, anyway, and in a few hours, after the town of Garmella had been rendered ruinous by the *Arali*, he would know for sure.

CHAPTER TWENTY

"MR. BELL!"

Ramon gave three loud thumps on the front door and then took a step back on the portico and stared up, trying to get a view of the windows above and any movement inside. But the house was too high, and even if Winston Bell were in his bedroom peeking down at them through a curtain, there would have been no way to tell from the front porch.

"What about around back?" Tony asked. "Maybe the old man left one of his thousand windows open somewhere."

Ramon gave the front of the home one last inspection and then said, "It's worth a shot."

The two men went left around the house, Ramon checking the security of the garage door on the way—locked—and within moments they were standing on the outside of a ten-foot high gate, iron, with thin flat slats that ran top to bottom, designed in a way as to give no place for a foothold. Inside, between the fence and the mansion, the vast yard was anchored in the center by an Olympic-sized swimming pool that was landscaped all around by tropical trees and rushing waterfalls.

"Came this close to buying this place," Tony said flatly.

"Yeah, me too."

"How the hell we gonna get in there?"

Ramon continued to scan the yard and house for weaknesses, some gap of opportunity that had gone unnoticed previously, and then he strolled the length of the fence in both directions. At the end of the second wing, he sighed and shook his head, contemplating.

"What's the plan, Sheriff? Gotta have a plan, right?" Tony's voice teetered on annoyance.

Ramon put his hands to his hips and turned away from the house now, focusing on the plush trees and the large, man-made lake, a small portion of which he could just make out through the middle of the canopy. He stared up to the sky in thought and then back to the ground, and as he did, his eye caught an anomaly in the distance, thirty yards out, just before the tree line. "Look at that," he said, moving slowly in the direction of the forest.

"Whatcha got?"

Ramon broke into a light trot, and within seconds, he was standing at the muddy tree line pointing at a pair of tracks that began at the edge of the grass and stretched out into the woods. "Look!"

Tony was beside Ramon a few seconds later. "Someone drove a car into there?"

Ramon shook his head. "Smaller. Golf cart, maybe."

Tony nodded. "Any idea what's back there?"

Ramon shook his head. "Not really. I know there's a private lake. But other than that, no."

"Well, hell, shall we?"

Tony and Ramon jogged through the woods for a quarter-mile or so, and when they finally cleared the tree line on the other side, they were met by the shoreline of Winston's private lake, which was as beautiful and serene as Ramon and Tony's day was chaotic.

"Wow," Tony uttered.

"Yeah, well, maybe when the house comes on the market again, you should make a better offer."

"No, thanks." Both men surveyed the area for several seconds, and then Tony pointed to a spot in the forest about fifty yards down. "Will you look at that."

"What?"

"See it? Looks like a deer stand. A helluva one too. Didn't peg old Winston for a hunter. Never seen him in my place before."

Ramon had lost the tracks of the golf cart ten yards or so into the woods, but as his eyes adjusted to the new coastal landscape, he located them again, a pair of treaded, sandy wires several feet down on the soft shoreline, leading in the direction of the tree stand.

"I'm gonna check it out."

"Okay, but let me call Allie first." Ramon had already clicked the call button on his radio, and he held up a finger, signaling to Tony, who was already halfway to the stand, to wait. "Tony, hold up."

"Catch up when you're done." Tony held his shotgun above his head, never turning, demonstrating he was well-equipped to defend himself against an eighty-year-old millionaire, if, indeed, he were hiding out in the hunting loft, waiting to ambush.

Ramon began to call for the gun-store owner again, to insist he wait, when Allie's answer rang through the speaker.

"Sheriff!"

Ramon heaved a sigh of relief at his deputy's voice. "Allie, where are you?"

"KD's. Looks like there was some activity out back earli-er. All clear now though."

Ramon decided not to describe his role in stated activity. "What are you doing there?"

"We just came from Carla's and I wanted to check it out. Found Josh's mom at the diner. Locked herself in the fridge. She's alive. Okay, I think."

"Thank god. And the baby?"

"Found him too. Also alive. He's...okay too, I guess. Be-lieve it or not." There was a pause. "Were you able to get a hold of anyone?"

"No. Haven't really had a chance to try. Far as I know the phones and internet are still down."

"Where are you?"

"Winston Bell's." And then, "Geez, Allie, I can't believe you were right about Maria's brother. Honestly, I didn't see much hope there."

"Yeah, well, I'll be honest with you, Sheriff. He doesn't look great. He's clearly not healthy. I don't know how much life is left in him. It's...quite the condition he has." There was a moment of silence and then, "What are you doing at the Bell place?"

"Ran into Tony Radowski."

"What? Where?"

"Long story, but he saved my life."

"Wow."

"And he also had a curious idea."

"Yeah?"

"Yeah. Thinks these things have something to do with the Grieg, and that Mr. Bell's interference these last few months isn't a coincidence. He doesn't know what the connection is, but we figured a couple of questions were in order."

Allie was quiet.

"You still there?"

"Just taking in the new data, trying to put the pieces together."

"You have some pieces to add?"

"I've got one, at least. One I think is pretty solid."

"Yeah? What's that?"

"Well, it seems pretty obvious they don't like loud noises. You noticed that, right?"

Ramon did, but he wasn't sure what it had to do with the telescope. "Yeah, I think that's right. But I'm not sure what difference it makes, since they don't seem to get hurt by the bullets that make those loud noises."

"Right, but I don't think it's the bullets; that's the point. I think it's the *sound of the bullets* they don't like. And I don't think it just scares them either; I think it causes them actual pain." There was a delay, and then, "At least..." Allie broke off the thought.

"At least what?"

"I don't know. At least it did at first. Caused them pain, I mean. But I think maybe the sound isn't hurting them as much anymore. From what Josh and Maria described. I think they're getting stronger. Or maybe that's not the right word. More resilient, maybe. I don't know, I'm rambling."

Ramon gave his deputy's words a moment to land, and then he said, "Well, it's new intel, something to work with, so I'll take it. Josh and Maria, are they okay?"

"Yeah, they're fine. Had some moments though."

Ramon continued watching Tony until the man finally disappeared into the woods in the direction of the hunting stand. "I've gotta go, Allie, but—"

"Yeah, go, we'll get on the way now. Be there in a few minutes."

"No," Ramon blurted automatically. "Don't come here."

"What do you mean? Why?"

"You have kids with you, Allie. And now a baby. And I'm guessing a woman who needs more than a warm blanket and a rub on the back. You need to get them out of here."

"Yeah, that's not an option, remember? There's a sinkhole the size of Rhode Island in the middle of 91."

"I remember, Allie, but you've got to try. We can't...we can't all die here."

Allie was silent for several seconds, and Ramon could sense her debating another retort as she moved away from the car and the prying ears within. Instead, when the radio crackled again, she said with a whisper, "Okay, Sheriff, what's the plan?"

CHAPTER TWENTY-ONE

ZANDER'S BACKUP PLAN to gas the town was one he'd given great thought to over the last six months, and as he considered the execution of it now, he thought it ingenious. It was only a backup plan, of course, in the event he was wrong about the *Arali* and where they would go once the collections were done; but in any case, by the end of the day, the air above Garmella would be poisonous and the land un-inhabitable.

The explosions would occur at a number of strategic points around the town, and, if all went to plan, would set a half-dozen houses—each of which had been staged as methamphetamine labs—ablaze. The blasts would be significant, and once the structures were lit, the fire would eventually jump to the surrounding homes, creating a domino of flames that would burn for days.

The result of this conflagration would be the release of large quantities of pseudoephedrine, as well as a number of other toxic gases, all of which would render the town a waste land, at least for several days following, depending on when the emergency vehicles arrived, which, with the sinkhole un-repaired, could be as long as a week.

And once the investigation began and evidence of the labs and the budding meth empire was uncovered, only the conspiracy theorists of the world would continue looking for explanations beyond what science and forensics had concluded.

And for those handful of souls who did survive the day, the mind-altering qualities of the chemicals in the air would be the only reasonable explanation for their hallucinations, at least as far as the FBI would be concerned, if not the survivors themselves. Mass hallucinations were a well-documented phenomenon, and little time would be spent searching for blurry black creatures that possessed the ability to control minds.

But Zander's plan wasn't perfect. The catastrophe unleased by these amateur chemists seeking their fortunes through the ruination of the lives of others wouldn't disguise everything. The lack of corpses would be a mystery. Where were the bodies of those who hadn't perished in the fires? It was a question that any agent worth his salt would be forced to pursue.

But that question would be one for the criminals to answer, the meth cookers and amateur gangsters. And Deputy Gloria Reynolds was the perfect mark.

Zander, Tehya and Ouray had staged her house earlier that morning, the moment she left for the station, preparing the various kettles and pots of ingredients that made up the insidious recipe. Hers was the last of six houses they had arranged over the last several days—the first five of which were empty—and though it had taken great effort to clear out the squalid room in the deputy's home, the three had worked quickly, diligently, and within ninety minutes, the lab was set and ready for detonation.

Zander had also made the decision to keep Deputy Reynolds alive, imprisoning her during the slaughter in the one place he thought the *Arali* were unlikely to search. His reasoning for not killing her was that if at least one person from the fictitious meth ring was alive when the police arrived, it would benefit him and his associates in the end. He needed a culprit, someone with authority and connections, and, if possible, a personal life that was shaky and tattered, qualities that would make the story of their drug dealing at least plausible.

Zander had monitored all five of the Garmella officers over the last six months, and in the end, the choice had come down to the two female deputies, both of whom were single, which, Zander knew, would be essential to staging the home. But the hoarding qualities of Deputy Reynolds separated her from Deputy Nyler, since it suggested not only some level of despair, but mental illness as well, the latter of which would be a valuable characteristic once the officers began their questioning.

And when the evidence finally led them to the deputy's house—and her lab—whatever story she told to them would be dismissed as the rantings of a crazy person. They would interrogate her for days about the disappearances of the people in the town, insisting on the name of the drug lord to whom she answered, or perhaps the middleman that connected her with the head of the cartel. And, of course, the deputy would have no answers, since the entire scenario was an invention, a Potemkin village of methamphetamines. In the end, she would be arrested and tried, and then either acquitted, institutionalized, or sentenced to prison, any of which suited Zander just fine.

But even with all the planning, with all the cover and contingencies for which Zander had prepared, the pieces wouldn't fit entirely. The investigations into the labs and fires would continue for months, years maybe, and since the site of the impending disaster occurred in the home of the Grieg telescope, even more attention would be paid than usual.

In the end, however, he doubted any of it would matter. The *Arali* would stay this time; Zander could almost taste that truth on his tongue. Garmella's population was too small; the creatures needed more than what the town could provide. Each visit over the last fifty years had seen the *Arali* increase their consumption, and Zander knew one day—almost certainly this one—the souls of the town wouldn't quench them, and the *Arali* would continue their destruction, fighting the draw of solar noon until they were satiated.

The Arali.

It had been twelve years since he had given his sin to the beings, and as he recalled the moment now, sitting quietly in the back of the audit truck, he could feel the sense of fear again, the desire. Back then he was young, scared and naïve, and the doubt he'd felt as he stood in front of them—doubt that his offer to them was indeed the prize the god-like beings craved—had been like a large stone lodged in his chest.

But Zander had always been clever, and just as his plan for the events of this day were meticulous, so too had he planned for that encounter as well. He had insured against the possibility that his spoken sin would be faulty, unsuitable; the bones of his parents were buried still, deep in the earth at the edge of his tribal homeland.

Zander grieved his mother and father deeply—at the time of the murder and even still—but he never regretted the crimes, not for a single day since their commission. And it wasn't just because of the reward of this extended life, it was because of the time spent in the presence of the *Arali* themselves, and his longing to experience them once more.

And, ultimately, forever.

He had spent only minutes with the creatures during that first encounter at the far edges of a Siberian town, but every second since still teemed in Zander' cells like warm bourbon, and even now, with so many years having passed, whenever the thought of confronting them again entered his mind—which occurred several times each day—his mouth filled with his saliva, his brain with dopamine and endorphins.

"Zander, we're here."

Zander blinked twice and looked to Ouray, and from the middle of the back seat he stared coldly through the windshield at the palatial home of Winston Bell, which sat high on a hill just beyond a cluster of trees in the foreground.

Zander considered the qualities of the man inside now, and though Zander had every intention of honoring his end of the deal, he doubted Winston Bell would survive the experience. There was a quiet arrogance in the old man, a subtle over-confidence that eclipsed whatever intelligence and desire for life he possessed. And this would be his undoing. Even when a man's intentions were genuine, Zander knew, there were few in this world who could reach the oily bottom of their souls. For most, such a place was simply too cavernous to find.

But Zander would escort Winston Bell to the *Arali* nevertheless, and while the dying man stood before the towering creatures, he would have the opportunity to sell his sins, to purge his evil to the nether creatures in exchange for a life of wellbeing and longevity.

"Look, Zander," Tehya barked.

Zander saw the police cruiser a second after the words left his associate's mouth, and he instructed Tehya to stop the truck just before it cleared the trees of the property and exposed them on the road.

"Is it her? The one who stopped us earlier? I knew we should have..." Ouray stopped short of expressing his gruesome wish, not wanting to anger his leader. "She suspected something the moment she saw us on the road. She—"

"It's not her," Zander interrupted. "It's the sheriff."

"How do you know?"

"I suppose I don't. Not for certain. But Deputy Nyler seemed to be in quite a hurry. She was almost frantic. And it wasn't in a rush to get to Winston Bell's house." Zander paused, recalling the encounter from earlier, and then he added, "And even if I'm wrong, we were correct not to pursue her."

"What?"

Zander stared out the window now, measuring his next steps as he absently explained himself to his subordinates. "If she called in our stop, which she almost certainly did, and then disappeared moments later, who do you think they would have come looking for?"

"But then they know we're here now. In Garmella."

Zander shrugged. "The deputy questioned us, and we gave appropriate answers. Answers consistent with our audits. There's no reason to suspect we had anything to do with what's happened here today. Even if the officers do make it out alive."

Ouray digested Zander's answers, a shade of doubt in his eyes, and then he said wearily, "The police. They're all still alive. Why? How?"

Zander shrugged slightly. "It is the nature of the job in this town. The hours, that is. They left for work before the *Arali* arrived. This was not unexpected, though I supposed there is a lesson here." Zander let his mind drift again to future collections, determined not to let whatever morals there were to be gleaned from this day evaporate from his memory. "And we don't know about the brothers. I suspect we have nothing to worry about where they're concerned."

Ouray stared at Zander, the reverence for his boss' wisdom now glimmering in his eyes. He swallowed. "What do we do, Zander? What do we do now?"

Zander smiled. "We will see things through as they've been planned. This is not a crisis. The police have come to question Mr. Bell, just as they have for most of the last six months. But they won't find him. Not there. Not if he's taken the proper precautions." Zander looked at his watch. "Solar noon is still eighty minutes away. We have time."

"But...what if they've already finished their collections? What if the *Arali* have already gone?"

Zander knew the anxiety Ouray was feeling, as he, himself, had felt it too the day of his only experience with the *Arali*. The fear that all their work would be wasted. That not only would they fail to discover the full faculties of the creatures, but that they would fail even to witness them at all.

"They will take the time they have," Zander answered calmly. "And when they fail to satisfy the full breadth of their cravings, they will advance to the sinkhole before proceeding to the town beyond." Zander said this last part with no uncertainty, as if he had concrete evidence about how the *Arali* would behave once the collections were done. "But we made a deal with Winston Bell, and we will honor it as such. He will be given the chance of an offering, granted he arrives by the scheduled time."

There were several beats of silence in the truck before Tehya finally spoke. "Do you truly believe it?" she asked, referencing Zander's claims of the *Arali*. "How can you know, Zander?"

Zander gave a crisp stare to Tehya, his eyelids narrow and heavy. "I just know."

And he did, if not intellectually, he knew it in his heart. The *Arali* had become his life's work. Whereas Tehya and Ouray continued to bask in the history of the creatures, Zander pushed beyond the stories and myths to the science. It was he who had tracked them, had deciphered their patterns and their draw to the telescope (though *why* they were drawn to the devices he had yet to learn). Tehya and Ouray had recruited him, that was true, but Zander was the tip of the spear now, the one who had embedded them into the Grieg system and devised the plans that had seen this day come to fruition. His associates were the past of the *Arali*; Zander was the present and the future.

"What do we do now?" Ouray asked. "Where do we go?"

Zander gave the question several seconds of consideration and then looked up and said, "Deputy Nyler is expecting us to be at our house by the lake. So let us not disappoint her."

CHAPTER TWENTY-TWO

Allie sat in the cruiser, fixated on the front of KD's Convenience as she focused on her conversation with the sheriff. Maria was feeding Antonio a bottle in the seat beside her, while Josh continued to monitor his mother in the back seat. Deedee was still drifting in and out of sleep, shivering at times, fighting to get her body temperature fully stable.

Allie wanted to reject Tony Radowski's theory out of hand, but the notion of the telescope's role in the calamity rang, if not true exactly, at least interesting. Possible. Winston Bell's activities over the last several months were odd to be sure, uncharacteristic of someone who had been so reclusive and ordinary for decades. That combined with the fact that the black monsters had arrived in *their* quiet town, home of one of the biggest telescopes in the world, certainly made for quite the coincidence.

But Allie had her instructions now—her orders—to drive out to the sinkhole and guide her party down the road to Simonson, which was a little more than nine miles away. The bad news was with the sinkhole spanning the width of the roadway, they had to *walk* to the next town; the good news was the trek was almost entirely downhill.

"What was that about the sinkhole?" Josh asked from the back, his voice little more than a whisper.

"Sheriff ordered us to go there and then walk out of town," Allie replied without hesitation, matter-of-factly, as if the instruction were a normal part of her daily routine. "He wants us to head down to Simonson on foot. And then send back help."

Josh was quiet, and Allie knew he was weighing his mom's condition and her ability to pull off such a trek.

"How's your mom?"

"I'm okay," Deedee said, a tone of relief in her voice, as if she'd been through the middle of hell and was now coming out the other side. "Could use a cigarette though."

Allie smiled and glanced in the rearview. "Yeah, me too. And a drink."

Deedee caught Allie's eyes and grinned back. "Gotta walk ten miles first though, huh?"

"Looks that way. Can you do it?"

"Guess we're gonna find out."

Allie noted a strength in the woman's voice that she hadn't heard before, and by the time the group reached the sinkhole several minutes later, Deedee was sitting up straight with her arm around Josh, pulling him tightly to her body.

Allie nudged aside two of the cones in the blockade with the grill of her car, and then she pulled the cruiser to within five yards or so of the crater. She stared silently past the hole to the slope of the open road beyond, the empty street taunting her with its offering of freedom and escape. "Hang here for a minute," she said.

Allie exited the cruiser and walked slowly toward the hole, the stench from earlier hitting her again almost instantly. She studied the scope of the gaping black chasm again, noting that it extended utterly to the cliffside on the right, leaving not an inch of pavement to get by in that direction. To the left of the cavity, where the road dropped off precipitously into the valley, near the spot where Allie originally thought Derek Zamora and Amber Godwin had gone over but now suspected otherwise, the hole had eaten up the entire roadway as well. However, along that same edge, on the opposite side of the guardrail, just before the earth disappeared into a freefall hundreds of feet down, there was a narrow pathway of stone, about the width of a single brick, which looked sturdy and durable, bolstered by the earth, certainly capable of handling the weight of a person. And they would have the guardrail to hold for balance as they made their way the thirty feet or so to the other side. They could do it; Allie had little doubt about it.

She studied the pathway for several more seconds, calculating and re-calculating, ensuring she hadn't missed anything in her estimations, and then she walked back to the car and leaned in through the open window of the driver's door, resting casually on her forearms. She looked to the back seat at Josh and his mom. "You guys ready?"

Josh and Deedee looked at each other and paused, their eyebrows raised, questioning each other's readiness. After a few beats, they both nodded in unison.

"Good. But know this: it's not going to be the easiest walk you've ever taken. There's space for footing, but you won't want to let go of the guardrail. And—as always—don't look down."

"Sounds great," Deedee answered sarcastically.

Allie looked at Maria. "How 'bout you, corkscrew?"

"How?"

"How what?"

"How can I walk that with Antonio? I can't hold him and the guardrail. What if I fall?"

"You won't fall. It's plenty wide for your tiny feet. And if you want, I'll walk Antonio over and then come back."

Maria paused and stared into Allie's eyes. "Come back? What do you mean?"

Allie's shoulders slumped as she sighed. She hadn't planned on revealing her intentions just yet, though obviously it wouldn't have been a secret for much longer. "I'm not going with you. The sheriff was right to send you guys down and get you to safety, but I'm going back. This is my job, and this is my town. There may be others who need help. Those auditors I stopped, for example; I promised I would check on them."

"Then I'm going with you!"

"Maria, you can't."

Maria looked down at her brother and then back to Allie, a tear now hovering on her cheek. She wiped it away. "Antonio isn't going to live much longer. I can hear it. In his breathing. He'll die on the way. It's too far. Too hot."

Allie had tried to ignore it, but she had heard the decline too. Since they'd left the diner, there was a different sound to the baby's breathing, an arduous wheezing noise coming from his lungs. It was as if his encounter with the creature had debilitated him, drained him of whatever energy he'd been accessing to stay alive this long.

"And his eyes are starting to roll and get dim. He won't make it to Simonson."

Allie felt defeated. "What do you want me to do, Maria?"

"Send Josh and his mom, just like you said. But let me help you. I don't know how, but I can help. I have to."

Allie closed her eyes and stood tall, and then she tilted her face to the sky, searching for an answer there, knowing there was none to be found. She looked out again to the sinkhole and beyond, and then back toward the town before focusing once more on the inside of the car and Maria. "Okay, you can come back with me, but you *will* stay in the car. The whole time. Unless I say otherwise. Got it?"

Maria nodded and focused again on Antonio, who was coughing now, struggling to breathe.

Allie waited for a protest from Josh in the back, but none came from the boy, and she silently opened the back door and ushered him and Deedee out, leading them to the place where they would cross from the city limits of Garmella to the freedom of Interstate 91.

Josh went first as Allie stood at the foot of the walkway and watched the boy make the tightrope walk across the footpath with relative ease, just as she suspected he would.

Deedee was next, and she, too, despite her recent bout with hypothermia, demonstrated agility across the treacherous route, though Allie could see the white exploding on her knuckles as she gripped the top of the gunmetal guardrail. When she was safely across, she raised her arms high like a victorious prize fighter and then hugged Josh with a visible showing of relief.

Allie gave a thumbs up and Deedee and Josh waved in unison, sad smiles on each of their faces, realizing there was a better-than-not chance they would never see Allie again. "Good luck, deputy," Deedee called out.

"You too."

Deedee looked to the ground for a moment, and when she looked back up, there was a grimace on her face, distress. "Will you do me a favor?" she said, choking out the words.

Allie nodded, "Of course."

"If...somehow you find my husband—Ray—will you let him know...that I'm sorry. And that I love him."

Allie frowned and nodded. "I will."

Josh tilted his head up. "Tell him that from me, too. Especially the part about being sorry."

Deedee looked down at her son but said nothing, and Allie simply nodded again, knowing there was little chance she would find Ray Bronigan alive.

She gave a final, half-mast wave and then turned and walked back to the cruiser, entering it like a car thief and shifting it into reverse with veracity, squealing the tires on the pavement as she and Maria headed back toward town.

CHAPTER TWENTY-THREE

Ramon knew something was wrong before he started up the ramped walkway of Winston Bell's deer stand, but Tony wasn't answering his shouts, and since there was no one to call for back up, he was committed to entering the stand alone. He held his Glock in prayer in front of his face, his eyes fixed on the thin, rectangular windows that surrounded the hexagonal structure. But the slats were too narrow, and from his position, he couldn't see a thing.

He followed the second segment of the L-shaped ramp until he reached the top where a six-foot high fence had been constructed, the barrier clearly used to cordon off the structure from any critters who might amble up the slope seeking food or shelter. But the gate to the fence was open wide, allowing passage to the main structure, and Ramon stepped through and turned right toward the narrow opening of the stand doorway.

He saw Tony immediately, back-straight in an armless school chair, his hands laced and resting atop his head as if he were gazing at the ocean from a chaise on the lido deck of a cruise ship.

"Tony!" Ramon whispered and then instantly regretted it.

Tony bowed his head slightly and then looked straight again, slumping his shoulders in a deep sigh. He then leaned to his left, a sideways nod of sorts, and Ramon knew it was a signal.

Ramon shifted his eyes left and then took a quick step inside the deer stand, turning toward the wall to his left as he did, his pistol outstretched, prepared to unload the bloated clip on the ambush coming from the corner.

But the space was empty, and when the ambush came, it was from the opposite side of the room. The muzzle of the rifle poked the back of Ramon's skull a second later, and he slowly dropped his pistol and raised his hands high and wide. From his periphery, he saw Tony begin to stand.

"Sit down, Mr. Radowski," Winston Bell instructed, his voice stern though shaky.

Tony followed the order and kept his position in the chair, but he lowered his hands to his lap and sighed, shaking his head. "I'm sorry, Sheriff. You were right. We should have stayed together. Guess that's why you're the sheriff." He paused and then said solemnly. "He said he'd shoot me if I didn't give you the wrong signal. Didn't feel like I had much choice."

"Not your fault, Tony."

"It's the fault of both of you, in fact," Winston said. And then, "Why did you come here, Sheriff? All that's happened today, and here you are at my house. My stand on the lake. Why?"

"Just wanted to ask you a few questions, but it looks like I already got my answer."

"And what answer is that?"

Ramon lifted his chin high and turned slowly, his hands still high and unthreatening. He was almost daring the old man to shoot him, which he was seventy-five percent sure he wouldn't—not odds Ramon would have taken on a normal day—and when he was facing Winston and still breathing, he said, "You did have something to do with this. You helped murder a town full of people."

Winston Bell swallowed and shifted his eyes from Ramon, and then he steeled his nerves again and locked the sheriff's stare. "And how would I have done that, Sheriff? I've been here all night. The rain brought me down here. I thought the sound of the downpour on the lake would help me sleep."

"I don't know how, exactly, that was second part of my question. My friend Tony thinks your interference with the telescope had something to do with their coming. Somehow drew them here." Ramon squinted and quivered his head. "What are they, Winston? Do you even know?"

Winston's eyes bloomed, his lips parting slightly. "You've seen them?"

Ramon scoffed and nodded. "You could say that."

Winston swallowed nervously as he suppressed a smile. He then pointed the gun toward Tony and jerked it toward the door. "Let's go," he ordered, "we don't have a lot of time."

CHAPTER TWENTY-FOUR

ALLIE DROVE WITH PURPOSE toward the opposite edge of town where the Brandt house was located, watching the desert landscape quickly populate with houses as she reached Oak Street and the small section where downtown Garmella began.

"Where are we going," Maria asked, rubbing her brother's forehead with the tip of her thumb. Her voice was low and sullen as she stared absently at the world outside.

"To find Sheriff Thomas and his friend. But I have to follow up on something first."

"Those people from the truck?"

"That's right. They said they were staying at a house by Kelly's Market. Just gonna swing by and make sure they're okay." Allie's intentions were a bit more targeted than just a follow up as her suspicions of the three had continued to grow since their encounter. But Maria was focused on her brother, and she didn't need the details.

As Allie reached St. Patrick's, her gaze was caught by the spire of the cathedral looming above the square. The structure first invoked images of Sunday school as a kid and Christmas Eve mass, but they were quickly consumed by thoughts of the creatures, of the demons that had ascended from the depths of Hell to bring ruination to the world above.

"Demons," Allie whispered. "Demons from Hell." As the words fell from her lips, she felt a burn of belief—of truth—in her heart, truth that Heaven and Hell were real, that God was somewhere in the universe watching. But as quickly as the satisfaction of reality set in, it was replaced by an overwhelming sense of fear, a terror of the magnitude she had never felt previously. It was indescribable.

"What?"

Allie turned to see Maria staring at her. "Nothing, honey," she answered, and then, "Look." Allie pointed to the jagged bill of a synthetic swordfish that rose above Kelly's Seafood Market, which was a half block from the Brandt house, on the opposite side of Oak. She slowed the cruiser and turned into Kelly's lot, and then guided the car around to the back of the market, hidden from the view of the street. She parked and opened the door.

"Stay here. I'll be right back."

Allie exited the car and quickly walked toward the front of the restaurant, and then, suddenly, she stopped and turned, flashing a forced smile and a reassuring nod to Maria through the windshield. But Maria's eyes were a beacon of sadness, and the girl held Allie's stare for only a beat before focusing back on her brother as she slumped low into the passenger seat until Allie could no longer see her above the dashboard. Allie considered returning to the car, but in that moment, she heard a voice echo from across the street, the new silence of the world carrying it like a virus through the air. Allie couldn't make out the words, so she stooped low and quickly dashed across the street until she was only twenty yards or so from the front of the house, hidden by a row of hedges.

"We can't wait anymore," a voice said. Allie knew instantly it was Zander, the younger of the men from the traffic stop. "We've run out of time. We can't be late for them."

"Why did we come back to begin with?" the woman of the group asked. The question was followed by a long pause, and Allie could almost feel the danger in Zander's eyes at the questioning of his subordinate. "I'm sorry, Zander. It was not for me to question."

Another pregnant silence and then, "We needed the detonators, and..." he paused. "She was one more to feed to them. One more for their collection."

AS SHE ENTERED THE wide-open straightaway of the interstate, Allie floored the accelerator and headed for the town entrance.

She didn't know for certain the van was headed for the sinkhole—and she couldn't very well follow them from any significant distance—but as she weighed the other possibilities, she couldn't think of another destination. She had always suspected the unusual crater was instrumental in the day's happenings, and now she was just about sure of it. And when she crested the hill by the cliffside at the edge of town, just at the point where the crater became visible from the roadway, all doubt was erased.

The first thing she saw were the creatures, the black forms rising tall in front of the sinkhole, hovering there like shadows over a grave. In front of them, facing the creatures, were Zander and his associates. Beside them was Winston

Bell, who looked to be standing slightly in front of the other three, closest to the creatures, facing them as if he were on trial, being judged by the beasts.

Allie was rapt for several seconds, but she recovered quickly and pulled the car to the shoulder, parking it out of sight behind one of the large desert evergreens that lined the side of the road. She craned her neck desperately, trying to get a view of the small crowd of people at the chasm, and though the car was now hidden, Allie had no visibility from the spot; she could only see the top of the van from her current position. She needed to get eyes on the scene.

Allie lifted a scolding finger to Maria, a warning to stay put; but Maria didn't see it, focused as she was on Antonio, her face still warped with distress. Finally, she looked at Allie, her eyes tear-filled, a bulge in her throat. "He's dying."

Allie frowned and put her hand to Maria's face, nodding. "Okay, honey. Just hold him. Keep him close to your body. Let him feel your heart beating. Love him." She removed her hand from the girl's face and used it to unclip her pistol. "I'll be back. I need to get a better look at what's going down out there."

Maria nodded, and Allie quietly opened the door and then stepped down to the dirt shoulder, barely closing the door to its first hitch before hunching her back and jogging forward to a cluster of shrubs twenty feet or so ahead. Once at the new hidden location, Allie stopped and stooped again, now peering through a new set of bushes that gave her a near-perfect view of the sinkhole and the bodies surrounding it. And with the breeze coming at her, she could hear the words coming from Winston Bell as if he were speaking them from only a foot away.

Ramon and Tony were nowhere to be seen, but Allie assumed they were in the cruiser, hopefully alive. She prayed it was true.

Winston Bell, on the other hand, stood tall in front of the creatures, facing the shimmering beasts like an orator speaking to a crowd of hundreds, his shoulders and chin high as he recited some tragic event of his past.

CHAPTER TWENTY-FIVE

"HER NAME WAS DIANA Modesto, and my intention was to rape her."

Winston spoke slowly, enunciating each syllable just as he'd rehearsed a hundred times, his eyes locked on the three creatures that he had dreamed of every night since that first morning Zander and his team arrived.

They were more than beautiful, beyond terrible; they were the culmination of every mythical being he could imagine, godlike in their majesty and size, their lack of visual clarity somehow enhancing their splendor.

The beings had latched his mind almost instantly, without warning or introduction, but Winston was prepared, and he knew when it began to let the memories flow through his mind without resistance, and to allow them to reach the end of the reel before drawing out and focusing on the one in particular.

And when the film finally ended, Winston conjured the memory of Diane Modesto once more. He summoned the shape and smell of her body, the sounds of the serene setting, bringing to life the event at the Christmas party for what he hoped would be the final time in his soon-to-be-long life.

But he didn't waste time on the backstory or the build-up to the evening; instead he got right to the crux of the confession, unleashing the desire and harm of his polluted heart to these demons—these *Arali*—of Perdition.

"I grabbed her. I forced her to me. I rubbed my groin and body against her and brought her to the ground with the intent to penetrate her. She got away from me—I didn't have the strength that night to restrain her—but if she hadn't, I would have done my worst to her."

The moment he uttered this statement of guilt, the words he believed communicated the worst his soul had to offer, he glanced toward Zander, who immediately looked away as if Winston had disappointed him.

Winston's face flooded with the burn of adrenaline at Zander's reaction, and the doubt and fear that he'd tried so hard to suppress over the last few months suddenly gripped him again.

"It...it isn't that what I did was as bad as...I..." He looked at Zander again, desperate now for the words that would put him back on the right path. "What is it?" he cried. "What do they want me to say?"

Zander looked to the ground and then back to Winston, sadness in his eyes now, a frown on his face. He shook his head. "I'm afraid you've failed, Mr. Bell. Just as I feared you would."

"Failed? How could I fail? This is my crime! This is the evil in my heart! You told me to find it and I did! Who else can say what is *my* sin?"

Zander let his eyes linger on Winston for several beats, allowing the elderly sinner the opportunity to discover the answer for himself. But Winston could only stare back in desperation, his eyes sodden and feeble. "You've sacrificed an entire town of people, Mr. Bell. Instead of warning them, you've killed them. And you've done it all for yourself."

"What? No, I—"

"Hundreds of people died today because of you, Mr. Bell, and you facilitated those deaths based on nothing more than a promise from me. Do you not think that is the sin they desired?"

The obviousness of the statement hit Winston like an armored tank, and as he opened his mouth to accept this new felony as gospel, to speak this new truth to the demons who now controlled his future, the blood inside him instantly thickened, and within seconds, his veins and arteries shattered like glass.

Winston Bell's organs and bones, his tendons and muscles and skin, all turned to black in a broiling wave, and then his corpse collapsed to the ground like a used fireplace log, bouncing slightly before turning face down onto the pavement.

CHAPTER TWENTY-SIX

ZANDER STEPPED IN FRONT of the *Arali* with the confidence of his immunity, knowing that he had paid his sin to the creatures years ago and was, if not safe from their wrath, at least shielded from it.

But he had always desired more from them—and to offer more—and his research, warped and biased though it may have been, had led him to believe that if he could provide the sins of others to the *Arali*, sins that they knew had been offered to them by Zander, they would extend his life even further, perhaps all the way to immortality. Or at least close to it.

"I have others to offer," Zander said with a smile, a glimmer in his eyes that resembled that of a young man seeing the love of his life for the first time.

Zander turned to Ouray and nodded; his was face stern like a drill sergeant's, and the elder man quickly complied to the tacit order, striding like a soldier back to the cruiser. He opened the door and grabbed Tony Radowski by the arm and pulled him outside, and then nudged him from behind with an elbow as they marched to the spot where Winston Bell had stood with confidence only minutes earlier.

Tony faced the *Arali* with his chin high, and then he cleared the terror from his throat and swallowed. "Which one of you ugly fucks did I shoot earlier?" he asked, lifting a finger and pointing to the creature on the right. "I think it was you." He shifted the finger to the middle *Arali*. "Or maybe it wa—"

Tony Radowski suddenly threw his hands to his forehead and squeezed his eyes closed, pressing his hands at his temples. His mind began to strobe in a surge of memories: His days in the army—the best of his life; the eighteen months he did in Coconino for assault; his cellmate who Tony had killed one night with a bedsheet following a lightly veiled threat and a wag of the bastard's tongue.

Zander stared at Tony patiently, waiting for the images of the man's life—which Zander could only assume was a long and sordid one—to finish playing in his head.

Finally, Tony exhaled in a gasp and raised his head, opening his eyes now and staring at the *Arali* with a bit more fear and deference than earlier.

"Give them what they want," Zander whispered aloud, knowing the *Arali* were making the same request in the man's mind at that very moment. "Give them your evil."

Tony turned away from the monsters and looked down at the fried corpse of Winston Bell below him. Finally, he turned to Zander and said, "Fuck you and fuck them too."

Zander's shoulders slumped at Tony's words, and he sighed in disgust and weariness.

He took no pleasure in Tony Radowski's screams of pain, or his death that followed a half-second later.

CHAPTER TWENY-SEVEN

ALLIE SQUEEZED HER eyes shut at the sight of Tony Radowski's destroyed body collapsing to the pavement, and she instinctively kept her hand hovering just below her mouth, ready to stifle a scream if one emerged. But she kept herself together and forced herself to take several slow breaths, trying to keep her mind focused on what she could do to help.

"Get the sheriff," she heard the man from the audit truck command again to his elder counterpart, and when Allie saw Ramon being pulled from the cruiser and marched forward toward his execution, the fire of her convictions re-ignited, and she cleared her mind and cocked her weapon. A second later, she emerged from the shrubs and into the roadway like an ambushing jaguar.

Allie assumed there were weapons somewhere at the scene, but she'd yet to see one being brandished, so she walked straight ahead with alacrity, her weapon pointed at the back of the older man who was still shoving Ramon toward the sinkhole. She kept her gaze down, averting her eyes from the monsters hovering just beyond, their bodies like the glossy air above a hot grill. Instead, she focused on the assailant and called out, "Let him go! Now! And put your fucking hands as high as they can reach!"

The man didn't turn toward Allie, but he clearly sensed the gun on him, and he released Ramon and raised his hands as instructed.

From the corner of Allie's eye, she saw Zander make a move toward the truck, and she shifted her gun in his direction. "You move another inch and you've got two rounds in your head a second later. Got that?"

The man froze and raised his hands as well, and as he gave a single nod of understanding, Allie thought she detected a grin appear on his face.

Ramon turned slowly toward Allie and shook his head.

"How'd you let this happen, boss?"

"Dammit, Allie, I told you to go."

"Yeah, I can see you have everything under control, Sheriff, but, you know, I thought I'd help out anyway. You're welcome."

"Where are the kids?"

"They're all on the way to Simonson," she lied, the words suddenly sounding as if they'd been spoken in a dream. "Just like you..."

Allie suddenly lost the ability to speak, her brain no longer signaling the words to her mouth; her thoughts, normally like drifting clouds in her mind, felt as if they were now swirling in a vacuum.

"Don't let it get inside you, Allie. Keep your mind clear. I don't know how, but..."

Allie never heard the rest of Ramon's sentence, and her mind was now fully into the movie of her life, with thoughts and memories sparking in her brain like flint. The last sound she heard from the outside world was of her pistol hitting the street.

In what might have been several minutes but was likely only seconds, the spinning reel in her head reached its end, and Allie suddenly heard a voice in her head, questioning, the tone demanding and cruel.

Tell me your evil.

Like the primal instincts of earliest man, Allie reacted to the danger, and she instantly brought the request to the front of her mind. There was perhaps a second of hesitation as she gathered the story in her mind, and then she spoke the truth of that day on the yacht as if she were telling it to a priest.

"I didn't really know her that well," Allie began. "Cassidy and I met maybe a week before at a party. I was a freshman and she was a junior. And she was funny and beautiful, and I was impressionable, so, when she invited me to come along with her and a couple guys she knew, one of which had a boat, what was I going to say? She seemed like the kind of girl who was on a boat every weekend, and I wanted to be a part of that world. I guess I had a girl crush."

Allie's face was stoical, at ease, and though her thoughts weren't exactly her own, she knew she was safe in that moment, on the path to redemption.

"Cassidy was sunbathing nude on the stern that day, which I didn't know until I came from the bow and saw her there. I kind of froze and just stared at her. I don't think I'd ever even seen another naked woman before, not in the flesh anyway, and certainly not someone who looked like she did. She was so carefree. I just wanted to be near her." Allie paused. "But I also didn't want to embarrass her. Or myself. So, I just stood there staring at her. And, out of nowhere, Cody appeared. I guess they were in the cabin below, but suddenly he was just standing above her, hovering there, and Cassidy didn't even make a move to cover herself or anything. Cody was questioning her about something; I couldn't hear what they were saying, but I could see she was kind of shaking him off, laughing but also kind of annoyed, like she just wanted to be left alone. It was late in the day by then, and everyone had been swimming and drinking and now everyone was kind of winding down." A tear began to streak down Allie's cheek. "But Cody and Mark had other ideas."

Allie felt the full thrust of her sin now—the personal crime which she'd hid in the deepest part of her conscience for nearly two decades—and for the first time in her life, she began to weep openly about her part in the assault of Cassidy Mayes.

"I heard her screaming outside the door, and I knew what was happening, but I didn't do anything to stop it. I wanted to—God, I wanted to be that brave—but I wasn't. I'm not. I'm scared. I'm scared all the time. Then and now." Allie paused again. "I believed they would kill me if they knew I had heard, and certainly if I tried to stop them. I really did believe that. They couldn't have two witnesses. One girl's claims were tough to prove, but if *I* was a witness, if I could testify to what I'd heard, that would have changed everything. And if I had tried to physically stop them..." She paused. "So, I turned away. I just walked back to the bow of the ship like the coward that I was. And I just stared out at the sea and cried, knowing my life would never be the same after that day. Cassidy was ruined, and so was I. Afterwards, when it was over and they were coming up from the cabin, I pretended to be asleep. And then when we got back to shore, I waited for Cassidy to tell me what had happened, but she never said a word. She just got in her car and left. Sped off in her little VW bug, and it was the last time I ever saw her."

Allie let the final emotions of the experience run through her, and then she opened her eyes and stared at the beasts, defiantly now, daring them to question her sincerity, to find something she held in her heart that was darker than the story she'd just told. And when she felt her mind break free of the grip and belong to her again, she knew she was safe.

Except that wasn't entirely true.

In the real world, beyond the hold of the creatures, the man who had surrendered to Allie moments earlier now faced her, a semi-automatic rifle in his hands.

"Congratulations, Deputy Nyler," the leader said, his face a mask of gleeful surprise, prideful even. "The *Arali* seem pleased with the authenticity of your sins. That is a rarity."

"But it's not enough, is it?" Allie replied, now understanding her fate rested beyond the creatures and was, in fact, in the hands of these fanatics. "You're going to kill us anyway?" Allie looked down to her pistol which was on the ground, several feet in front of her. She contemplated a move, but she had no chance of reaching the weapon with an AR-15 pointed at her head. "What do you get out of this?"

Zander smiled and turned his head slightly, as if giving the question some earnest thought. "I will be here long after your youngest niece or nephew has grown old and died. And had you lived beyond this day, that reward would have been yours as well."

Allie shook her head, confused. "What are you saying?"

Zander shrugged. "You have been blessed with this unique experience, deputy. The *Arali* bring quite profound destruction wherever they surface. In a very short span of time. But for those fortunate enough to exist in the place and time of their arrival, and then to possess the strength to feed them that which they desire, life's greatest reward can be realized. And it is yours now, if only for a few moments longer."

Allie fought to doubt the man's words, to dismiss them as the rantings of a lunatic; but that she was standing in front of these three demons—and had listened to their voices in her mind, craving her darkness—she had no choice but to accept his assertions as true. Which meant that though she may never learn the truth for herself, Josh one day might, having reached the threshold of his sins and was now currently trekking down Interstate 91.

"And soon, others will have the opportunity as well."

Allie felt her heart seize at the menacing words. "What does that mean?" she choked out.

Zander smiled. "The *Arali* have more collections to make."

"What?"

"This town," Zander said, extending his hand as if introducing Garmella for the first time, "it is far too small to satiate them. As perhaps is Simonson."

"What are you saying?"

"When they are done here, they will move on this time. I know it for certain now." Zander stared at the sky, smiling. "It is well past solar noon, and yet here they remain." And then, "I can't know it for sure, but perhaps the *Arali* are here to stay. Perhaps forever this time."

"You have to stop them," Allie said, at which point the man beside her kicked her at the top of her left thigh, bringing her to her knees. Allie dropped to the street in a grunt.

"Allie!" Ramon called, unleashing a scream as loud as he could remember, holding his deputy's name on his vocal cords until they burned.

And as the shout resonated through the desert air, the *Arali*, who were fewer than thirty yards from Ramon, began to writhe and twitch for a moment, shifting erratically like the movement of flipbook animation. Zander shuddered reflexively and as he stared up at the demons, his face a veil of concern.

Ramon caught the look and turned back to Allie, and then he screamed her name again, even louder this time, ending it with a piercing, high-pitched coda. The creatures reacted with similar unease, and Ramon knew Allie had been right about the sounds.

"Stop!" Zander said softly, putting his hands in front of him as if hoping to bring order back to the scene that he'd controlled so well a minute ago.

"Scream, Allie!" Ramon yelled to his deputy. "Scream as loud as you can!" Ramon looked back to Zander. "Loud noises are like poison to them. You know that, don't you? That's why your man isn't going to shoot anyone. You're afraid it will hurt them. You're afraid they'll leave."

Zander turned toward Allie, who had picked up where Ramon left off and was now shouting at the *Arali* as if she were trying to scare off a grizzly. The *Arali* continued their sways of pain, but as effective as the play seemed at first, Allie noted how their distress was already showing a bit less vigor and animation.

"Don't test me, Sheriff," Zander warned, but his eyes were searching frantically now, bouncing back and forth from the *Arali* to Allie and back to Ramon.

"But I bet there's one thing you didn't figure out about these things," Ramon continued.

Zander turned to Ramon now, his eyes wide, daring him to describe something he hadn't already thought of.

"Allie don't stop!" Ramon ordered, and then he turned back to Zander, emboldened with his secret. "You think these things are in Garmella because of the telescope, don't you? You think they're somehow attracted to signals from space or something?"

Zander said nothing, revealing his answer.

"But your wrong. They're here—in Garmella—because it's *quiet*. Just like every other town with a radio telescope. That's how you knew, right? That's how you knew they were coming? Probably mapped out the places where these things have been before and tracked them here?"

"It *is* the telescope."

"No. Winston Bell knew it too. He just went along with the theory because of the prize you offered him. His interference was useless, unnecessary."

"That's not true."

Ramon shrugged. "It is. Your monsters don't like loud sounds, that's all, and I'll bet the constant blast of cell phones and radio waves is like acid to them."

Zander looked to the ground in thought, his breathing heavy, and then he looked back to his treasured *Arali,* weighing the possibility that what the Sheriff had said was true.

"Ramon!" It was Allie, out of breath. "Ramon it's not working anymore."

"What?"

"The screaming,"

Zander stared to the creatures, assessing the news.

Ramon began to scream again, but the *Arali* barely moved this time.

"Yes," Zander whispered. "It *is* the noise. A poison." He paused. "But they're becoming...inoculated." He looked to Ouray now and nodded, his eyes full of fervor and hate, and the man with the gun raised it high once more, preparing for Allie's execution.

Allie opened her mouth to scream, but her throat had nothing left to give, and she squeezed her eyes shut as she waited for the bullet to enter somewhere in her skull.

And then a high-pitched shriek of near ultrasonic levels split the air, and Allie instinctively looked toward the creatures, who were now writhing and twitching again, this time with an agony suggesting they'd been set ablaze.

Ouray lowered the rifle and turned to the creatures as well, and within moments, all five living members of the sinkhole congregation watched in horror and fascination as the forms began to change slowly from their glistening bodies of dusky gray to something solid and black, twitching and jerking with erratic rapidity.

"What is happening?" Allie whispered.

And then she saw another figure move beside her, just over her left shoulder, and as she turned toward it, she saw Maria walking past her.

The girl strode confidently forward, toward the sinkhole and the creatures still floating above it, cradling Antonio out in front of her as if he were the messiah. She didn't shift a glance in Allie's direction as she passed.

Ouray noticed Maria as well, but he could only stare at the girl, confused. He looked to his boss for instruction, but Zander was just as mesmerized by the girl as he, and his face, that had shown a desperate concern earlier, was now a ball of panic and turmoil.

And when the twelve-year-old girl finally reached the edge of the sinkhole and held Antonio forward, the man who had orchestrated the unspeakable crime on Garmella, Arizona finally understood what was happening.

He screamed with pleas of torture for Maria to stop, but before the echo of his cries had dissipated, it was already too late.

CHAPTER TWENTY-EIGHT

"NO!"

Zander was fewer than ten yards from the girl now, and when he finally realized her motives, he sprinted toward her, his arms stretched forward, reaching for the bundle in her arms.

But Ramon had seen the twitch of Zander's reaction before he took a step, and before the villain could reach her, the sheriff threw his body into Zander's exposed rib cage, knocking him to the ground like a linebacker.

Zander scrambled to a sitting position and turned now to Tehya, who seemed not to have noticed what was happening with her comrade, so mesmerized was she by the *Arali* and their apparent anguish.

But it was more than just pain the *Arali* were demonstrating; the forms of the creatures were diminishing now, both in size and color, and Zander looked desperately up to Ouray, who, though fixated on the *Arali,* still held the rifle in his hand. "Shoot her, Ouray! She's killing them!"

Ouray met his boss' gaze and snapped back to the present, and then he lifted the rifle again, this time aiming it at the back of Maria's head. He closed his free eye and steadied the sight as he wrapped his finger around the trigger.

And then Zander heard the pop of a pistol, and a second later he watched Ouray's body crumple to the ground, the exit wound of the bullet from the deputy's sidearm like a third eye in his associate's forehead.

Zander struggled to his knees when he heard the command for him to freeze, but his legs were like wet pasta now as he watched helplessly the destruction of the beings to which he'd committed his entire life.

"Oh god, no!" he whispered. "Leave!" he screamed toward the monsters. "Leave!"

But the *Arali* were now latched onto the baby's mind, just as they had latched onto the minds of possibly thousands of people over several millenia. This time, however, it was they who were controlled. The child was killing them from within.

It was the first taste of innocence for the *Arali*—Zander knew it as certainly as he knew the names of his murdered parents—and the pure, sinless virtue of the baby before them was nothing short of annihilation. The sounds of the world had been a poison to the demons, but they had adapted to the weakness quickly. There was no adaptation to purity, however; it was the toxin of God Himself.

Within minutes, the forms had shrunk to the sizes of small men and the color of anthracite, and the once towering beasts who had raged through the town like cyclones now stood like impotent statues in an abandoned park.

"Shoot them," Maria said, stepping to the side, never turning to see Allie move in closer to her targets.

"Gladly."

With three quick pops, Allie shot the monsters in succession, each bullet exploding the black figures to dust before sending the crumbs of their figures into the air and down into the chasm behind them. Not a sound came from the beasts as they disintegrated, and the hole behind them simply absorbed their remnants as the ocean absorbs rain.

Zander stood now, his face white and astonished, and despite Allie's order of 'Don't move!', he walked to the edge of the sinkhole and stared down into the gaping chasm, despondent and disbelieving. He turned to Maria, who stood less than ten feet away, a look of awe upon his face now, having replaced his expression of misery and hopelessness. He then turned and met Allie's eyes, followed by Ramon's, and then finally he looked at Tehya. His eyes softened on the woman and he gave her a sad smile, and then he took one more step and plummeted into the sinkhole.

CHAPTER TWENTY-NINE

"ARE YOU SURE ABOUT this, Maria?" Ramon asked.

Maria nodded, and with permission granted, Ramon shoved the spade of the shovel into the dirt, breaking ground on Antonio's grave in the back of St. Patrick's Catholic Church.

An hour later, just as the whirr of the rescue helicopter began chopping above them—a sign that Josh and his mom had made it to Simonson—the tiny burial hole of Antonio Suarez was finished, and Ramon, Allie, and Gloria listened quietly as Maria said a prayer for her brother.

And then another voice called out, muffled and distant.

In unison, the three lifted their heads and looked at each other. "You heard that right," Ramon asked.

Maria and Allie nodded, their eyes wide and terrified.

Ramon turned and stared up at the church, and within seconds, the voice boomed again, this time with absolute clarity.

"Help!"

"Gloria?" Allie asked quietly to Ramon, and then realizing she was right, she shouted her name with what little of her voice she still had. "Gloria, it's Allie!"

"Allie?!" Gloria begin to cry, her sobs a combination of emotions that included joy and fear, confusion and disbelief. "It wasn't me! I swear to God! I know those people are trying to use me, but I didn't do anything! I don't know why they're doing it, but I swear I'm not involved!"

"It's okay, Gloria, we're coming!"

Before the chopper had landed, Gloria was free, and the four survivors made a pact simply to tell the truth of what had happened the morning of June 12th in Garmella, Arizona, though each would have slightly different versions of the events, especially Gloria Reynolds, who spent most of the day locked in a cell in St. Patrick's Catholic Church.

And if no one believed them, well, that wasn't any of their concern. Josh and Deedee knew the truth, and certainly other survivors would be found as well, though perhaps that wasn't so certain after all. As of yet, they hadn't seen a soul.

And there was Tehya, of course; how much she would tell, Ramon couldn't know, but he was beginning to re-think his position on waterboarding.

Ramon walked with Allie from the grounds of the church to the street, where the chopper had set down, idling.

"Do you believe him?" Ramon asked.

Allie didn't hesitate; she knew what he was asking. "I guess we'll know in a hundred years, right? If I'm playing racquetball with my great-great-grandkids and everyone else I know is dead and gone, that'll be the answer."

Ramon laughed. "I guess."

"But if those things are really dead, maybe that means 'the reward' dies with them."

Ramon shrugged. "Are you gonna tell Josh?"

Allie nodded, as if she'd already thought about the question. "I don't know." She squinted and cocked her head. "Something tells me he already knows. I think *I* would have known. Whether Zander told me or not."

Ramon pursed his lips, giving the statement its due consideration, and neither spoke another word as they walked to the rescue helicopter rumbling in the middle of Interstate 91. Within moments, the chopper was off the ground again, preparing to carry away the only known survivors of a town that had been suddenly cursed, capriciously, as if on the impulse of some malicious god whose wish it was to thrust Garmella, Arizona into the middle of a nightmare.

As the chopper rose quickly into the air, Ramon kept his eyes focused on the ground below, watching the sinkhole that had kept his town hostage shrink until it was little more than a puddle in the middle of the interstate. He raised his head and stared at Allie and Gloria, both of whom were also studying the ground below.

Ramon glanced at Maria, who was already fast asleep, and a thin glaze of tears welled in his eyes as he speculated about her dreams in that moment.

Ramon then closed his own eyes, and within minutes he was also asleep, dreaming of puddles and the splashing of raindrops.

THE END

DEAR READER,

Thank you for reading They Came with the Rain. I hope you enjoyed it. I would be grateful if you would leave a review for it on Amazon. It doesn't have to be long. A simple, "I liked it!" is enough. That is, if you did like it, which I hope you did!

OTHER BOOKS BY CHRISTOPHER COLEMAN

THE GRETEL SERIES
Marlene's Revenge (Gretel Book Two)
Hansel (Gretel Book Three)
Anika Rising (Gretel Book Four)
The Crippling (Gretel Book Five)
The Killing of Orphism (Gretel Book Six)
THE THEY CAME WITH THE SNOW SE-
RIES
They Came with the Snow (They Came with the
Snow Book One)
The Melting (They Came with the Snow Book
Two)
The List (They Came with the Snow Book Three)
The Ghosts of Winter (They Came with the Snow
Book Four)
THE SIGHTING SERIES
The Sighting (The Sighting Book One)
The Origin (The Sighting Book Two)
The Reappearance (The Sighting Book Three)
Standalone Novel

They Came with the Storm

Made in the USA
Middletown, DE
12 September 2020